Praise for Katie Porter's
Vegas Top Guns series

"The writing duo that is Katie Porter knows erotica."
~ *RT Book Reviews on* Double Down

"When I finished, I may have bounced in my chair a few imes with glee."
~ *Smart Bitches, Trashy Books on* Double Down

"Readers who are looking for handsome pilots and long, un-filled nights will love this sassy read, sure to get your jets ff!"
~ *Library Journal on* Double Down

"Every once in a while you finish a book, smile and say: low that's what I'm talking about!"
~ *USA TODAY on* Inside Bet

"The eroticism in this novel is exquisite, vivid and daring. ive stars and a fist pump!"
~ *Book Lovers Inc. on* Inside Bet

"I can't recommend *Hold 'Em* or this series more highly if ou like action, romance, humor and some steamy encounters."
~ *Sizzling Hot Book Reviews on* Hold 'Em

"Exploring femdom sex, Katie Porter leashes readers by the ecks and keeps them riveted from page one. A must-read!"
~ *Fresh Fiction on* Hold 'Em

Look for these titles by
Katie Porter

Now Available:

Came Upon a Midnight Clear

Vegas Top Guns
Double Down
Inside Bet
Hold 'Em
Hard Way
Bare Knuckle

Club Devant
Lead and Follow
Chains and Canes

Hold 'Em

Katie Porter

Samhain Publishing, Ltd.
11821 Mason Montgomery Road, 4B
Cincinnati, OH 45249
www.samhainpublishing.com

Hold 'Em
Copyright © 2013 by Katie Porter
Print ISBN: 978-1-61921-356-2
Digital ISBN: 978-1-61921-087-5

Editing by Sasha Knight
Cover by Scott Carpenter

First Samhain Publishing, Ltd. electronic publication: September 2012
First Samhain Publishing, Ltd. print publication: August 2013

Dedication

To BC & SG
My temptation and salvation

Acknowledgments

We deeply appreciate our families' unflagging support. Credit for much of our sanity is owed to the Group That Shall Not Be Named. Gratitude to Dana Gautier for saving our butts about the motorcycles and for being such a great asset to our work. As well as being our incredible cheerleader, Fedora Chen was an amazing proofreader on both this project and Inside Bet. In addition, we offer thanks to Sarah Frantz, Rowan Larke, Zoe Archer, Patti Ann Colt and Kelly Schaub for their friendship, and to Kevan Lyon and Sasha Knight for their amazing enthusiasm.

Chapter One

Captain Leah Girardi loved her time in the flight simulator. Not every pilot did. She figured that when Big Daddy Air Force was being stingy with the jet fuel, the simulator was as good as it got. Besides, the full mission simulator was almost like the real thing. Best video game ever.

But as much as she liked it, a few hours spent in there tended to take the oomph out of a girl.

By the time she walked into the 64th Aggressor Squadron's hangar, she was worn out. Her back ached, her eyes were blurry and her neck was as tight as it ever got. Luckily she only had to report in to Major Ryan Haverty and she was good to go. She ought to be home in about twenty minutes. Fifteen if she pushed her motorcycle as fast as she shouldn't.

Fang's office was barely bigger than a cubicle, but he had it to himself. He looked up from his stacks of paperwork as Leah dropped into the spare chair. "You up to date?"

"Yep. Everything's straight. I came through with flying colors."

"When don't you?" He clicked away on his computer for a second.

"Never. Because I'm awesome." Leaning forward, she snagged a framed picture from beside his monitor. The woman behind the glass was an elfin-featured redhead. "Aw, so cute. Does Cassandra know she rated desk space already?"

A hint of a blush spread over Ryan's cheeks. It was still bizarre to see him in a real relationship. Leah, Ryan, and their third friend, Captain Jon Carlisle, had been a solid unit. They still were, but Ryan and Jon had both added girlfriends to the mix.

Leah didn't like to admit how much it bugged her. Not because she begrudged them their happiness, since they both totally deserved it, but because it had become wickedly apparent she had no one. A nagging frustration and ridiculous sense of boredom pervaded her waking hours when she went home alone.

She was a fighter pilot, for Christ's sake. A *female* fighter pilot. She needed to be better than perfect.

But when she wasn't in the air, she was bored.

She wiggled the picture under her chin. "So...does Cass know?"

"Yeah," he said on a slightly awkward chuckle. "She caught me printing it off."

"You two are so adorable, I think I might die of a diabetic coma." She put the picture back on the desk then stretched her legs out and crossed them at the ankles. She was still stiff from four hours in the flight simulator. "But why'd you want me to come by? Everyone else got to go straight home. You're crimping my four-day."

"Don't pout," he said dryly. "It's unbecoming of an officer."

She stuck her tongue out. "Spill."

Pulling a dark blue folder out from the bottom of a teetering stack of paper, Ryan released a chuffing breath. "We've got a new pilot. He just showed up today."

"Don't say it," she warned.

"I'd like you to be his point of contact."

She flopped back in her seat. "I *knew* that was what you were gonna say. Come on, Fang, don't do this to me. It's Washington's birthday on Monday. Four-day weekend. I have plans."

"And what exactly do those entail? Getting shitfaced and calling me for a ride?" He lifted his eyebrows. Ryan was generally a nice guy. Buff, and so clean-cut he should've joined the Army just to be in the 82nd, the nickname of which was the All Americans. There were times Leah remembered why he was the boss.

"I've been good lately," she said, *and even more freaking bored as a result.* She'd gotten too near to inappropriate with an ineligible guy at the yearly Air Force Ball. Luckily Ryan and Jon had hauled her out of there before she got too far flirting with an executive officer's husband. They'd also chewed her a new one. Quite the night.

It had been a bit of a wake-up call.

She'd barely had a drink since. Just a few beers now and then.

"I really don't want to spend the whole weekend dragging some random guy all around Vegas trying to find him a place to live."

"Then we're good on that front," said a voice from the doorway behind her. "I'm already locked down. Had my household goods delivered this morning."

Leah went stock-still, like her engines had shut off. She gripped the padded arms of the seat. And her heartbeat... Yeah, she could admit her heartbeat went into overdrive. Hardcore.

She knew that voice.

It had been a long time—six years, as a matter of fact—but that didn't matter. When a woman's strongest memory of a man was his voice in her ear telling her that he loved the way she smiled when she came, it tended to be memorable.

Ryan smiled past Leah. "There you are. Templeton, I'd like you to meet Captain Leah Girardi. Also known as Princess Leah."

Her eyes narrowed. She was tempted to deck Fang. Princess might be her call sign, but that didn't mean she liked it.

Ryan kept talking as if he didn't feel the death threats she was telepathically sending his way. "Princess, this is Captain Mike Templeton. Call sign Strap Happy, right?"

She made herself twist in the seat to look. Seeing him would only get worse the longer she put it off.

11

In the absence of any logical thought, a creative string of curses assembled in her mind. The man looked better than ever. Good enough to nom down on. A few times.

When Leah had last seen him, Mike had been...cute. Kind of adorable in the way he hadn't yet grown into his lanky hands and tall height.

But now...

He wore the usual olive-green flight suit, but he filled it out like whoa and damn. His shoulders had gotten wider—way wider—while his hips were as narrow as when she'd wrapped her ankles around him. He'd even matured through the face, his jawline sharper. His eyes were still that unforgettable neon blue, silently laughing at her. Constantly.

He grinned at her. "Leah and I go way back."

Leah sent up a silent prayer that he'd leave it at that. She and Ryan had also briefly dated what felt like a century ago. Since that time, she'd called a moratorium on sleeping with fellow pilots. It was hard as hell to be taken seriously in the sky when the guys thought she was also a throttle groupie.

Forcing herself to stick a hand out was easier than she'd expected. "Hey, Mike." Even her voice had a more tranquil pitch than she'd feared. "Where you been hiding yourself?"

He shrugged, took her hand and shook it. As he drew away, he trailed his middle finger down her palm.

No way in hell would she admit the shiver that worked past her shoulder blades. Or the way her nipples tightened. Thank God for the thick-ass layers of her flight suit.

"Been here and there." Thankfully, he positioned himself along a triangle between her and Ryan's desk, so she could assess them both. "Few tours over Iraq and the 'Stans. How'd you get lucky enough to hide out here so fast?"

Poof. Tightened-nipple problem fixed. She slumped back into her seat. Nothing killed her attraction faster than condescension. Her teeth ground together, but she kept the smile on her lips. "By being better than you, obviously," she said in a syrupy-sweet tone.

Ryan folded his hands over the folder. "Are we going to have a problem here?"

The laugh lines spreading out from the corners of Mike's eyes were new. "No problem at all. In fact, it's almost like being home again."

Ryan wasn't stupid. He scrutinized them both, finally landing his gaze on her. A firm glint of warning sparked in his eyes. He'd been on Leah's ass to clean up her act for a while now, arguing that she was due to have been major a year ago. Sparring with a fellow squadron member wasn't going to win her any gold stars.

"So," he said slowly, glancing at Mike. "Strap Happy? How'd you get saddled with that?"

Since there was nowhere else for him to sit, Mike leaned those freaking wide shoulders against the wall. He put on a gee-shucks grin and darted Leah a look out of the corner of his eye. "You know how it is. Get caught with one tiny riding crop and there's no shaking the jokes."

She coughed into a fist to hide a hot rush. Her thighs loosened—just a fraction—before she clenched them again.

Mike into the kinky stuff? No way. What a joke that was.

Hell, not once over their three-month relationship had she been able to tease him into giving her the kind of fucking she'd wanted. Although the sex hadn't been bad by any means, it hadn't been a rocking good time. Sex that was all sweetness and slow touches had its time, but occasionally Leah needed something meatier. Rougher.

Mike hadn't ever managed to cough it up.

"So if Templeton already has a place, it sounds like there won't be much for you to do, Leah," Ryan said. "You've lucked out. Maybe show him the clinic and the BX."

Leah lifted her eyebrows. "Are you kicking us out, Fang? What, you got a hot date?"

"I've got a hot date every night," Ryan said after a laugh. "Because I am one lucky son of a gun. Now out. I need to lock up."

Reluctantly, she cranked out of her seat.

Mike still looked just as good. Fuck. *So* not fair that men only got hotter as they got older. Even his smirk better fit his angular features.

As she walked through the near-empty headquarters with Mike at her side, Leah passed an uncomfortably nervous hand over the slick sweep of her hair. Still knotted up right and tight, not a strand out of place. She couldn't wait until she could get home and let the heavy weight down. Who knew how long that would be now.

She slipped on her dark-as-hell sunglasses as they stepped out into the parking lot. Even in mid-February, the Nevada sun was bright—shocking after the dim shadows of the cool building. Unseasonable heat made her flight suit cling damply to the back of her neck.

Mike still looked as cool as a cucumber. His hair was longer than it used to be, the golden brown coming way too close to his ears. The length revealed a hint of curl she hadn't remembered. Without a haircut before Tuesday, the higher-ups were going to give him hell. But far be it for her to point that out. He knew the regs. He had to. He'd already been a fighter pilot when she'd been fresh out of commissioned officer training.

"I know you only made captain two years ago," she said.

He raked his fingers across his scalp. The move thickened his biceps to a seriously unfair degree. "Sets a guy back when he can't fly for a year. Torn ACLs will do that. I was lucky the surgery worked. Didn't realize you were keeping tabs on me, Leah."

"Small community. Hard to avoid the shit." She turned her gaze out to the far-off horizon. A C-17 was lumbering into the air just over the rows of hangars. "I've got more time in grade than you."

"So?"

Like he didn't know what she was talking about. He'd been absently dismissive of female pilots when he and Leah were involved. Apparently chicks in jets didn't even rate enough to get worked up over.

"So," she said, as if speaking to a child. "I've been a captain longer. I want to know the same thing Major Haverty did. Are we going to have a problem?"

Chapter Two

So, the princess wanted to piss on a few trees and mark her territory. Fine by him. Already she looked ready to spit gnashed-up teeth. Those clipped, precise syllables might fool other people into believing she was unaffected, but Mike only smiled. He liked the idea that he'd already crawled underneath her skin.

"No problem, Captain Girardi, ma'am." He tried his best aw-shucks shrug. "I know my place."

"Can it, Templeton. The major's assigned me to be your friendly neighborhood tour guide, so that's what I'll do. But you pull any crap with me, and your adjustment to life here will *not* go smoothly."

She turned on her heel. Exit stage left.

Mike stood in the parking lot with his arms crossed, but he needed a minute to breathe. And grin. Because, holy damn, she was turning him on. He had issues with women officers in harm's way, but he couldn't help the jolt of arousal that came from being dressed down by one.

As he walked after her, crossing the nearly deserted parking lot, he indulged his salacious smile. Although pissing Leah off might not do any favors for his prospects with his new squadron, he knew what he'd be thinking about that night. The pointed, haughty tone of voice. The snap and flash in her whiskey eyes.

What would she do if she knew?

He remembered her as a newly minted officer, barely twenty-three, with soft cheeks and ambition higher than a skyscraper. Even then she'd had her eyes turned heavenward, set on becoming a pilot. Mike hadn't given it much thought. After all, her chances had been slim.

Fit and graceful, Leah had realized her ambitions. That power quickened his blood.

But hell if he was going to let her jerk him around by his dick, even if she had no idea of her effect. Play was play. Work was still work. The idea of women flying in combat, even in a teaching capacity, rubbed like a rusted file against everything he'd ever believed.

"How's your family?" he asked, his long strides easily closing the distance. "Still racing?"

Leah flashed him a frown. He'd almost forgotten that their three months together had been more than sex. They'd talked. Sometimes. Her father had been a professional driver on the Motocross Championship, with her older brothers following suit. Speed was in her blood.

"Not so much," she said. "Chris had an accident a few years ago that took him out of Supercross, but he and Jake and Dad all run a bike shop now. Yours?"

Mike shrugged, taking note of street names and landmarks as they walked. "Tom made partner and has a six-year-old girl. Shannon moved to New York after she got out of design school. Mom's convinced she'll either wind up lesbian or knifed in an alley. I'm not sure which she'd think was worse."

That got a laugh out of Leah. She touched her hair again. The scraped-back regulation bun did no favors for luscious deep brown hair that used to be cut chin length. The severe style put her features front and center. Her big doe eyes were classic while her lush mouth was crooked at the corner. She looked like she constantly held back a tide of dirty thoughts.

"There's the BX," she said, waving a casual hand toward another quiet parking lot. It wasn't exactly the most professional orientation Mike had ever received. "And down there, that building behind the water tower—that's the officers' club. They have a barber."

"Is that a hint?"

"Yes."

The idea that she'd been checking him out that closely made his guts take notice. "What's the club like?"

"Same as any. Dull. Everybody out to impress."

"So you would recommend...?"

She shifted her weight onto her back foot, looking him up and down. "Are you asking me where I go for a good time?"

"No, *before* the good time."

Leah narrowed her eyes, but it was like being threatened by a kitten. The only genuine rise he'd dragged out of her had been about her flying. "You can lay off the innuendo, Templeton. I'm not interested."

"Why, you got a guy? Hell, you could have kids by now for all I know."

"I don't see how that's your business."

"Come off it, Leah. I see a former lover after, what—six years? I'm just curious how your life's been."

"You know that whole two-wars thing going on? I've been busy."

"With ivory-tower types here, sure."

Leah's mock indignation flared into something hot and sharp. The skin above her eyes relaxed, her lids going heavy with condescension. A sneer shaped her crooked mouth. She looked like a snotty, angry sorority sister.

"I've done four tours," she said coldly.

"Um...good?"

Of course he'd known. Small world and all that. Their particular corner of the military was a clubby bunch, always up in each other's shit. Frankly, he was surprised he hadn't run into her before this evening.

"You know, Mike, you've got a lot of nerve pissing me off in the first hour you're on base."

"I should've waited?"

"Well, let's just think about the possibilities, shall we?"

Mike permitted a slow smile. "Please do."

She seemed intent on taking the moment seriously. "This isn't flying sorties over the enemy. To be honest, it takes a helluva lot more skill."

"Sure," he said. "I find it hard to imagine mortal danger. Much easier just to get hit in the face with the real thing."

As she advanced, her whiskey eyes sparked with a fire that had Mike thinking really, *really* inappropriate things—probably why he was baiting her so badly. Forget the politics and the morality of women as combat pilots, he just wanted the rush of reaching for something dangerous. Leah Girardi was a lit cigarette near a gasoline spill.

She didn't rail or rant. She didn't lose her cool. Every minute effort to hold her temper in check stretched across wide cheekbones. Passion *and* control. Mike couldn't think too long about that combination or he'd embarrass himself with a hard-on in the BX parking lot.

"You're new here, Captain," she said, emphasizing his rank. It irked the shit out of him that she had seniority. "And it's the weekend, so I won't dog on you too hard."

"Yet."

"*Yet.* Because you've got a lot to learn before you climb into an F-16 for the Aggressors. No one goes up without the major's say-so, and he listens to me."

Mike didn't actually voice what he was thinking. Sporting a black eye all weekend held no appeal. For a flash, he wondered about the connection between Leah and Major "Fang" Haverty, and why a tickle of jealousy snaked between his ribs.

"So while the rest of us are up in the air come Tuesday morning," she said, "your butt will be in the simulator."

"Like hell."

"You think you can read a few manuals on enemy combat tactics and fly like one? If you do, we're going to have an even bigger problem than your attitude."

"You're the one busting my balls."

She punched the tip of her finger against his sternum. "Every eight weeks we get another batch of hotshots in here.

Other branches of service, other nations. All of them are great pilots with the same piss-poor attitude. They think they already know everything. Our job, Captain, is to show them their weaknesses. That means knowing our opponents until we can fly like them in our sleep, until it's deep muscle memory." Leah tossed up her chin, looking him dead in the eye. "So, yeah. You and that simulator are gonna get to know each other *real* well."

She headed back toward the hangars as the sun slanted long and low across the land. Mike forced himself to follow. His feet were heavy, weighed by his misgivings. Gut instinct and courage were all well and good. He had those in spades, with no doubt as to how he could handle himself during the big show. Anything that smacked of school, however, had his C+ gray matter cringing and looking for an opportunity to play hooky.

Beyond the looming workload, the mere idea of spending weeks, possibly longer, to get into the head of the enemy was almost...sick. He knew it wasn't a logical reaction and that red force squads were responsible for improving allied pilots from all over the world. Didn't mean he was into those kinds of head games. He'd spent the last eight years as one of the good guys.

Had he got his way, he'd still be flying over Afghanistan. Brass, however, had decided otherwise. The next time he took to the skies, he'd be wearing a red star on his helmet and ripping through the air in an F-16 painted the same gray camo as a Russian MiG. That held about as much appeal as shoving a lit blowtorch down his shorts.

Still. Leah didn't need his shit. In her way, she was trying to help. He'd liked her all those years ago and didn't relish the idea of flaming out in the first few minutes.

"Hey, Princess," he called, jogging to catch up. "Truce?"

She glared at him. "Whatever. Just take this seriously, would ya, Mike? What we do here is important."

"Understood, Captain Girardi. I am yours to mold."

"Cut the crap." The hangar parking lot was quiet as she glanced around. "Where's your ride?"

Mike nodded toward his bike. "The BMW over there by the hot pink toy. Yours?"

"The hot pink toy."

He should've known. The Ducati street bike had Leah written all over it—sleek and flashy. But the custom pink paint job made it a chick's bike. "What's the engine on that thing? Maybe six hundred ccs?"

"Almost eight fifty, thank you very much. A hundred and forty horsepower."

"Huh."

She sighed. "Fine. I'll bite. Yours?"

"It's the S1000RR. A hundred and ninety five horsepower."

"Good for you, Strap Happy. Feel better? You've got the bigger dick."

"Sure as hell hope so."

"Didn't you used to be Zoomy or Speedy or some other stupid call sign? What's the real deal with the new one?"

God, she looked sexy. Forget the sweaty flight suit and the shellacked hair. The pop of her hip against the seat of her bike made him remember how her body had felt under his hands. Toned but soft. Strong but lush in all the right places. She'd tasted amazing. Other lovers had trickled across his history in the years since, yet he still recalled her salty sweetness—so uniquely Leah. Not even one-hundred-twenty-proof moonshine hit his brain faster.

But they'd never been quite right for each other. Something hadn't clicked. Mike had a good idea of what that was, considering what he'd since learned about his own needs.

He shoved his helmet on his head, doing up the latch with a smile. "Wouldn't you just like to know, huh?"

"Yeah, I would. Because I know for a fact that whips and chains weren't your deal."

"You had three months with me, Leah. You didn't learn everything."

"Right," she said, dragging out the word. She grabbed her helmet too, which matched her bike's hot pink. "And I'm sure all the good stuff was there in your foot locker. Just never got around to it, eh?"

Mike indulged in an even broader smile. She was hot shit, no doubt. But on this topic she had absolutely no idea what she was talking about. Hell, he hadn't had a clue either. Not back then. Four months under the tutelage of a very patient, very exacting mistress had revealed sides of himself that had always lurked in shadow.

Leah jumped on her bike and fired up its sweet little engine. Olive drab pulled snug over her ass. The quasi hard-on he'd been sporting gave a twitch when he imagined her straddling him that way.

"I thought you were going to show me the clinic," he shouted.

"It's on the way out. Think you can keep up?"

Mike threw a leg over his bike, enjoying how she watched. A playful sizzle lit her wide baby-doll eyes. He kicked his S1000RR to life. Buzzing vibrations shook up through his spine. For a moment they just sat there in the parking lot, gunning the engines, showing off. A laugh started up in his chest. He glanced over and found that same daredevil laughter shaping Leah's crooked lips into a full-on grin.

She spun the Ducati in a hard arc. The back tire squealed. A jolt of fire shot through Mike's bones as he tore out after her. The wind against his face was pure energy. Pilots were adrenaline junkies down to the cellular level, and he was no exception. Nothing topped speed.

Other than the idea of Leah holding his riding crop.

What he'd told Major Haverty about his revised call sign was true. Only the crop hadn't been to use *on* a woman. Used *by* a woman was so much hotter. Maybe if he were very good and very patient...

Skidding to a stop outside another innocuous base building, she gave it a flippant wave. "And there's the clinic," she shouted over their loud-as-hell bikes. "Your tour is finito."

The crazy-cool glint in her eye dared him for more. "Where will you be tomorrow night?" he asked.

"Paulie's," she said simply.

Then she was off, tearing down the road toward the base's main gate.

Chapter Three

By Friday night, Leah wasn't looking forward to the rest of the weekend. She'd had jack shit to do all day. After cleaning her apartment in the morning, she'd read the newest Vince Flynn and still had hours left to fill.

She'd called Jon and Ryan to see if they wanted to go out, but they had prior commitments. Jon and Heather were going to some French foreign movie—and Leah really didn't want to know why he'd started laughing when he'd mentioned it. Ryan had been headed out the door to visit Cassandra's dad in Henderson, even though Cass was working late at the gallery. Family time? That one was beyond strange, but whatever. Leah could find something to do on her own.

So Paulie's it was, just like she'd told Mike. Not that it had been an invitation. Mostly her default answer for Friday nights.

Only a couple blocks away from the Nellis main gate, Paulie's was a tidy little hole-in-the-wall joint. When Leah cruised in around twenty-one hundred hours, only about half the tables and booths were filled. No one was up on the karaoke stage. Templeton was nowhere to be seen. Maybe he'd be too wiped out from unpacking boxes to make an appearance.

Unfortunately, the idea of him spending the day moving in led to ideas about him hot. And sweaty. And standing under a steaming shower, washing off the dirt. What would all that new weight through his torso look like when stripped bare? She pictured a rivulet of water dribbling down between his pecs and soap bubbles outlining his abs.

Even when they'd been together, he'd been cut. Not buff, but lean enough that every muscle had stood out in stark definition. Now...

Now, she had to get her brain up out of her panties. That was a crash waiting to happen.

Besides, the fact that his body was bigger meant nothing about the methods he used in the sack. He'd still be all sweetness and light, wasting that wickedly naughty grin.

Slipping into an empty booth, Leah pointedly didn't look at the table they staked when the whole crew showed up. Sitting there by herself would be silly. She waved down the waitress who wove through the tables with an empty drink tray balanced on one hand.

"Hi, Princess," Theresa chirped. "Your boys abandon you?"

She couldn't even get away from her call sign with civilians. But then, Theresa hardly counted since the majority of the clientele at Paulie's were airmen—none of whom hesitated to whip out the cinnamon-bun-hair jokes. She smiled at the blonde. "They're turning into respectable members of society."

Theresa shook her head with mock disappointment. "It's a crying shame. Two flyboys like that getting tied down."

"Women all over the city are in deep mourning."

"Don't think I'm not one of them." The waitress winked. "Now what can I get you?"

Leah wound the end of her long ponytail through her fingers then drew it over her shoulder. She wanted a margarita, heavy on the tequila. But she'd ridden her bike, and it'd be rude as hell to call Jon or Ryan for a ride when she knew they were occupied. "A Dr. Pepper," she said on a sigh.

"Coming right up, sweetheart." Theresa disappeared on a swish of hips.

With no one onstage to laugh at, Leah pulled her phone out of her pocket to amuse herself with a flying game. Even she knew that she was a little obsessed.

When Theresa came back, she set the plastic cup on the table in front of Leah. "Here you go."

"Cherries, even?" She grinned up at the waitress. "Don't tell me you're so desperate for a pilot that you'll pick up a chick?"

Theresa laughed. "All joking aside, you pilots are too scary psycho for me. The cherries are from the guy at the bar. He said you'd know what it was about."

Leah knew who she was going to see before she even jerked her head around.

Mike leaned backward against the bar with his elbows hooked on the edge. She'd almost managed to convince herself that his newly impressive body had been a trick of the flight suit. Apparently not. Simple blue jeans showed off long legs with thick thighs. His dark T-shirt was on the snug side, probably since he knew exactly what he was showing off.

She raised the cup of soda in a silent salute. Only being friendly to a new squadron member. It was the right thing to do. She'd been the new girl on base plenty of times herself.

After Mike lifted his beer bottle in response, she turned back to face the stage. It wouldn't do to let the poor boy think he had a chance. Of course, her act would be a lot easier to carry off if someone were up onstage singing. She drummed her fingers next to her glass.

Really, she was thinking about the cherries. He still remembered that she'd liked them. Mike had always laughed when she'd pulled the jar out of her fridge to drop a couple in her sodas. She might have a sweet tooth, but she earned it the hard way by running almost every morning.

Then there was the time when they'd put a few cherries to an entirely different purpose. That remained one of their most memorable nights together. As he decorated her with the cold, sweet treats, then nibbled them off, Mike had made her feel almost...worshiped. As if he adored her body. It had been tantalizing and a little freaky at the same time.

"This seat taken?" he asked, sliding into the booth across from her.

She sat up straighter, shaking off the wisp of memory. That was then and this was now. He was a team member.

"By all means."

"I never figured you for a solo partier."

She took a sip of her drink. "That'd be the reason for the Dr. Pepper. Thanks for the cherries, by the way."

God, his smile was wicked. His lips were finely drawn, but mostly it was the way his eyes sparked at her. That bright blue had followed her around way longer than they deserved.

"I couldn't resist," he said.

She wasn't following that line of conversation. No thankee. "I assume you've been busy today? Settling in?"

"You know it. When you don't carry a lot of crap around, it makes it easy to unpack. I'm almost done already."

"Unbelievable." She laughed. "I hate moving. All the decisions. I still have a few boxes stuffed in my storage space."

His boots brushed by her toes as he stretched out his legs. He hitched one arm across the back of the imitation red leather seat bench. "So this is Vegas on a Friday night? I'd expected bigger. Flashier."

She rolled her eyes. "This isn't the Strip. That's where all the crazy people congregate."

"Then I'm doubly shocked you're not there."

"Oh my, I'd forgotten how terribly funny you were," she deadpanned.

She half-expected him to grouse at her. He'd always been touchy at any implied lack. But something about him was more...at ease than before. His laid-back cool made her want to shake him up, just to see if she could. He only laughed.

"Haven't you been to Vegas before?" She wasn't sure why she asked. Maybe curiosity, but a lot more of filling time. It wasn't like she had anywhere else to be or anyone else to talk to.

"Nope. Been into Nellis for Red Flag before, but I was too busy getting my ass shot down every day to see the sights." He offered it as a quip, but she saw it for what it was. Another attempt at a truce.

So she'd take it. Life at work would be easier if they weren't at each other's throats. "That seems like a shame. I bet you could tear up the town. At least you've got plenty of time now."

"That I do." His gaze turned measured, burning into her. "So what do you say? Wanna head up there with me?"

"Oh, no way. That's just asking for trouble."

He looked at her from under his brows, smile stretching even wider. His tongue slicked across his bottom lip. "Don't say you're scared, Princess. I think that might start the apocalypse."

She blew a breath out, short and tight. Everything inside her was warning that this was a bad idea. Reckless. Stupid.

She'd been acting like a saint for so damn long. Being a good girl didn't fit her skin. Biting back yawns on a Friday night was *so* not her idea of a great time.

She ran her finger around the rim of her glass then dipped it in her mouth to lick off the drop of dark soda. Mike's eyes blazed brighter, even in the carefully dim lighting of the bar, as he tracked every move. He tightened his grip on his beer bottle where she noticed a plain silver cuff on his right wrist. His shoulders hulked up a few inches as he tensed.

Oh, she was bad. Nasty, even.

Really, going out with him wouldn't actually mean anything. It wasn't like she was an easy lay. Never had been. She had fun, but she was always picky about her partners.

"The day the tourists scare me is the day I give up my commission and buy a Camry."

"There's nothing wrong with a Camry," Mike teased. "My mom drives one."

"My point exactly."

"So you and me. On the Strip." He dangled the possibilities like an apple before Eve, all tempting and obviously bad intentions.

But he wasn't pushing too hard. He leaned back in his seat as if waiting for her to come to him. Only his sharp-edged smile reached out to her.

The thing was, under that smile...

He looked almost wistful. Maybe? It was hard to put a name on the lurking emotion. She'd never been able to get inside his head.

Really, Leah would be doing him a favor by heading out to tourist land with him. He might have friends in the squadron already—she didn't keep that close of tabs on him to know—but maybe he hadn't found a chance to meet up with them yet. He had to be as bored as she was, not to mention frustrated after a whole day spent unpacking boxes.

"All right," she said slowly. "If you really need a babysitter to keep you safe from the tourists, it seems the least I can do. In the interest of squadron morale and all."

He nodded. An obviously fake solemn look pulled his mouth down. "Right. Big bad ol' me needs help keeping safe."

She slid out of the booth and tucked her hands into her back pockets, totally confident he'd be right behind her. She shook her ass as she walked, just a little, just to show him what he wasn't getting.

Outside, she drew to a stop. His BMW was parked right next to hers, meaning he'd known she was there even before walking in. She didn't like having been blindsided.

Worse than that, she didn't like how much she appreciated his bike. All red on black, it was huge. A man would need long legs to be able to keep that thing upright, and a hell of a lot of control to keep it moving. Mike had that control now, and she wanted to pick it apart piece by piece. Something unnameable set up a low-level heat between her legs.

She shook it off. They'd been down that road before, and she'd only been disappointed. Not happening again. Mike could be a great friend though, if she could concentrate. "Where are we going?"

Mike scooped up his helmet as he gave her another one of those mixed-up smiles. He shrugged into a worn black leather jacket that fit him like his jeans—like those clothes had never been meant for a body other than his. "You're the expert around here. Why don't you tell me? I'm at your whim."

No way. She was not thinking about the tingling thrill those words gave her. No chance.

"Gambling," she said abruptly. "You haven't been to Vegas unless you've gambled."

Chapter Four

As Mike pulled up to the light, he grinned over at Leah where she'd stopped alongside him. He'd poked fun at her bike on principle, but it was a badass machine. Quick and agile, it made up in maneuverability what his engine lost in the busy, crowded city streets. Choked with Friday night revelers, the Strip might as well have been a parking lot for how much speed they could manage.

She revved her engine, ready to rip up asphalt, then her black-tinted visor snapped back toward the intersection. Mike turned away from how her thigh flexed beneath khaki cargoes. He answered her with a sharp twist of the throttle. Vibration gunned up his arms as he leaned forward.

The light turned green. Their back tires squealed. The heady, happy stink of burnt rubber swirled up and around. Slammed back by the laws of weight and motion, Mike pressed hard against the sudden burst of G-force. It wasn't exactly a jet, but it was nearly enough to tide him over.

A hundred yards ahead, they had to slow down. More traffic.

With a glance to his right, Mike caught the flash of Leah's frustration in the way she smacked the gas tank between her knees.

She angled her head toward a valet line outside Caesar's. Mike nodded and followed, content to let her lead—for many reasons. The foremost at that moment was making sure she didn't ditch him. Friday nights were hard enough in a new town. The prospect of losing a relatively friendly face was made all the more serious because, *damn*, she was a fine woman.

Leah killed the throttle and swung her leg over. She ditched her helmet, shrugged out of her flight jacket and handed the whole lot over to the valet. With a mental shrug, Mike did the same and added a crisp twenty too.

"Have you ever been here?" he asked as they climbed the steps to the main entrance.

She nodded. "You stay here long enough, you make the rounds."

"How long have you been here?"

"Three years."

"Shit, that's forever."

"I know. I'm *so* fucking bored." She looked him up and down when he grabbed the door for her. "But I love the job too much to volunteer to move. I'll stay until they kick me out."

She pushed past but grimaced at her reflection in the glass. Mike watched as she ducked out of the flow of pedestrian traffic. Frowning, he followed to where she stood against a chest-high urn decorated in Roman-style mosaics.

"What?" he asked.

"I hate helmet hair."

She reached back to grab the rubber band from her messy ponytail. The motion drew her breasts up and pressed them flush against her baby-blue camisole top. Although the material was thick enough to be worn as a shirt, the shape and size of her nipples were perfectly visible—hard nubs after the thrill of the ride. She intensified the subtle torture by letting her hair down and giving it a good shake. Soft falls of dark, dark brown curled around her shoulders. The ends brushed the tops of her breasts.

Mike's mouth turned desert dry. She'd been a new officer last time they met, doing everything possible to be taken more seriously. This...

Nothing about her seemed grasping anymore. A little wild and a lot stir-crazy, sure, but that eager young officer had been replaced by a seasoned one.

He cleared his throat and looked away, intent on being good. She'd been doing her best to make him feel welcome. Just squad mates. In return, he'd do his best not to come in his pants at the thought of burying his nose in that dark, lush curtain.

Leah scooped up the loose ends and set about redoing the ponytail.

"No, wait," Mike began.

She stopped mid-motion, hands at the back of her head, breasts high. "What?"

The words were on his tongue, but he didn't have the right to say them. It wasn't his place.

Colleagues. Ex-lovers. That was all.

"Never mind. Forget it."

She dropped her hands, wearing a look of exasperation. "Tell me."

A subtle frisson made his hands flex. He was beginning to adore that tone of voice. "I was going to ask that you leave your hair down," he said evenly.

Something dark and curious swept across her expression. He was not so hopeful as to think she understood what he wanted from her. Not yet. She hadn't given his cuff a second look, which made him think the subtleties of his particular bent were beyond her experience.

But she seemed game enough to flex her muscles—if only as a woman in the position to tease.

"Well, then," she said, one finger twirling a loose end. "Ask it."

Maybe she thought he wouldn't. Maybe she assumed he'd make it into a joke. Yet for Mike there was nothing simpler than answering a woman when she asked what he wanted.

There wasn't much space between their bodies, for the sake of staying clear of other guests. He chose to shrink that distance even farther. But not too much. From morning to night, Leah Girardi probably had guys on her like bugs on flypaper. He was in no mood to be just any guy.

He *was* in the mood to catch a hint of her scent and the subtle touch of her body heat. He'd grab a little sample before he locked it down again.

"Leah," he said, gaze trained on her mouth. Looking her in the eye would be too challenging, which he didn't want at all. "Will you leave your hair down?" He paused for a heartbeat. "Please?"

Her lower lip had strayed from its partner, parting. Dark brows quirked a fraction. She smelled of something floral mixed with a faint trace of gasoline and leather. Heat from her body pulsed along the bare skin of his forearms, even warming his T-shirt.

She dropped her hand. "Whatever," she said, but Mike caught the swallow that constricted her throat. "You have very good manners, Michael."

With a nod and a slight shimmy, she angled away from him and toward the main lobby. Dark hair trailed behind her, the ends of which brushed where the lace edge of her camisole touched naked skin. He could only stand there, body frozen, heart hammering, as he tried to find his composure.

She'd called him Michael. And she'd done as he asked.

The two intimacies together were enough to shift the ground beneath his feet.

"You coming?" she called from across the faux-marble monstrosity.

After sweeping a hand over his mouth, Mike stifled his grin and joined her. She wasn't anything to him yet. Not more than a bundle of memories from six years ago, layered with the complexities of finding himself her colleague. But his body was clear for take-off. He was already beginning to wonder what Leah would be like as his mistress, where being granted any request from such a woman was a treasured gift.

The flashing thrill of their bike ride was long gone. He sank into an easy calm that belied his keyed-up body. This was either going to happen or it wouldn't. The decision wasn't his to make. She would grant permission if the time came. Mike followed her through to the casino, mentally releasing himself into her care.

"Pick your poison." Leah opened her arms to the casino floor. Hundreds of people shared space with gaming tables and a circus worth of noise and lights. The buzz and clink and ring of the slot machines filled every silent hollow. "Anything you want."

Mike ignored the invitation. That's not how he wanted to play. "I suppose it depends on how much we have to lose."

Laughing, Leah shook her head. "Not much then."

"More trouble in paradise, Miss Flying Ace?"

"We live for the speed, not the pay." She swiped a tendril of hair off her cheek. "I've been going out with Jon too much. Need to remember that not everyone has a limitless store of cash."

Her casual mention of another man cooled the hard-and-fast run of his libido. "Jon?"

"Jon Carlisle, call sign Tin Tin. He's freaking *loaded.*" A sneaky grin shaped her lips. "You'll meet him Tuesday."

Mike humored her with a nod. The exchange reminded him just how much history he was coming into by joining the Aggressors. By military standards, these pilots enjoyed long, long assignments to the same unit. That meant stronger than usual bonds between the pilots, and even more difficulty when forming romantic attachments within a squad.

"Poker, then," she said. "Might as well start with poker."

That found his humor again. "Are you serious? You have just about the world's worst poker face."

"I'm not talking about me. You have unreadable down to a science. Let's go make money."

After a quick stop at an ATM, they exchanged cash for Caesar's chips and found a table of Texas Hold 'Em. Mike took a seat, with Leah scooched in beside him.

Unreadable, eh? He wouldn't have called himself that, not in a million years. But then, he'd been carrying around "Strap Happy" for three years now, always with a straight face—or better yet, with a knowing smile. The world wasn't exactly on

35

board with what he enjoyed in his off hours. Much easier to keep it cool and let folks assume they knew what aroused a guy like him.

"You're not going to be much help if you're sitting beside me," he said.

"You think I'll peek and give something away?"

"If you peek, you *will* give something away."

"Fine. I'll sit here and send you good-luck vibes."

Mike anted up, smothering a snicker. "You do that, Princess."

Two cards were dealt to each of the six players by a fifty-something Hispanic man with a thick mustache. Briefly Mike wondered how many people the dealer had seen come and go. Even in one night he must face-off against hundreds of gamblers intent on a big payout. Some people might've been intimidated by those sorts of odds, but not Mike. He'd made his living battling much tougher challenges for much higher stakes.

"The big blind is ten dollars," the dealer announced. "To you, sir."

Mike acknowledged his responsibility with a mere flick of his eyes. Poker was a way of life where he'd been stationed outside of Kabul—where waiting was a helluva lot worse than any sortie. Waiting for orders. Waiting for news. Even right then, that moment, he was waiting for his stay at Nellis to truly begin. Might as well kill time the old-fashioned way.

He lifted the corner of his cards, catching sight of an ace of clubs and a five of diamonds. Betting continued as the dealer turned the three flop cards face down, and then again as he revealed the turn—a queen of spades. Mike had already sorted out his competition from his marks. His only real opponent was a short balding man with a bright red birthmark across his scalp.

Leah, however, was proving quite a distraction. She ordered Mike a beer and herself a Dr. Pepper, then proceeded to pick at his bottle's label. He was able to relegate her to background motion—barely—until she touched his silver cuff.

His whole body tensed. She obviously didn't get it, but the cuff was a silent proclamation of Mike's preferences. He was a sub. Plain and simple. Giving his sexual power to a woman was his biggest turn-on, and seeing Leah touch it, her expression somewhat curious, laid a foggy blanket over his ability to think.

"It's pretty," she said quietly.

Mike cleared his throat. "You're not helping my odds here."

"Not my money to lose."

"How generous of you."

"Who gave it to you?"

With a hand to his temple, he tried to reclaim his strategy for the next round of betting. Leah's knee brushed his thigh, blowing that aim all to hell.

"Call." Mike wasn't exactly sure if that was wise. Nothing about the evening reeked of wisdom. But she was touching his cuff again. The fit of his jeans became considerably less comfortable.

"Who, Michael?"

"You assume someone gave it to me," he said roughly.

She shrugged. "Of course I do. It's too nice. So...?"

"A friend." That was as far as he would go with thoughts of Georgia. One day he might reveal more to the right woman, but for now those four months as her lover were his alone.

"And the final card." The dealer flipped up an ace.

If one more ace waited in the flop, Mike had a chance. He couldn't begin to calculate the odds because Leah had thrown him off his game. So he called, then matched when the bald man upped his bet.

The dealer nodded. "Reveal your cards, gentlemen."

The bald man had managed a respectable hand—two pair with queens high. Mike turned over his ace and five, hoping for the best. Not for the first time that evening, he gave himself over to the whim of fate. He couldn't have survived the last few years without that simple act of faith.

The dealer revealed the flop cards. A third ace gave Mike three of a kind.

Leah squealed. Nah, that wasn't right. She wooted like a drunk hippie girl at a Dave Matthews concert. Then she hugged him round the neck, planting a swift kiss to his temple.

Mike sat there, dazed, extremely turned on and happy to let Lady Luck take the night.

Chapter Five

Leah loved winning. She loved it best when she rocked it out herself, but standing at Mike's side when he took the hand was almost as good. Messing with his head while he tried to keep his mind on the game didn't hurt.

She only meant it as a tease—a little taste of what he couldn't have anymore. That was all. So she kept touching him.

Mostly she trailed her fingers through the slightly too-long hair across the back of his neck. To get that shaggy, he must have taken a nice chunk of leave before showing up at Nellis. She liked the novelty.

What she *really* liked was how he shuddered when she scraped her nails over his skin.

He obviously tried to power through it, winning two more hands and losing one to the older dude across the table. The muscle at the back of his jaw ticked in response.

She was so freaking cruel. To both of them really since nothing could come of it.

The moment in the lobby had meant...something. Mike had steadily watched her mouth as he asked Leah to leave her hair down. He'd been so polite, despite the way his voice hit a rumbling pitch that had made its way down her torso. Lower. Between her legs.

Plenty of guys hit on her. A lot of them had even been fellow squadron members. One of the reasons she was so close with Ryan and Jon was their ability to ignore that she was a chick.

Technically, Mike hadn't even hit on her. He'd asked for such a simple thing. Yet no man had ever been so respectful. Or intense.

The bracelet hadn't helped, either. Well, calling it a bracelet was entirely too feminine. The dully polished silver had barely registered to Leah until his strange reaction, as if she'd poked at a tender spot.

It had been six years. By no means did she think that Mike had spent them locked alone in his bedroom—though that image had its own naughty appeal. After all, she certainly hadn't been alone.

Neither had someone given her a silver cuff that she still wore.

Hot possessiveness slunk through her muscles and made her eyes narrow.

As if moved by their own power, Leah's fingers walked down his arm. The thick muscles and tendons rippled under her touch. She traced the edge of the silver cuff. It was strange. Snug as hell. She could barely wiggle the tip of her index finger between his hair-dusted skin and the metal warmed by his body.

He slanted her a look from those sharp blue eyes. A hint of a grin pushed laugh lines across the top of his cheek. "You're like a dog with a bone, aren't you?"

She shrugged. "Curiosity is one of my biggest failings."

"I don't know." His long fingers stacked and restacked chips into tidy piles. "There's something to be said for exploring boundaries."

"I guess that's why we're fighter pilots, right?" She made herself pull back.

When he chuckled, his thigh bounced against her knee. He shook his head. Streaky gold-brown hair dipped across his temple. "That wasn't the type of boundaries I meant."

"Right," she said. "Because you're so edgy, aren't you?"

He stretched until his mouth brushed the curve of her ear. That her hair was down made the move more intimate, creating a screen from the world. "Wouldn't you like to know?"

"You are *all* talk, Michael Templeton. Remember, I know that for a fact."

His eyes shifted to a deeper blue. Less neon, more devious. "Facts change. After all, Pluto's not a planet anymore."

She laughed, a little relieved that the tension had somewhere to escape. Her nipples had been drawing too hard for comfort. Mike was a buddy now. He'd have to be since they were going to work together.

Wouldn't that just bite her in the ass, if teasing him ended up teasing her. She'd been told all her life that pushing as hard as she did would come back to smack her someday. But there was something different about Mike now. Something she couldn't name. She wanted to take him apart to figure him out.

"Call," he said to the dealer, when she'd barely paid attention. Oh, that was no good.

She edged deeper into his space, near enough that she could smell the faint hint of his cologne. The warm notes of the scent were sultry and went straight to her brain. And deeper. He hadn't worn cologne six years ago. Then he'd been all about Ivory soap.

Had his friend given him the cologne too?

"So what have you been up to, Mike?" The question popped out of its own volition. "Are you dating anyone?"

Amusement was back in his bright blue eyes as he silently laughed at her again. At least this time it wasn't about her ambition.

"If I were, do you think I'd let you lean all over me?" He flipped his cards over as the dealer called. He'd lost.

Maybe she *was* getting to him.

"I am not leaning all over you," she lied. "I'm trying to peek at your hand."

"I thought we agreed there'd be none of that."

"I'm getting bored."

His eyes widened to a degree that ought to be comical. But he also parted his lips on a faked gasp of surprise. Oh. This was bad. His mouth had her thinking dirty things.

She leaned away from him. Not happening. She might like risk, but there was a difference between risk and ridiculous.

"We can't have you bored," he murmured.

She forced a laugh. "You really have no idea. Bad things will happen. Mayhem will ensue."

"Promises, promises." His eyes had gone that deeper blue again.

Weird. She didn't remember them being so changeable before. Then, he had been all bright amusement, in deeds as well as the way he looked at her.

The new Mike wouldn't let her relax. His easygoing attitude, contrasting with the black leather jacket he'd worn on his big-ass bike, was almost more than she could take. And the fucking silver cuff. Only a completely confident guy could carry off something like that.

The way that only added to the yumminess of him? Yeah. She should be heading way deep into ignoring land.

Then he touched her.

Nothing like the rough grabs she'd dodged on occasion. His gaze focused on the bare inch at her waist revealed where her camisole had twisted on one side. The skin over his cheekbones tightened. He trailed two fingers over the waistband of her cargoes, brushing her hipbone.

A shiver worked up her spine. She locked it down as fast as she could. But not before it reached her breasts, making them feel heavier. Fuller.

"Hey, now." She threw the words out as lightly as she could, adding in a neutral smile. "I thought we were trying the friendship thing. That means no touchies."

"Yes, Captain." His smile was back, but it looked more miserly. Sharper at the corners. "I guess you're going to be giving me a lot of orders soon."

What the hell was that strange tone of voice? She had never been very good at reading undercurrents. When a man just said what he wanted, she could decide whether to take him up on it.

"Besides," he continued, turning back to the poker table. "You seem to feel quite free to touch me."

She wound her fingers through his shaggy hair. Pulled. The move was light, but his shoulders tensed again. Even through the material of his T-shirt, she saw the twitch of thick muscles arrowing down his spine. "That's different. I'm the chick."

"All right," he said on a laugh. "That is definitely it." Gathering up his chips, he stood to his full height.

"Aw, come on. I was just starting to have a good time."

He stalked through the casino, dodging a stooped old couple with matching white hair. "Yeah. I could tell."

She sauntered along by his side. The night was taking on a heady edge that had her contemplating bad things. Or maybe very good things.

She'd changed over the last few years. If Mike didn't come up to scratch, she could always take what she needed. No more coy playacting and hoping he would man up. Worst-case scenario had her finishing herself off, just drinking in his newfound gorgeousness as she fingered her clit.

Down, girl. All her lady bits needed to shut the hell up. Banging a coworker would be the fast track to staying a captain forever. A short relationship with Ryan fell under the category of mistake—one they'd been able to keep on the down low. Any more risk than that and she'd pull a reputation.

But damn if she didn't want to take a chance. She lived for risk. Lived for adventure. She never would've thought she'd associate that taste of the blade with Mike.

The way he prowled through the busy casino said maybe she'd been wrong. His profile was sharp, his stride powerful.

A kiss of the forbidden.

The grin he slanted at her didn't help. "Now what?"

She nibbled her bottom lip as she looked around. What said Vegas? What hadn't she done sixty billion times in order to stave off the boredom that chomped at her? "Wanna strip naked and run through the fountains?"

He stopped dead, letting streams of people split around him. King of the freaking world. The way he studied her shot down to her toes. "I almost believe you'd do it."

"Almost? Just try me. I bet you're the one who'd chicken out first."

He lifted his eyebrows, his smile spreading slowly. He bent his head toward hers. God he smelled good, like she could just scarf him down.

"Don't be so sure of yourself, Princess."

"You forget. I *know* you." She walked off. Not like she had any real destination in mind. Just away. The dude was being really unfair, tempting her with a taste of something he couldn't choke up. "You're nothing more than a big teddy bear."

Out of nowhere, Leah found herself hustled behind one of the giant urns that decorated the foyers. Holy crap, how did that happen? She'd barely felt his hand across the dip of her spine before, *whoosh*, she was exactly where he wanted her.

"Has anyone ever told you that you should be careful who you tease?" He loomed over her, his voice dark and low, but she didn't feel intimidated. *Way* beyond strange. She felt...protected, as if he was putting his body between her and the drunken crowds.

Leah made herself shrug. If the way she tucked her hands in her back pockets pushed up her breasts, too bad for him. "I've heard it. But I'm still not scared."

"No? The whole whips-and-chains joke?" He planted a hand on the curve of the urn's rim, right at her hip. "It ain't a joke."

She laughed. It bubbled up from her chest and spilled out without warning. He didn't join her. His bright blues burned into her. Hot. Tempting her to believe.

He couldn't possibly be serious. No chance on that one.

"Prove it, Michael."

Chapter Six

No matter the larger scope of his desires, Mike really wanted to kiss that smug look off her face. She was so sure of herself.

And frankly, she'd put her money on the right pony. If judging by past experience alone, he wouldn't have thought much of their prospects either. They hadn't been fully formed people back then—still too young and uncertain.

He watched the corner of her mouth, the crooked place where her top lip angled higher than its flip side. Risking the ruin of a potential friendship was right there, in the urge to claim more. He wanted permission to think of that quirking mouth as his. Looking at it all day long, hampered by the "just colleagues" label, would leave him in a serious nut twist.

Kissing her was off the table. The best way to help her eat her words and her bright, teasing laughter was to show her how much he'd changed. His needs were so much deeper now.

Straightening, he forced a calming breath into his lungs. "My place, then?"

She rolled her lips into her mouth, as if trying to work sensation back into numb flesh. He knew all about that—numb everywhere except for where his cock swelled. He'd almost forgotten about that other piece of jewelry he wore, until mental and physical arousal collided around a rush of blood.

"You're serious?"

Mike shoved his fists into his jeans. No touching. Not without permission. He'd already done more than he'd planned, but holy fuck, she'd been messing with him. A slip of skin at her waist had seemed a sanity-saving liberty after an hour enduring Leah's oh-so-innocent flirtations.

The flirt was still very much at play, but her lighthearted attitude was proved a lie by the looks she slid down his bare arm. The backs of his triceps, the bulge where his biceps dipped toward his elbow, the tracks of muscle down his forearm—her lingering admiration was as strong as a caress.

Chin to his chest, he angled a sharp gaze from beneath his brows. "Yes, I'm serious. But it's your call. Who knows what sort of demonic implements I have waiting for you."

Another laugh. She shoved a restless hand through her unbound hair. He liked that. The nerves. It was a fair sight better than the *no way in hell* sign she'd been posting at the karaoke bar.

"You know, I've been trying to figure out what's different about you," she said.

He blinked. "And have you?"

"Sure, Captain Comedy. You've decided you have a sense of humor."

"Yeah, that's it."

"Fine. Whatever. Let's venture into the dungeon, shall we?"

With a quick thanks to Lady Luck, Mike nodded.

As if walking Leah to dinner, he offered his arm—the bare arm she couldn't stop drooling over. His hopes for the evening amounted to very little more than worshiping her body, but having her appreciate him in return gave him a crisp thrill. Pleasing her in any way, even with something as basic as how he looked, tingled down his spine.

He was going to have a fucking hell of a time riding his bike with a hard-on.

Valets brought the motorcycles around, looking mildly ridiculous in their matched uniforms. Their smiles made Mike laugh. Just two young guys doing their workaday job in Sin City. He was glad the bikes gave them a grin.

Leah caught his eye, sharing his mirth. She was just plain *fun*. Six years ago, her every waking breath had been plans and strategies and the hard edge of ambition. In truth, it had left him cold. Now he could almost forget what awaited them both come Tuesday morning. Him in a simulator. Her in charge.

She shrugged into her flight jacket, as if unconsciously reinforcing Mike's realization. Pilot. Colleague.

Boredom was making them both fools.

"Leah?"

Pausing, her hands wrapped around her helmet, she tossed loose hair over her shoulder. God, she'd do that if she were riding him—that sharp flick. He swallowed back a groan.

"What?" she asked. "Chickening out? That doesn't bode well for your future as an Aggressor."

He grinned at that. She had no idea.

Screw it. Tuesday was a long-ass ways away.

Jacket on, helmet on, he gunned the throttle. One of the valets gave him a thumbs-up, which made him grin all over again. He angled his bike around the semicircular driveway. Leah's squealing engine revved in reply, right on his tail.

The Strip was almost painfully bright, all neon and shimmer. Leah rode beside him. Her posture was taut and low as if she'd been the professional motocross racer, not her dad. Did she take nothing by half measures?

For the sake of their evening together, Mike hoped not.

The traffic thinned as they continued back toward base, giving him time enough to wonder if he'd read her wrong. Maybe his hard-up arousal had been feeding him signs that weren't there. She was just fucking with him. It wasn't like she had any idea what really awaited her at his place.

No whips, unless you counted the corded tassels on his flogger.

No chains, unless you counted the locks on his wrist restraints.

And none of that was meant for her.

If a woman didn't go for power, the whole prospect might seem damn strange, or even a turn-off. He hadn't made that mistake since meeting Georgia, but he didn't like the idea of misreading Leah so badly. The evening wouldn't be a complete loss, no matter what happened, but the hard ache in his chest and the itch under his skin wanted more than a passable hump.

If for no other reason, he wanted her to know how much he'd changed. He knew they could be amazing together.

The pink terror of a bike zipped past him. Leah flipped him off then gunned it again. Mike laughed. He couldn't hear it and could barely feel it, but his laugh was deep and rich. Doubt fizzled to nothing. If ever there was a woman who liked being in charge, it was Princess Leah.

He leaned low over his BMW and let the engine get its growl on. Easily he pulled alongside her and even edged ahead before backing off. The power was there. The sheer blunt muscle. He didn't need to blow her out of the water to make the point.

A minute later they hauled ass out of the city. The environs just outside Nellis were the type preferred by military the world over, tidy and small. Mike turned on to a side street, amused when Leah had to double back to follow. A few wan streetlights seemed like caveman times compared to the glare of Las Vegas Boulevard.

He steered into his driveway. Leah killed her engine almost in tandem, leaving the night air of that tiny neighborhood suddenly quiet. Her laugh followed as she stripped off her helmet. "Shit, that was fun."

Mike banked the hard shudder brought on by her satisfied words. "Keep it down, will ya?"

"Says the man on the Harley." She eyed the little single-car garage as if she'd never seen one before. "Really? Like, a real house?"

"Why not?"

"Your secret isn't whips and chains, Michael. It's a wife and three kids."

"You keep hedging like this and I'll assume I was right."

She went toe-to-toe with him, chin up. Although she wasn't a short woman, she barely came up to his collarbones—more to do with his height rather than her lack of stature. "Right about what?"

"About you being scared."

Daring her was like cutting a line for an addict. She seemed unable to resist. Her baby-doll eyes took on that heavy-lidded condescension, telling him he wasn't worth noticing. He stifled the urge to back down and apologize. After all, he stood a better chance of getting what he wanted if she were slightly...pissed off.

Just a little.

"I don't get scared, Templeton. You should know that about me."

"Everyone has limits. Secrets. Dark places."

"Well, that is why we're here, isn't it? C'mon then, dungeon master."

She led the way up to his front door. *She* led *him*. Mike hid a grin behind his fist.

He flipped on the overhead light in the entryway, groping around in the unfamiliar space.

"So why the full-on house? Most single guys go for the bachelor pad deluxe."

"Complete with locker-room-stank smell? Not my style." He hung his helmet and jacket on a couple of pegs and nodded for Leah to do the same. "You want something to drink?"

This was a test, even if she didn't know it. If Leah ordered a double Jack and Coke, he'd give up on the idea of anything too elaborate. Rules were important. Rules like no drinking. Both parties needed to know the boundaries and when to stop. He wouldn't hand his keys to a girl drenched in alcohol, and he wouldn't hand over his body either.

Leah slipped out of her flight jacket with a shrug. The scent of warm leather clung to her. "Just a soda. Whatever."

"Cool," he said on an exhalation. "Come on in."

She followed him through the near-empty rooms, looking everything over. He didn't have curtains yet. No blinds. The best he'd managed in the bedroom was a heavy blanket over the curtain rod. Their footsteps echoed on the hardwood. The nearly empty house was fit for ghosts to haunt.

Mike grabbed two cans of Coke Zero out of the fridge, which didn't contain much else. Half-and-half for his morning coffee. A jug of milk for cereal. Lunch meat and condiments. His cabinets didn't look much better. "I'd offer you a glass but I can't remember where I put them."

"No problem."

She tabbed it open and took a swallow. Mike found himself staring at the flex of muscles along her throat. He wanted his mouth right there, sucking.

"But no, seriously," she said. "Why a house?"

He leaned against the countertop, stretching his legs. "Maybe how I was brought up. You know, the rhythm of seasonal chores."

"No mowing here."

"You have no imagination. I bet I can get some grass going." He swigged a few gulps of Coke, glad for a moment to regain his composure. If he could breathe, he could do this right. "Owning is out of the question, obviously, but I like something that sort of pretends to be normal."

"A man's bungalow is his castle?"

"Sure. Why not."

And he waited. No way was the first move going to be his. Her frustration and slight edge of confusion showed in her nervous energy. She was an active, buzzing sort of woman anyway, but without purpose she turned downright fidgety. "So?"

"So?" he echoed.

"You got me here."

"True."

She took a deep breath that showed off her rack. Nipples still tight. Goddamn.

"So why haven't you tried to kiss me yet?"

Mike pinched his fingers around the lip of the countertop. "Because you haven't told me I could."

The hauteur was gone. So was any obvious frustration. She narrowed her eyes, using her gaze as a pickax to dig into his brain. He opened up to her inspection. He had nothing to hide. Not anymore.

"What is this about?" she asked carefully. The tone of her voice was soft, slightly awed, as if she perched on the edge of understanding.

Mike's throbbing dick was begging for her to make that leap.

"Come on. Let me show you something." He pushed away from the counter and walked with stiff legs to his bedroom. Sitting on the bed, he forced his body to unclench. *Breathe.*

She stood in the doorway, casually leaning against the frame. But she teased the ends of her hair—a nervous tell. "Mike, talk to me."

He resisted her command, instead nodding to his bedside table. When he'd unpacked his gear that morning, he certainly hadn't thought he would be using it so soon. "Open it."

After a moment's hesitation, she sauntered forward. "Ah. Your proof, I suppose?"

"Sure."

Leah slid open the drawer. Her mouth opened on a quiet noise. Eyes wide, she flashed him a questioning glance. He only shrugged.

She reached in, hands unsteady, and removed a length of leather studded with decorative rivets. A tiny padlock dangled from one end.

His wrist restraints.

Mike swallowed. Hard. He could barely hear past the rushing whirl of blood in his ears. That pulse matched the throb in his cock. For what he hoped would be the last time that night, he took the lead. When Leah turned to him once more, her expression a mess of questions, he lifted his arms and presented her with his wrists.

Chapter Seven

Leah had been to the Grand Canyon twice. She'd scooted right to the edge, letting the yawing depth reach up to suck at her limbs. She'd gotten tingly both times, her head splashing gray on the danger. Such a tiny guardrail had kept her from falling into disaster.

Standing in front of Mike while he quietly held out his wrists was like watching that guardrail fall and splinter. The rush to end all rushes.

The past twenty minutes had been nothing but one long tease. She'd ricocheted up and down, pinging around like a gone-wild piece of shrapnel. Even the zing of riding her bike hadn't been enough to calm her down. An intense ride usually cleared her mind. Not this time.

Mike was serious.

He wasn't.

He was yanking her chain. Trying to be something he wasn't.

Then she'd slid open the drawer. Lengths of leather and circlets of silver were perfectly arranged. Padlocks graded from smallest to largest lined the front wall of the drawer, each mated with its keys. There was a leather-handled flogger and a damn ball gag, as well as a few toys she couldn't identify, some of which were spiky and intimidating.

He hadn't known where his drinking glasses were, but she didn't have a single fucking doubt that he could recite the entire contents of this drawer.

Leah's knees had gone weak. Wet heat spilled down to her pussy. For a long, charged moment, the only sounds in his little house were inhalations and exhalations. They were breathing almost in tandem, both of their chests rising and falling.

The single lamp in the room was on his nightstand. Light draped across the open drawer, making the contents gleam, but not enough reached Mike. His eyes were more shadowy than ever and even more difficult to read. She gripped the leather so that the dull metal rivets bit into her palm.

A single step brought her to stand within his outstretched legs. Her other hand rose slowly, shaking now, to touch his hair. She twisted the thicker mass at his crown. His eyes drifted nearly shut. His outstretched hands folded shut, fingers tucking into his palms. At the casino she'd constrained herself to teasing the ends of his hair. She'd wanted more.

If Mike had already opened up this much, how far was he willing to go?

She couldn't help but yank harder, much more covetously than she'd risked while sitting at the poker table. Already she was walking a fine line of temptation. He shuddered again, feeding whatever it was waking up inside her.

"Exactly what are you offering me, Michael?"

His eyes flashed open. The grin that slipped across his mouth looked a little faked. A little forced. As if he were way more nervous than he seemed. His eyes were that deep, deep blue again. "What do you want to take?"

Holy Christ, the possibilities. The trust he was placing in her hands—her shaking, tingly hands. If she fucked this up... She didn't think she'd ever forgive herself.

"Take the cuff off," she said abruptly.

No sweet talking. No pleases. Just a harsh order that came from the heat twining through her body. She wanted to wrap the leather and metal around his wrist, but she wanted the other cuff gone first—the one someone else had given him. The one he'd still worn, even when he knew the odds were high he'd see Leah that night.

Fuck if he didn't immediately obey. There was a rough-hewn clasp on the tender inside of his wrist that flicked open with a deft, practiced move. Still, he set it carefully on the nightstand, shutting it up so that it rested in a perfect circle. The metal was dull but managed to gleam in the low light.

Without the circlet, his wrist looked both stronger and more naked. Bared.

Until she curled the black leather around it.

God, her hands knew what to do all on their own. She didn't have to think it through. The small silver padlock slipped back through the hasp and shut with a tiny click that sounded ridiculously loud in the quiet room.

Sealed.

Blowing out a tensely held breath, she needed to look away from him as she set the key on the nightstand. Steady blasts of power had her tingling all over, not just in her soaking panties, but in her lungs, her head, her stomach. She was fully involved in a way that had been out of reach for so long. She'd been so damned good lately.

Apparently Mike would be her reward.

When she looked back at him, she found his gaze focused on her mouth like a laser beam. His tiny smile still quirked, until he licked his bottom lip.

They were all mixed up. They hadn't even kissed yet, and she'd closed a leather cuff around his wrist. But then, he'd already revealed his keystone.

She only needed to give her permission.

Delving both hands into his hair, she tugged until his face was tipped up. Another step brought her so near that her breasts brushed his collarbones and his skin-warmed T-shirt.

"Did you know? Back then?" She didn't want to ask but she did anyway. If he'd known about all this, about all they'd been missing, and never told her...

She'd make it very bad for him. In a damn good way, of course.

His thick throat worked over a swallow, his Adam's apple bobbing. "No. I didn't figure it out until three years ago."

That still gave him three years on her. Three years of knowing exactly what he wanted and what he was looking for. The fear of failure had never been her friend. And this was too important to screw up.

She felt suddenly, strangely alone—disconnected from the depths he had probably explored for years. "Touch me."

Immediately his hands looped loosely around her hips. Rough thumbs dipped under the waistband of her cargo pants, stroking over her hipbones. That naughty grin of his spread across his mouth.

"What is it?" She scraped her nails lightly under his hair, across his scalp.

He shook his head, but she only tugged tighter. She was really coming to like the slightly shaggy length of it. It would be a damn shame when he cut it before Tuesday.

That realization trickled ice water down her spine. What the hell would she do once they were back at work?

She pushed away the dose of reality just as fast as it popped up. This time was for them. For experimenting. Any consequences would wait—hopefully until much later.

"Spill it," she said. Her voice had taken on a crisp, warning tone she'd only ever used on unruly airmen who thought they could do a half-assed maintenance job on her plane just because she was a chick.

Mike's smile only grew wider. "You're taking to this rather well."

"I am, aren't I?" She traced two fingers down the sharp lines of his cheekbones, then back over his ears. This scenario fit so well, as if she'd cracked open a part of her psyche that had always been there. Waiting. Lurking. "I take it you like orders? Being told what to do?"

"To an extent," he hedged. "I've got limits. Hard limits. Things I won't do."

"Tell me." She didn't want to break this tension before they even got started. The slow burn was threatening to send her up in flames.

"No marks that show when I'm in uniform."

Fuck if that didn't send another pulse of heat through her bones. The converse of it—what he wasn't saying. That he'd allow her to mark him in other ways.

His thumbs kept up small strokes over her hipbones, delving deeper. Her stomach sucked concave on a particularly tempting shiver.

"No permanent damage, of course. I don't enjoy blood play, so no breaking the skin." His gaze dropped from hers. "The rest...we could probably discuss later. Most of them involve third parties."

She curved a hand around the underside of his chin and tugged up. "No, keep looking at me. I like the way you watch me."

His fingers gripped the top of her ass. "How do I watch you?"

"Like you're hungry. For me."

"That's because I am."

That did it. She went flying over the edge of the canyon, spun wild on the absolute rush of his faith.

She wrenched his hair. "Kiss me." Another order. They spilled out of her mouth more easily each time.

"All you had to do was tell me," he growled.

He stretched up and she leaned down at the same time. Hot. Fast. Immediate. A coming together of more than lips, more than his tongue in her mouth. Their teeth clicked together. Hard.

She moaned into him. His hands spread across her lower back. The blend of cold metal and warm leather scraped her skin. She bit his lower lip, which gave slightly under her teeth.

Leah pulled back, gripping his silky hair when his mouth tried to follow her.

God, it was like she'd been waiting six years for this force. This energy. Every move he'd ever made was recast as a silent promise of that moment...

Leah reached out and found the matching cuff in the drawer. It locked around his other wrist with another quiet click she could barely hear over the whooshing in her ears. Lacing her fingers through his, she pulled his hands into the small space between their bodies to look at the matching cuffs. Strong, rough wrists. Taut tendons. A light dusting of golden hair. All of it bound, as he'd allowed her to do.

"Fuck, that's hot," she breathed.

"You're telling me."

She kissed him the second time, taking his mouth with hers. Her fingers clawed under his T-shirt, then yanked it up over his head. She held back a soft moan when she finally saw him bared.

He looked every bit as good as she'd thought he would. The thick, heavy curves of his pecs were dusted with a whorl of golden-brown hair. His tightly sprung abs weren't just a six-pack but a freaking *eight*-pack. She wanted to bite her way down his body and scrape her nails over the rows of tiny ligaments that bound his ribs to his stomach.

With her hands at his shoulders, she pushed him onto the mattress until he stretched out sideways across the wide space. He *let* her, leashing all that latent strength.

She crawled onto the bed, over him, kissing him the whole time. Her knee grazed over the thick bulge of his cock, all wrapped up in his jeans. She paused, then deliberately did it again. A little hint of danger. She absorbed his full-body shudder.

Even through the thick denim, he was huge. His cock seemed bigger than she remembered, but maybe that was his excitement. He was masculine enough to club things, all full-on Neanderthal, but he didn't. He was holding back, obviously reining himself in. Waiting on her. Waiting on her commands.

Her thoughts hit her so strongly that she needed to press flat against him, edging her knees out to straddle him. She laced her fingers through the bands of the leather cuffs and pinned him down with his wrists by his head.

She took another kiss, even rougher this time, trying to steel herself for what she might do next. Nothing prevented the wild-fire heat that roared up once she fitted her pussy over his cock and rocked. Twice. God, that felt so damn good, like she could come from the pressure alone.

Taking a deep breath, she forced herself to pull back. Her tongue slicked over her bottom lip, drawing in his taste— sweetness from the sodas, plus a salty bite that was only him.

"Michael," she purred, intentionally grazing her nipples over his bare chest. "You do realize I'm going to do very bad things to you?"

Chapter Eight

Mike had lost the rhythm of his own breath. It pressed out of his lungs in fits and hot gulps. Every inhalation brushed his naked skin against Leah's lush breasts. He wiggled his fingers, which tingled almost to the point of numbness.

"Yes," he rasped. "I realize that."

She was going to do bad things to him, and thank Christ for it. The razor blade of the last few moments had dulled, replaced by a different sort of danger. No more worry about whether he'd misjudged her—only a calm hunger as his arousal spiked.

Relief came first. Then anticipation. His pleasure was another person's domain now. That simple release held an appeal he'd never been able to explain. From it he found the most satisfaction.

"You're shaking," she whispered, her voice somewhat awed.

"I am."

"Is it me or the getup?"

"Both."

She leaned in close and licked him from the notch at the base of his throat up to his chin. His evening stubble rasped under her wet tongue. "Explain it to me."

"If I didn't want you and trust you, I wouldn't have asked you to open that drawer." He swallowed. "The right woman plus the right moment."

"The right woman, huh? I like that."

As if to prove the point, she shoved down on the restraints she held, sinking the backs of his hands into the lightweight comforter. Her mouth pushed over his. She angled her head so that their lips matched. No wasted space. No room to maneuver. He took her kisses as she offered them—fierce, hard, greedy. The sweep of her tongue over his sent a hot jolt down to his guts. The hard-on he'd been sporting half the night was a beast now, eager to come out to play.

But that was her choice. Her decision.

Mike sank into the freedom of it. He let his mind drift on pure sensation. She still tasted of Coke, but that was giving way to the woman beneath. Her breath fanned across his cheek as she dove in for another frantic kiss. He wanted to tell her she could slow down. He wasn't going anywhere. Yet he remained quiet, absorbing her eagerness like the burn of three fingers of bourbon.

She released his hands and sat up. With a quick toss of her arms over her head, she was topless. Just like that.

A clutching noise grated out of his throat. His upper body jerked as if he'd been struck. Christ, to receive pain from this woman...

He yanked that idea back down and shoved it away. He'd lose it if he got ahead of himself. Keeping control around Leah was going to be difficult enough without supposing more.

"Oh, that was fun," she said with a laugh.

"What?" He didn't sound like himself. Wrapped and wound, he was a turbine pushed to overheating.

"Seeing your face. I could do anything, couldn't I?" A bright smile turned those crooked lips into a masterpiece. "I could touch myself right now without even letting you out of your jeans. I think I could get off just watching your face."

"But you won't."

She painted her hands across his abs in a slow, worshipful slide. Her fingers thumped softly over every rib. "You hope."

"You won't," he said again with more force. The only thing he had over her now was experience, and even that was likely to be fleeting. She'd wrapped his wrists as if she'd done it for years. "Otherwise it'd be like having an entire buffet laid out for your pleasure, but you stick to a bologna sandwich."

"So you're my buffet?"

"That's how you're looking at me. Turns me on, Princess."

She tweaked his nipples so hard that he flinched. "No. No 'Princess'. Not here."

His laugh felt good, just a small release to the pressure. "Noted." He caught her gaze again then ducked his eyes. "It turns me on, Leah."

"But *you* don't look at me. Why not?" She smiled and licked up from his navel—all wet and ticklish and sexy as hell. "Wait, don't tell me. Permission again?"

He nodded. Her hair brushed over his abs, and the angle of her torso intensified the push of her pussy against his rock-hard cock.

"Well, here's the deal, Michael." He couldn't suppress the shudder that worked down his spine. Leah tipped her head to the side. "What...? *Michael?*"

Rolling his eyes to the ceiling, he fought for calm. Fought to breathe.

"That's it, isn't it? You like your full name." She grinned against his stomach then bared her teeth. At that sweet scrape, testing such sensitive skin, Mike made fists. She tugged the waistband of his jeans. "Are you listening to me?"

"Yes, ma'am."

"Oh, I do like that." She tugged again, which focused his attention where he most wanted her fingers. "Here's the deal, Michael. I *want* you to look at me. Whenever you want. I give you that permission. Understand?"

"Yes, ma'am," he said on a long exhalation.

He indulged. Because Leah Girardi was a beautiful woman. Her lean thighs bunched around his waist, clasping against his with every movement. The breasts she'd bared were full despite her trim physique, tipped with coffee-and-cream areolas and pert, almost small nipples. Mike swirled his tongue over his lower lip as if licking her flesh.

"That's right," she whispered. Her fingers clenched along the V line of muscles that arrowed down from his hips. "Do you like what you see, Michael?"

"Yes, ma'am."

"Good boy. But now it's my turn. I want you naked."

Mike sank deeper into the arousal that was quickly chipping into his brain, making inroads toward his control. Sinking in was easier than fighting it. He absorbed it like any extreme sensation—pleasure or pain, hot or cold, fear or desire. At that moment they all felt like Leah.

She thumbed open the top button and wrenched down his zipper. No grace. He relaxed even further. They were in this together. A partnership of sorts, despite the lopsided control.

"Up."

Mike boosted his hips. The jeans took another time or two to give up on his ass. Leah's look of concentration and wonder held him enraptured. So much of what he wanted was in that expression.

"Damn, you're built," she said with a laugh.

Another chuckle from Mike. He definitely felt like her own personal smorgasbord, complete with caviar and mimosas. "Thank you, ma'am."

"Keep up that *ma'am* stuff. Very nice."

Leah's hand trailed down the front of his boxer briefs. Dark brown baby-doll eyes widened. She made a little "O" with her mouth then slid her forefinger inside the elastic band. Mike tensed. His limbs shook. She lifted her gaze to watch his face. That tickling rub turned sharp as she scraped his skin with her nail.

Mike breathed through his mouth. She did it again, and he bit his back teeth together, resisting the hard, primal pull that demanded more. Throw her down. Open her legs. Drive deep.

"That is a beautiful thing to watch," she murmured.

"What is?"

"Your face. Holding back. Being good for me."

"I'm trying."

"I know. And you deserve a reward." She dipped her whole hand into his briefs. Her damp palm closed over his shaft.

Mike's hips rose involuntarily. He thrust into her closed fist.

"Be still." Her no-nonsense tone froze every muscle.

She nodded once. Funny how such a small measure of approval set a fire in his chest.

"Now relax," she said.

Doing his best, he forced each muscle group to unfurl the gathered tension. Between his shoulders, down his spine, in the bunching of his abs—then lower to his thighs, ass, calves. Even his toes. He shuddered on a slow, slow exhalation.

"Very nice, Michael. I'm impressed."

"Thank you, ma'am."

Apparently a lot more confident about his control than he was, Leah resumed her exploration of his erection. The treasure she found there, and Mike's pleasure in seeing her shock, was a twin jolt to his nerves.

"My, you are full of surprises." She caressed the ring that banded his cock just beneath the head. "Do you wear it all the time?"

Words swam just outside of his comprehension as she kept petting.

"Michael. Answer me."

He fisted his fingers in his hair. "Not on duty. Can get distracting."

"I can imagine. It's lovely. Who bought it for you?"

"I did."

"Good. Then it can stay." The "O" was back, shaping her mouth as she admired him. A hot wave of tingles flushed his naked body. His skin felt too pinched, too sharp. "I wonder what it would feel like for me."

"Try it."

"Ask me," she said.

"For what?"

"What it is you want."

God, he couldn't think. Drums pounded behind his eyes. He watched, transfixed, as she swirled a drop of fluid around his head. "Not going to last long that way," he gasped.

Leah eased back on her heels. "You *will* last. My orders. Got it? If you come now, I get up and walk out."

"You haven't been doing this long enough to bluff."

"Try me," she said tartly.

She looked like a Valkyrie or a demonic ballerina, all soft features and fierce control. He didn't want her to go—positive, suddenly, sure that she meant what she'd said. So he locked it down. He had a raging hard-on to end all hard-ons, but getting her permission was what he really wanted. Satisfying the fierce, biting need of his body was a secondary concern. He'd indulge once she gave the say-so.

Because she would. Eventually. He just had to hold out that long.

"Now, back to what you want, Michael. Tell me."

He imagined thrusting his dick between her beautiful lips. Balanced between what he wanted and what he didn't think he could control, Mike forced out the words. "I want you to know what my ring feels like in your mouth."

She grasped him fully. A spike of light hit behind his eyes. Gritting his teeth, he twisted his hands in his hair again—the way she had.

"You had such good manners earlier, pretty boy. Where have they gone?"

"My apologies, ma'am."

"That's a start." She slipped off the bed, poised between his tense thighs. "Go on."

"Will you take me in your mouth? Please?"

"Much better." Again she swiped her thumb over his head to swirl the fluid. Then she licked her palm, slowly, starting at the fleshy pad. He shuddered, clenched his fingers.

She stopped mid-lick. "Now wait a second, Michael. I didn't say you could tug your own hair."

She shimmied up his body, slinking her breasts along every inch of skin along the way. Fingers twined with his, she pulled his hands away from his head. The points of her elbows held his forearms in place as she petted the hair back from his temples. "This is mine, isn't it?"

"Yes, ma'am."

"Like the rest of you?"

"Yes, ma'am."

"Good. Up to the headboard."

Mike's chest clenched as she scooted back to the bedside table. She frowned as she peered into his collection. For a moment their playacting dropped away—just a bit.

"The length of chain," he said softly. "Lower right corner."

"Thank you." She took the opportunity to shrug out of her cargoes. A flaming pink thong the same shade as her motorcycle threaded up her toned ass. "Condom?"

"Medicine cabinet over the sink."

He lay there on the pillows, stripped of all clothes except for his briefs. His arms remained outstretched where she'd left them. Waiting, grabbing at the last threads of his control, he admired the shake and bounce of her body as she snagged the box of Trojans.

"Good," she said, returning.

"What is?"

"You watching me. And holding still. Very good, Michael."

Pleasure fizzed under his skin. He was coming to need that feeling, knowing he'd satisfied some expectation of hers—no matter how small. It was his reward for letting go.

For another fleeting moment, she lost her composure. She stood by the side of the bed, nude except for her thong. The length of chain rested in one palm, the box of condoms in the other.

"What is it?" he asked.

"I..." Whatever doubts she'd briefly wrestled met their match. She stood straighter. "We'll need a safe word, don't you think?"

Chapter Nine

Leah knew what BDSM was. No doubt. It wasn't really possible to be an adult without soaking up some peripheral knowledge. Most of the images she'd seen were of women on their knees, collars wrapped around their tiny necks and thick cocks in their mouths. None of that had tripped her triggers, so she'd figured the kink scene wasn't for her.

Standing beside the bed with a length of cold, implacable chain in one hand and a box of condoms in the other? No—even better than that. Looking down at Michael fully extended on the bed, waiting on her pleasure?

Oh yeah. That did it. Majorly.

So she whipped out what knowledge she had. Safety first. That meant a word she'd have to obey, though she guessed they wouldn't go quite that far. He had three years of experience on her and an entire drawer of stuff, some of which she'd never seen.

All of it added up to making a safe word a bit of a game, but one she'd gladly play.

"Well?" she prompted, smiling. "A word?"

The lovely muscles bisecting his abs jumped and twitched. She put the box of condoms down on the side table, then edged one knee onto the bed. The chain he'd pointed out was on the small side, with spring clasps of matching delicacy. They'd hook right into the hasps on his cuffs without needing to remove those rough little padlocks.

Biting her bottom lip as she concentrated, she trailed the links up the center of his body. The end in her hand had warmed, but what slid against his skin had to be chilly. Jarring.

"I'm not continuing until you give me one." Her voice sounded throaty. Totally new. She was riding a fine edge of control.

His shoulders twitched again. He still didn't pull his arms down, though it was obvious how much determination that required. "How about red? Green will be good, keep going. Red, stop immediately."

"I draw the line at making you ask 'mother may I?' That would be creepy." She chuckled quietly as she hooked one end of the chain to his wrist. It helped her to ignore the fact that yes, she was strapping up a totally hot dude—a guy about whom she'd complained wouldn't know how to fuck rough if he had his balls in a vise. Hell, maybe that would've gotten them to this point way faster.

His grin was wide and playful. But a little wild too. "We definitely aren't shooting for creepy."

Intentionally she slid naked breasts across his shoulders, drawing out the movement for maximum contact. She threaded the chain through his headboard, which had obviously been selected—or even made—for play like this. Multiple heavy oak slats stood between the center and corner posts.

Despite all Leah's teasing, her torments, and the way she kept raking her nails down his torso, Mike stayed still. Patient. He watched her the whole damn time, as if she'd become the center of his sexual universe.

Christ that was hot.

She pinched his nipple, lightly at first, until his eyes flashed and his lips slightly parted. He liked that. So she flicked the edge of her nail over the flat disc. His hips jumped.

She grinned on a heady surge of power. "You're very responsive."

"It's situational."

"So you don't walk around with your shirts driving you nuts all the time?" She swept her hand down his body in a fast stroke then took hold of his eager cock. He was so hard that he brushed up against his navel, peeking out from under his boxers. One long stroke nestled the base of her thumb against his jewelry. "How about this? Is the ring always on your mind? Reminding you when you think about sex?"

He shuddered, and it was an obvious strain to keep his hips down like she'd ordered.

"Good boy," she cooed. "Now, answer me."

"Yes. Every time my dick twitches even the slightest bit, I notice."

The rawness of his expression was almost enough to make her explode. His lips were drawn. The skin over his cheekbones was flushed red. She rewarded him by stripping his boxers down off his hips. His cock bounced free. A tiny drip of precome on the tip shone in the low light.

She straddled his thighs. The dusting of his hair tickled the tender inside of her legs.

"When you saw me in Paulie's," she said slowly. She couldn't help but wrap her fingers around his thick length. He was so damn hard for her. "Did you feel the ring then?"

"Fuck, yeah." His eyelids drifted to half-mast on a sigh, but he didn't stop watching her. "As soon as you turned around and looked at me."

Such honesty deserved another reward. She nodded, licking her lips absently. A single flick sent her hair spilling back over her shoulder.

Leah had never minded giving head. Many women seemed to consider it a chore, or something to push past before the fun stuff started. But she'd always dug the feeling of power of having a guy at her whim, under her control.

This was so much more. With Mike laid out before her, arms stretched above his head and latched to the headboard, Leah *throbbed* with power. Just...mind-blowing. His hefty cock nudged toward her on an involuntary twitch. She nuzzled her cheek against his shaft then scraped her nails through the neatly trimmed hair around his balls.

A taut ligament at the top of his thigh was just begging for a nibble, so she set her teeth to his hot skin. Bit down. Licked against the red mark she'd left.

Through it all, he stayed so tightly tethered. He didn't even tug on the thin chain holding him to the bed. It was all him. His restraint. Given to her.

She ringed her tongue against the smooth loop of metal tucked under his head. The shiny silver had been warmed by his hard cock—something for her to play with, to slide under her lips as she sucked him into her mouth. God, he tasted good. Clean, with just a hint of salty. Manly in the best way.

Her fingers found the smooth stretch of his lower abs where his torso angled toward his groin. She reached past his stomach and pinched his nipples once, twice, matching the rhythm of her mouth over his cock.

"Christ, Leah," he growled. His thighs pulsed subtly between her knees. "I'm not going to last long if you keep that up."

She drew her mouth off him abruptly. Ringing her fingers around the base of his cock, she locked her grip until her knuckles dug into his groin. "What did you call me?"

He gulped, but his eyes only blazed brighter. Bluer. Almost fluorescent. "Ma'am, I meant."

"Much better." She freed the smile that had been collecting behind her lips. With a single nail tip, she followed the line of a vein along his shaft. "You have a pretty, pretty cock. Did I ever tell you that before?"

He shook his head. "No, ma'am."

"I'm not surprised." She hadn't been as self-assured as she was now, or as free with her words. "Do you know what I want to do with this cock?"

He made fists around the links that bound him to the heavy oak headboard. What a sexy picture of depravity he made. The comforter and pillows were regular masculine fare. A cotton blanket and white pillowcases. His wrists, wrapped in black leather and silvered rivets, stretched over them.

"Feel free to tell me what you want, ma'am," he finally said. The subservient words were technically right, but underneath lurked a tone she couldn't place, as if he was subtly taunting her.

She ignored it. Reached for a condom. Ripped it open. "You're lucky I'm in a good mood. Because I want to ride you."

He grinned. His hands opened and closed around the chains, but that was his only hint of edginess. She'd have to push him further to earn more of a reaction. But she didn't have that sort of time. If she didn't fuck him soon, her body would go up in a ball of flame. Already her pulse roared in her ears and between her legs.

She wrapped the condom down his long, thick length, all sorts of silly giddy that it was transparent. Through it, she could still see the gorgeous ring snugged up against the head of his cock.

Her panties were wet when she pulled them off. Soaked. At least she wasn't alone. Mike's hard-on practically jumped toward her.

She rose up on her knees and canted her hips back. Curling her hands around his shaft, she slanted his head to rub against her clit. Tiny shivers worked down her legs and up under her ribs. She bent her chin to her chest. Long hair slipped over her shoulder.

"Oh, that's good," she breathed. "I could come just like this, rubbing your cock on my pussy. Would you mind?" She flashed him a bright, shiny grin. "Oh, that's right. You've given up your say."

His stomach firmed into a perfect grid of muscles. The cords along his neck popped. Still he said nothing. His gaze focused relentlessly on *her*.

She liked that more than anything. Maybe a hidden font of vanity. Maybe the power trip. Whatever the reason, the result was good. Head-numbingly good. Dive-off-a-cliff-without-a-parachute good.

Rearing back, she planted a hand flat on the bed behind her. She angled his dick so that the decorative ring brushed her clit, over and over again, until she was seconds from coming.

She bit her bottom lip to drive back the threatening orgasm.

His hips jumped. His triceps swelled out in lovely lines of definition as he strained against his own will.

"Ah-ah," she breathed. Honestly, deep down underneath the warning, she was loving it, soaking up every bit of attention. She relished that she could push him to flinching, even when he was trying not to. "No moving until I say so."

"Please, ma'am. Let me move."

"Why should I?" She rubbed his cock head between her lips. Wetness soaked down to where her fingers circled his jewelry. "I'm enjoying myself. Immensely."

His grin was a dare extended and accepted, all at once. "Give me permission to move so I can fuck you the way you want. The way your body needs. Hard and fast."

She shuddered with full-body excitement. Her hand clenched his dick securely enough that he shook. Good. She didn't want to be alone in this.

"Have you been good enough?"

"You tell me, ma'am."

She reared up on her knees until the head of his cock tucked into her. "I have no idea, honestly. But you know what, Michael? I know for damned sure that I've been good enough for my rewards."

With her knees on either side of his hips, Leah spread one hand across his stomach, wishing her nails were more than blunted tips. She wanted to dig into him, to grab on and ride.

God, he filled her so well. Stretching, tingling, until she felt him all the way through her body in deep throbs. Head falling back, the tips of her hair brushed against her ass. That soft, teasing flick was a direct contrast to his penetration.

She ran her hands up his thickly muscled body then bent low to open her mouth over the thin skin covering his collarbones. With the smallest bite, he bucked under her.

"Now, Michael," she whispered. "Now you can move."

Chapter Ten

Her words were a starter pistol.

Mike surged. His hips flexed off the mattress, powering his body into hers. Holding back had been worth it. Even all those years-ago missteps had been worth it, just to hear her hard grunt. She took all of him easily, but with a pussy so snug that his brain dissolved away. Only a few titillating words lingered here and there. Heat. Slick. *Fuck.*

He had a point to prove. Mindless and bound, he also wanted this to be better, *hellaciously* better, than what they'd shared before. So he fought his gathering orgasm like he'd once fought to stay conscious during a particularly grueling G-force simulation. The body could be controlled.

He squeezed his hands into fists, right where the length of silver chain rattled against the headboard. With a deep inhalation, he forced his thrusts to slow. Now it was all about the grind, deep and long.

Leah moaned. "Shit, like that."

She nibbled down from his neck, toward the erect nubs of his nipples. Mike watched as she flicked out her tongue. He answered that tingling snap of heat with another long grind.

He had her permission to move, yes, but the act of fucking her was making him greedy. Wants that had been easier to hold back a few minutes ago became an unstoppable current. He wanted to palm her breast and use his teeth as she was doing now. Only after she was mindless under his steady attention would he suck deeply, so slowly.

Most of all he wanted to taste her. Mike could smell her arousal, could nearly imagine her sweet cream sliding over his tongue.

The measured pace of his hips took on a frantic edge. His chest ached from the burning breaths he couldn't inhale fast enough. Leah's panting, purring noises were going to drive him insane.

She reared up from his chest and flicked her hair back over her shoulder, just as he'd pictured. The fusion of possible and actual made him smile despite how his quest for control was ripping his body apart.

"Smiling, Michael? At a time like this?"

"Hell yeah."

With her hands pressed flat against his hips, just in front of her thighs, she applied pressure. Hard pressure. The sudden resistance made him fight all the harder to get up, get *into* her. Only her words killed the impulse.

"Stop, Michael."

He growled. His back arched off the pillows. Tensing against the chain for the first time—really testing its strength and his—he managed to do as he was told.

Hips still, lungs inflating his chest on quick inhalations, he was surprised by the wash of gray that covered his vision. He hadn't been this far gone in so long. She was playing him like a practiced mistress. The sweetness. The raunch. The power.

"God, have you any idea what that does to me?" she asked.

No matter how she praised him, her husky words held an element of threat that did vicious things to his guts. She was pleased, but only for now. He would have to keep proving himself.

Over and over. As long as this was the payoff.

"Now hold still. Still as you can. I want to bounce for a while." She added a seriously cute smile to her wicked intentions. Her thighs tensed. Using Mike's taut abs for support, she lifted almost to the point of withdrawal. He would've slipped free had he moved at all. But he didn't. Just bit his molars together and focused on the graceful inward dip of her navel.

Katie Porter

"That ring feels *amazing*," she breathed. "I can feel it all the way in, then all the way out again."

"I'm not hard enough for you, ma'am?"

She actually giggled, then arched until her hands were flat against the muscles of his thighs. "You're plenty hard, pretty boy. But believe me, this is an added bonus. Is it the same for you?"

"All the way in, then all the way out again."

Leah's smile melted into something more desperate as she continued to build speed. Her whole body was powered by those gorgeous legs and the sleek fitness of her midsection. Up and down, her body used his. All the while Mike battled the raging storm in his blood. Tidal waves and the engine of an F-16 had nothing on the force that crashed across his nerves each time her pussy swallowed him up.

She reached a hand between her legs, circling her clit with stiff fingers. He groaned, his ass gripping against another quick spike of arousal.

"Michael," she gasped, eyes heavy-lidded. "Fuck me."

His fists unclenched. Every muscle in his body relaxed then did as she commanded. Harder now, so much deeper, he met her body halfway with each thrust. She dropped down. He pistoned up. The fast staccato slap of sweaty skin mingled with panting breaths.

"Don't you come yet," she said, breathless. "I'm first."

"Damn it, Leah."

Even then, so close to completion, she retaliated. She braced her weight with one hand smack in the middle of his chest. With the other she grabbed the back of his head. Fingers threaded through his hair and she twisted.

"Try again," she gritted out.

Mike resisted. Seeing her pissed was whisking his brain into scrambled egg. He yanked his head to the side, nearly free of her grip.

She gave up on his chest. Fingers splayed, she caught his head with both hands. "Try again. With an apology."

76

Teeth bared, he continued to thrust. His hips would not be stopped.

Leah tunneled her fingers back, deeper, until she captured his whole scalp beneath the dull nubs of her nails. She flexed and at the same time clenched the muscles of her pussy. Mike grunted, letting out a forceful gasp.

"With an apology," she repeated, each syllable crisp. "Or you get nothing."

He'd lost it. Somewhere. All he wanted was permission to let go. She was asking for too much.

"Michael," she whispered against his mouth. "You've given me something wonderful here tonight. It fits me. It fits my skin. But this is the truth, pretty boy. You may have your three years' experience on me here, but I will stop right now and leave you begging if you don't apologize."

Proving the point, she slid up, up, until only the tip of his head nestled against the wet entrance to her pussy.

Whatever resistance Mike had left seeped to zero. "I'm sorry, ma'am. Meant no offense." He blinked. Shuddered. Groaned. "I'm yours to command."

"Good boy."

She dropped down on him again, holding nothing back. Thrust for thrust they met one another, rattling the chains, smacking the headboard against the wall. Leah's cheeks flushed red. Her hair was a tangled, sweaty mess. Straight and proud, breasts out, she rode him.

Her orgasm clamped the head of his cock then gripped his entire staff. Chin toward the ceiling, she bucked her hips against that jerking release. First a groan, and then a sharp, keening wail.

"Come now, Michael," she gasped, even as her shoulders danced beneath another shiver.

Mike's vision went hazy red. He'd been holding back, waiting so long, that the trigger for his release took a moment to find. Leah provided it, of course, although he couldn't know if it was intentional. She simply looked down at him with wide, awed baby-doll eyes and gave him a smile with those crooked lips.

His balls tightened, the head of his cock swelled again, and he exploded. The chains tensed as he came. The restraints held him as firmly as Leah's pussy. Roll after roll of hot light hit behind his eyes as his body shuddered and twisted. He sank deep, deeper into each pulse. A moaned curse slipped from his throat.

"That was pretty to watch," Leah said.

Her voice sounded far away, but she was right there, still straddling him on his bed. Mike tried to find a grin. Nothing happened. He could only close his eyes, licking his lips as the last tremors twitched through his body.

Carefully, Leah pulled free. She made a little rumbling sound in her throat, all satisfied female.

But something changed. She lay by his side, stretched fully, as a storm cloud shadowed her happy features. "Hey, that was okay, yeah?"

Now his grin was easy to find. Her sudden hesitancy was such a shift after her ball-busting performance and ten-mile streak of confidence. "A helluva lot better than okay. Leah, that was incredible."

She quirked a smile. "Fucking A, it was."

Mike cleared his throat with a slight rattle of the chains. He lifted his brows. "Help a guy out?"

Her beautiful smile broadened into a full laugh. He enjoyed the effect that had on her bare breasts. "Please tell me you don't generally pick up random chicks and let them lock you up. That could slide toward conduct unbecoming pretty quick."

"I told you, it's trust and the right woman. We have history." He shrugged. "It was worth the chance."

First she unhooked the chain from the hasps, unwinding it from the headboard. Mike gingerly pulled his arms down as blood rushed back. He hissed softly. Leah must have noticed because she took one hand in both of hers and kissed each fingertip, swiping her tongue along the sensitized pads.

His fingers in her mouth, with the leather still banding his wrists, was one of the most erotic sights he'd ever been privileged to see. Jesus, he loved her lips.

After those tender ministrations, she retrieved the tiny key from the bedside table and unlocked the restraints. Still nude, she arranged each piece back in the bedside table drawer, almost reverent in making sure she found their right places. Mike quickly discarded his condom, trying to shake that image. It was nearly too perfect to believe.

"Come here," she said gently from where she sat half-propped on the pillows. There was no mistaking the command in her voice, but she'd backed way off.

Mike padded toward the bed. He stood naked, curbing a grin as she devoured him with her gaze. A guy could get used to being appreciated so thoroughly. She opened her arms in welcome.

Sinking onto the mattress was easy after the night's exertions. He released a shaky sigh as she guided his head to her stomach. Her hands petted his forehead, his hair, his nape, softly, in a rhythm that soothed the last of his crazy, pinging nerves. That touch was a reward in itself.

Mike laid his hand on the curve of her hip, circling her soft skin. He stroked upward in silent thanks for what she'd done. Because he needed to. The leap she'd taken into unfamiliar territory was humbling. Sure, she'd enjoyed herself, but she'd had no guarantees. That she'd taken such a risk for him was incredible.

The breasts he'd only been able to admire now filled his hands. Full and perfectly shaped, they were meant to be caressed. Nothing overtly sexual in his touch now—just a gentle relearning of the body he'd once known.

"Are you staying?" he asked against her stomach.

"May I?"

He laughed and tickled up her sides. Leah jackknifed around a fit of giggles.

"Stop!"

Although the temptation to continue was great, Mike behaved himself. "Yes, you may."

But even his grin couldn't shake the strangeness of their reversal. Naked in bed, their bodies having just shared so much, he knew that his mind wasn't yet back to being his own. She could've said, "I'm staying," and he'd have handed over his toothbrush. That was the true risk of being with a dominant woman. Not the toys. Not even the sex. Coming back into himself as a man became more difficult with each encounter.

Which was why he'd indulged in so few.

They ended up under the covers. Leah reached out to shut off the table lamp. That shift gently rattled the headboard against the wall. Laughing, she snuggled in beside him. "Now I know the real reason you have a house instead of an apartment."

He found her mouth in the darkness, kissing softly, smiling against her lips. This was familiar territory for them both. They'd slept that way before, tucked together. The effect was so much stronger this time, with his body *and* mind so thoroughly satisfied. "Go to sleep, Leah."

Chapter Eleven

By the time Leah woke up, her position with Mike had shifted. She'd rolled onto her side, facing the edge of the bed, and he was wrapped fully around her. The sheets were soft, warm chains binding their legs. His chin tucked over her head. Against her ass burned the thick pipe of his erection, but she didn't think he was awake. His breathing was too smooth and deep.

Slipping out of bed meant unwinding his arm from around her waist, but she managed quietly. He groaned then rolled onto his back as she padded into the bathroom.

Barely unpacked, the room was stark and the tile cold under her feet. She splashed her face with cold water anyway.

What in the name of God had happened last night?

It had started innocently enough. Then her whole existence had gone *kablooey*. Up and off into the stratosphere.

She'd liked it, there was no mistaking that. More than liked it. She'd sucked the experience into her whole being, finding a hidden part of herself that had been starving. For years. And Michael was her sustenance.

That same rightness, that same fulfillment, made it even scarier, like she'd lost thousands of feet of altitude in one huge dip. Terrifying. She hadn't been trained to overcome this one. She was on her own.

Leah went through the motions of preparing for the day with a slightly sick chill over her skin. Even brushing her teeth became an event. Should she use his toothbrush? *Could* she, even? It seemed so minor after the trust he'd put in her hands last night. In the end, she scrubbed her teeth the best she could using toothpaste and the side of her finger, plus some mouthwash for good measure.

When she walked back into the bedroom, she found Mike awake. Watching the door for her. He still lay in bed, all lusciously tanned skin against the white sheets. Her gaze strayed to his wrists, one of which draped across his flat stomach. The other he'd splayed onto her side of the bed, as if he'd been reaching for her.

She held back a shiver, forcing her chin up and making herself smile. "Got something I can wear?"

He pointed to the double dresser across the room, which had a medium-sized flat-screen perched on top. If he held true to form, turning it on would go right to ESPN. "Second drawer on the left."

A slightly hysterical giggle threatened to spill out of her. Last night had combusted with the opening of a different drawer. In this one she only found neatly folded T-shirts. She snagged the topmost one and pulled it on. The hem barely floated to the tops of her thighs. She scooped her hair out from the collar. The strands were a gnarled, tangled mess, but there wasn't much she could do about it except fish a hair tie out of the pocket of her jeans.

Halfway through twisting it back into a ponytail, she turned to find Mike still watching her. His eyes were back to that default clear neon blue.

She slid back into the bed at his side. "You got a problem, pretty boy?"

"No problem at all." He bent low over her and brushed a tender kiss on her neck. That was the Mike she remembered. Reverent and soft. Enchanting at first, but eventually she'd needed more. On that morning, however, she found herself appreciating his gentle side. "You know, I could see your whole ass when you bent over."

She stuck her tongue out at him. "I meant to do that."

"Sure you did." He ducked out of bed, toward the bathroom, before she could land the pinch she'd intended.

Lying all alone in that huge bed, she stretched her arms up over her head, only to run her knuckles into the solid headboard. Boom, there she was again. Picturing him tied up and strapped down. For her pleasure.

God, it was debauched. But the last thing in the world she felt was bored.

Mike was still stripped butt-ass naked when he came out of the bathroom, but he headed for his dresser to grab a pair of dark green boxer briefs. "Do you want some coffee?"

So simple. So normal. A little reassuring. "Sure."

In the morning light, his house had a certain amount of charm. It had obviously started life as a tract house, but somewhere along the way had endured several upgrades. The floors were hardwood and ceramic. Through French doors off the back of the kitchen, she saw a tidy patio and a walled-in yard of hard-packed earth with a few scraggly weeds.

Mike fumbled through the cabinets before pulling down two mugs and turning on the coffeepot. Leah eased onto a stool at the high bar and soaked him in—mostly his long, thick stretches of muscle.

He smiled again as he handed her a full cup of coffee, then laid sugar and the half-and-half in front of her. "So I'm still your personal smorgasbord, eh?"

She doctored her coffee then took a deliberate sip. Good Lord, it tasted like bitter dregs. She held down her shudder and spent her time studying him over the rim of her mug. Intentionally. Letting the slow-burn heat weaving through her body and perking her nipples show through in her gaze. "You're all but naked. It gives a girl ideas."

"I love creative women." He drank his caffeine with only a little splash of the half-and-half. Just so...*normal.*

Something inside Leah faltered. Shivered with fear. She stirred her spoon in her mug, letting it clink against the sides. "How did this happen, Mike?"

The smirk curving his mouth matched his bright neon eyes—all teasing now. Her girl bits woke up at the thought of making him shift to that deep, deep blue once again. That blue screamed his arousal and hid it in dark shadows. What would it take? Her fingers buzzed with the need to find out.

"Do I need to give you a sex-ed talk? I thought you were a big girl."

"No, not sex ed," she said with a little laugh. "I've had plenty of that. But maybe BDSM 101?" She nibbled on her bottom lip. "Because that is what we're doing here, right?"

He scraped his fingers along his nape. "Yeah, you could say that. I'd prefer to say we're having a good time. Getting off." He aimed that volatile smile at her, the one that made her heart go pitter-pat like she were some type of idiot tweener. "Getting off majorly."

"But I don't know where the line is. Where we stop."

He shrugged. "We stop wherever we want to."

Her short breath was everything frustration. "Don't play stupid. I know you're not. I mean if I wanted to order you to feed me breakfast, would you?"

"If you really wanted me to, maybe. I'd think about it." He folded his arms on the other side of the bar and leaned into them. His brow wrinkled as he thought. "I don't know how to explain this simply though. I'm not a service sub or into humiliation. I don't want to be treated like a piece of shit. I'm still the guy you used to know. Outside the bedroom, at least."

"But in it, you're different."

She was too, it seemed. Already she was hungering for more. To give him commands and watch him obey. She craved the pretty, tormented expression on his face as she pushed and pushed, trying to find his boundaries, and the way his muscles twitched and popped as he held back.

"Yeah. I am." He lifted his head at that, steadying his gaze. Daring her to make something of it.

A heated pulse set up between her legs. The fact that he liked to be tied up while he fucked didn't make him any less of a man. He almost shimmered with strength and a pulse of arrogance.

Leah locked her knees together. She still had more questions.

"Is that a strict rule?" she asked.

"What? Which part?"

"In the bedroom." She smiled slowly then tucked the bottom hem of her borrowed T-shirt between her thighs. "Like, if I told you to get down on your knees and lick me right now? Would you do that?"

His eyes turned that dark blue. His smile faltered, replaced by something hungrier. More raw. "Are you ordering me to?"

"Not yet. So by in the bedroom then, you mean sexual situations only."

His nod was sharp, tense. "Pretty much."

"What about your other limits? You said last night they involved third parties."

"I'm not into guys. I'm not into forced cuckolding."

"What?"

He was back to smug again. Apparently he liked knowing more than her. Resolve made her spine stiffen. That situation wouldn't last long. She might have to take a field trip on her own. Brush up on the basics. It never hurt a girl to know her opponent.

"Being made to watch while you bang someone else," he explained.

She shook her head. "No, not for me." This tenuous thing between them was entirely too...*something* to add more people. Special, she supposed. Exotic enough as it was.

"I've got some other things I won't do too, but I have a suspicion they're not going to come up. Or I'll give you a red light if they do." The tiniest hint of a patronizing tone slipped into his speech. He was so damn confident.

But that didn't keep the power away from her.

She flashed out a hand and sank her fingers into his tumbled hair. Pulling gently, then with crueler intent, she drank in the wince that tightened the skin around his eyes. The only thing better was the way they darkened and how he slicked his tongue over his smile. His shoulders bunched as he pressed his palms flat against the scuffed countertop.

"It's strange," she murmured. "Even hearing you say 'red light' makes me want to poke deeper. See what street that light's parked at."

He leaned toward her, with only the counter separating them. "I'd like to see you try."

"Haven't you learned not to dare me?"

His laugh spilled out rich and full. Real. No playacting. "I kind of liked the results last time."

She narrowed her eyes. "Kind of?"

"Okay, immensely." His eyelids drooped to half-mast then he tacked on a "Ma'am."

Oh, there it was. That lovely, tingling rush of *yes, more.* She liked that entirely too much. "Come around here."

He obeyed immediately, but every step was measured. Calculated. The bastard knew exactly what his body did to her.

When Mike was finally standing in front of her, she opened her knees. Slowly. She still held the hem of his T-shirt down over her pussy, where deep heat bloomed. Easing her heels over the rung of the stool, she slid forward on the seat. Her bare ass skipped along the leather.

"On your knees." Her voice had gone husky, but she managed to keep it sharp. Cool.

He dropped and steadied his hands behind her knees.

She cracked his knuckles with a little pop. "Did I give you permission to touch me?"

"No, ma'am." He slanted his gaze up at her. "Not yet."

Leah couldn't help but laugh. "No, not yet." Her body was flickering to life, more every second. She lifted the T-shirt. "But *now*, Michael. Lick me. Make me come."

Chapter Twelve

Between being assigned to the 64th and his subsequent relocation, Mike hadn't been in the cockpit of a jet for six weeks. Didn't matter. Not right then. The rush of Leah's demand and the sight of her pussy in full daylight hit him like the smack of adrenaline at take-off. The neatly trimmed triangle of hair hid so many secrets. Her excitement, however, was not one of them. Wetness glistened along the supple skin of her inner thighs.

He didn't shake, didn't fold—not under the rigors of combat. But her exposed cunt and soft command stripped the resilience from his body.

The linoleum of his kitchen floor was hard, cold, unyielding against his bare knees. He focused on that small bite of discomfort to keep his eagerness in check. She was open for him, offering him the taste he hadn't been able to forget.

That eagerness meant he wasn't able to play as deliberately. He could've dragged it out, asked for small degrees of permission. Instead he took her order as *carte blanche*. Whatever it took to make her come.

He nestled his mouth along the smooth hollow on the inside of her knee. A tingling thrill arrowed down his spine when she flinched, her exhalation already ragged. The tiny signs of her jacked arousal were enough to keep him calm and submissive. Anything she wanted, *anything*, as long as she doled out the quiet assurances that she was just as whacked-out greedy.

With his tongue, he traced the graceful line of her quads, stopping to re-wet his tongue three times. Each time he stayed put and paid extra attention to that swath of skin. Kissing. Opening his mouth. Scraping his teeth.

Leah had stayed motionless until then, when her hands scooped lightly over his shoulders. A gentle petting to start. Only as Mike eased nearer to her center did her caresses turn to keen, deep strokes. The nubs of her fingernails raced shivers up his nape, into his hair, peppering goose bumps over his scalp.

The tendons along her inner thighs were as taut as cables. He focused on just one, to start. One perfect leg. He slid his hands over and around the resilient muscle, pulling the skin until it stretched tight. That's where he placed his mouth. No gentle caress of tongue and teeth—not this time. He sucked hard.

Leah tensed on a gasp. Her fingertips became dull daggers needling the caps of his shoulders.

Mike kept that pressure steady, sucking, taking more of her flesh into his mouth. She relented first, when two rough hands took hold of his ears. She wrenched his face to look upward.

"What did I tell you to do, pretty boy?"

"Make you come."

Her pupils dilated and her cheeks had gone bright pink. Such a telltale face. "I said to lick me. Now show me your tongue."

His mouth opened first, just a hint of slack because of the erotic surprise of her demand. He swallowed. Then he poked the tip of his tongue out, licking his bottom lip.

"That's what I want, Michael. Your tongue on my clit. Do I need to be more explicit?"

He grinned up at her. "No, ma'am."

That tingling numbness had returned, down his thighs and across the soles of his feet. He leaned closer. The breath he tried to control was a hot pulse against her moist, swollen skin, fanning back over his own face. Sticking his tongue out on purpose, chancing one last glance up at Leah's expectant face, he licked exactly where she needed.

Taste. Ah, God. Her body's hot wetness was a sweet thrill, almost mild—like weak tea with just a dash of sugar. He'd remembered so many things about her, always overlaid by his regret at how badly they'd fared as sex partners, but he'd never forgotten her taste. With all that had changed between them so suddenly, he basked in having the privilege again.

Over and over, he circled her clit. For some passes he kept his tongue soft and relaxed, just laving her sensitive skin, drawing her juices into his mouth with long licks. For others he flicked, teased, rocked back and forth. Her bunched nub became his focus, his entire focus.

Only when she opened her knees wider did he expand his territory. He stabbed his tongue into her pussy with taut little jabs. Leah laced her fingers together at the base of his skull, holding him there. Mimicking the thrust of a cock, he explored her, searching out the shudders and groans and sharp inhalations that directed him to her pleasure.

He grazed his top teeth over her clit with a renewed enthusiasm. Sweat cooled on his palms, making it a challenge to grip her thighs. He shifted his hold and spread his fingers wide over each ass cheek. She let go of his nape to grab the countertop. Balanced there, she arched even farther and wrapped her legs around his upper back.

Mike withheld nothing. He indulged her just as he wanted to, where their desires matched so perfectly. He slanted his gaze to soak up the restless shake of her head and how panting breaths pushed her breasts against the fabric of the T-shirt. Morning sunshine streamed over her skin. Every inch of her was golden, graced with a gleam of sweat.

"I'm coming, Michael," she whispered. "Damn, make me come."

The breathy words sounded all the more tantalizing because they were in his kitchen. Just the plain, ordinary kitchen he'd seen for the first time three days before. Now it would always be the place where he'd face-fucked Leah Girardi.

He plunged his tongue inside her once again, licking upward to find the spot that made her liquefy. She tensed on a groan. Her clit pulsed with a hard burst of release then kept pulsing in quick, sharp waves beneath his tongue. Her fingers wound in his hair, pulling, as her body gave him another wash of taste—this time the sleek fluids of her satisfaction.

A single bead dribbled down his chin. Only when her shudders calmed did he straighten and wipe that liquid streak upward. A glance toward Leah revealed her eyes weak with pleasure. He painted her wetness over his lower lip.

"Kiss me," she said roughly.

Mike met her halfway with her thighs still hooked across his upper back. She was so damn lithe and lean, but her mouth was all power. She licked across his lower lip with hard strokes. The taste of her mouth mingled with the taste of her pussy.

Christ, he was hard.

Only now, once he'd dispatched her command, did he realize what a monster his erection had become. The front of his briefs was slightly damp with precome. The ring he wore on his cock jolted him with every pulse of blood, every beat of his frantic heart.

"Ma'am?" he rasped against her mouth.

"Yes, Michael?"

"Please."

It was all he could manage. His knees were mush, turned traitor as a heady rush swept through his muscles.

"Please what?"

"I want to come too."

"I know you do. Soon. Take me to the bedroom."

Mike gathered her into his arms. The weakness he'd only just suffered fled with her words. She was grinning at him, her skin still flushed with a faint pink glow.

"Have I mentioned lately how much I enjoy your body?" Her question was followed by a nuzzle along his neck, then a quick bite. Nothing deep enough to mark him. He liked that she honored his requests. It wouldn't do to show up with a hickey on his first day with the Aggressors.

He returned to the bedroom and lightly set her on the floor. His cock, so hard and demanding, wasn't likely to let him be neglectful much longer. The exhilaration of making Leah come was the most powerful aphrodisiac.

"Kneel again," she said. "Briefs off."

This time he didn't need to suffer the sting of bone against a hard surface. Leah snagged a towel from the shower rack and laid it in the center of cleared space in his bedroom. She stayed there, crouched, and tossed a smile up over her shoulder.

"Down here."

"Thank you, ma'am," he said as the terrycloth cushioned his kneecaps.

Leah was there with him, almost eye to eye, as she smoothed a hand along his jaw. "Anything for my pet."

Jesus. That was almost too much. Such a name for him. It implied care and ownership, caresses and affection. Raspy shakes wiggled down his limbs, pooling in his fingers and toes until he couldn't keep still. Her energy stoked his.

Then she was gone. Without Leah's permission to move, he stayed right where she'd left him. The slow slide of his bedside table drawer poked at his arousal. Just that sound was enough to start his mind down devious, dangerous paths.

"Hands behind your back, Michael."

She knelt as he obeyed. Her breasts slid down the skin along either side of his spine. The T-shirt was gone, revealing bare nipples beaded to fine points. She looped the restraints around his wrists with smooth motions. Her efficiency sent his pulse through the roof. So adept, and so quickly. He'd had no idea they were in for this kind of time, not really, but it was spiraling him to far-off places.

She cinched his wrists together. Side by side. Pressed against his lower back. The position arched his backbone just slightly.

"You are beautiful, Michael," she cooed against his cheek. "Shall I tell you?"

"I like it, ma'am."

"I can't get enough of your chest. Your nipples. Your freaking gorgeous abs." She reached around from behind him, touching each place as she spoke. "Your chest hair makes me want to scrape and scratch." Fingertips splayed over his pecs, tunneling through his thatch. "Such a proud chest, even though you can't touch me. I like that. Very much."

Her praise washed over him like hot honey. Just the dark silk of her voice. Every nerve perked up, screaming for the touches she doled out in bits and pieces. On hands and knees, she crawled around to face him. Her curtain of hair, loose once again, was a messy tangle that revealed and concealed her face as she moved, as if even her hair was conspiring to tease him.

"And here," she whispered against his hard-on. "You know how much I like this, don't you?"

"Please, tell me more."

She licked up his length, from balls to head. No hands. Just her tongue. Mike clenched his teeth against that rip of sensation. She looped her tongue around his ring, tracing it, dipping along either side to sweep across his swollen flesh. All he could do was sink deeper, going to a place where he wasn't on the verge of coming over her face. The only problem was he couldn't find such a place. His reserves were so nearly depleted.

"Michael?"

Her breath against his groin was almost cool compared to how hotly he burned. "Yes, ma'am?" he gritted out.

"Do you enjoy pain?"

"I enjoy what you do, ma'am."

The words came automatically now, his honest subservience, because he was lost. Nothing made sense when he gave over to her whims. She would see him through. That was all he had left.

"I'm curious about it, about pain," she said, slowly kneeling belly to belly. "I don't even know if I'd like inflicting it. But I have a guess. I think I'd like to see you absorb it and swallow it into you. You do that, you know. I can see it on your face when you leave a little of this world behind."

"Have to, ma'am."

"I know, Michael." She kissed him so sweet and slow, as if already soothing him in advance of what was to come. "It turns me on."

His words were gone. All he could do was shake and wait and need.

"So let's see, shall we, pet? Let's see what you can take."

Chapter Thirteen

With whatever cerebral powers she had left, Leah thought maybe she should be more worried. Feel less sure of herself. A little shakier, as she'd felt in the kitchen when she'd quizzed Mike.

All that had fled.

There was only the heady intoxicant of power and control and curiosity. How far could she push this? What would make that tasty conflicted look reappear on his face? She relished seeing his mouth turn tight, his eyes go deep blue. The key seemed to be surprising him. Twisting his expectations into something different. New.

She arose slowly, drinking in the way his gaze followed her every move. Standing with her feet barely shoulder width apart, she lifted the heavy mass of her hair to let cool air drift over her neck.

Oh yeah, she was teasing him. She let him admire the up-tilted swell of her breasts and her nipples, which had curled into nubs. Because she could. Because it made his lips fall open and made his gorgeous, built chest rise on a potent inhalation.

He was trying so desperately to keep his control.

Except Leah realized that was her job now. Keep control. So he didn't have to. So he could let loose.

She walked around behind him, trailing her fingers over the sharp line of his collarbone. He watched her as long as he could out of the corner of his eye but kept his face forward, even though she hadn't ordered it.

"You're a good boy, Michael," she said quietly. "You try so hard. Do you know what that does to me?"

"No. Not really." His voice had gone rough and gravelly. "I only know what I hope it does."

Hidden behind him, she allowed her eyes to drift shut for a moment and let go of the shiver she'd been restraining. She was a mess—her legs trembling, her sex still swollen and hot from that rocking orgasm. "Tell me."

"I hope it makes you as sprung tight as I am." Bound behind his back, his hands curled into loose fists. "I hope it drives you crazy."

"It does, Michael." She leaned down to open her mouth over the heavy arch of his shoulder. Teeth clenched, she bit with enough force that the muscle jumped beneath her lips. She sucked softly on the flesh, knowing it wouldn't soothe much. Hopefully none at all.

"This whole situation drives me crazy," she said.

"Good."

She smiled against his skin. "Good?"

He looked back over his shoulder. His angular features had taken on an even sharper cast. Determined. But somewhat troubled too. "No one likes to be alone."

With two fingers, she pushed his chin back to face forward. She hadn't given him permission to look, but he deserved something for such a raw confession.

"You're not alone. I'm right here, pet."

Keeping her step light, Leah crossed back to his drawer—the tricks and treats she'd delved into so eagerly. She rummaged around as quietly as she could, wanting him to wonder. To anticipate. But nothing could prevent the subtle clink of metal on metal when she shifted a pair of handcuffs. Those might be interesting for the future, but they weren't what she needed now.

She took out three items one by one, touching the cool leather. The various hefts of them. God, that was good. They felt perfect, as if crafted to fit her palms, to weigh down the trembling lengths of her arms.

She returned to Michael, who hadn't shifted position. Only his fast-heaving chest and an occasional twitch of unsteady fingers gave away his restlessness. She eased down to kneel. Her breasts slid along his shoulder blades, firing tingles through her nipples. His ass fit the curve of her stomach, his flesh so smooth with just a light sprinkle of hair at the tops of his thighs.

His bound hands flexed against her ribs.

She skated her lips over his spine. Then she held the first item out for him to see. "Is this the riding crop you got caught with? The one you mentioned to Ryan?"

"That one was borrowed," he said with a shake of his head. "The one in your hand is one I bought."

Good.

How insanely possessive she felt. She'd have chucked it across the room had he admitted someone gave it to him. Instead she brushed a kiss over his other shoulder blade. Then nibbled.

"And this is a flogger, right?"

Nodding, he opened his hands across her torso. Long, powerful fingers stretched down her stomach. He pressed gently, as if he searched for a measure of connection. But then she did too, or she wouldn't be plastered across his back.

"Permission to tell you something, ma'am?"

"Of course. I like hearing you talk."

"A flogger takes a certain amount of practice. There's a method to it."

"And I don't know the method yet."

No question there. She felt ridiculously new to the whole idea. That didn't mean she would leave it that way. She'd never enjoyed feeling ignorant, and her knowledge wouldn't be lacking for long.

"All due respect, but no, ma'am. You don't."

"I could hurt you if I did it wrong? Hurt you badly, I mean."

"You could."

"We don't want that." She set the flogger behind her, out of reach, and held out the last item. "And what's this one?"

His body shook once. Apparently it was one he liked. "That's a slapper."

"Mmm," she purred. "I think I like the sound of that." She set the slapper down next to his knee where he could see it. Watch it.

Laying a hand flat in the center of Mike's back, she coiled her fingernails into him and pushed until he levered slightly forward. "Can you keep that position?"

"For a while."

"But you'll try, as long as you can. Because it will make me happy." She trailed her nails down his back and arms, hard enough to leave red streaks.

"Yes, ma'am." His measured words came out as a growl.

Leah wrenched her hand back and smacked down hard on his ass. No warning. No warm up. His muscles jumped. The thick curve of his quads spasmed. The tendons along the back of his neck stiffened in a way that held her mesmerized.

He didn't pull away, even when she again hit the firm swells of his ass, five on each cheek. The force of those strikes reverberated up her biceps, through her shoulders, feeding something wild held within her. Letting it loose.

"Do you like that?" She gripped each globe of his ass and squeezed.

"Yes, ma'am," he gasped. His control was coming loose at the edges. Unraveling. She was picking it apart, strand by strand.

"And you still want to come?"

His shudder ate at her soul—beautiful in everything he was holding back. For *her*.

"Yes, ma'am."

She could learn to love those words. So quickly. She was halfway there already. "Be good through these next strokes and maybe I'll feel like rewarding you."

The muscle at the back of his jaw ticked, right under his ear. But he didn't say a word.

She clutched the cool leather handle of the slapper. The edges bit into her palm because she held it so tightly, like holding on to herself. She had to make it good—for both of them, yes, but mostly for him. Wiggling back on her knees, she found the room she needed to swing.

Leah cracked the black leather strap against his ass.

The sound was a thing of beauty, filling her ears and her bones with satisfaction. But the way his muscles jumped before he could lock down again was even better. More fulfilling.

She kept the strokes light, almost soft. Mostly she listened to the musical sting of sound and his labored breathing. Red streaks still appeared across his skin. She could keep going forever.

Suddenly almost afraid of how far she could go, she dropped the slapper.

As soon as it clattered to the floor next to Mike's thick calf, her body came back into play. Roared its arousal. Her pussy was dripping wet, her inner thighs trembling. Her breasts were swollen, begging to be touched. Begging for *his* touch.

The clasp holding his bindings together came undone with a single flick, but she left the restraints around his wrists, unwilling to give up that pretty picture.

Whipping her hair over her shoulder, she darted around him and laced her fingers through his leather restraints. "Come here," she said, tugging him toward the bed.

The dazed look in his eyes set her off again. Thrust her even higher. She pulled him down over her, both of them landing together on the soft mattress. His massive cock pushed against her thigh as their legs tangled together.

She flattened her hands over the sides of his face then traced her fingernail across the fine line of his mouth. "Do you even know how perfect you look?"

He shook his head. Still dazed. Still a little gone, even as he hovered over her, locked on his forearms. "You, ma'am. You're gorgeous."

"You even say perfect things. It's almost too much."

She brushed a kiss over the inside of his wrist, right below the warm leather. After groping for a condom, she unfurled it over his hard cock. A tiny laugh burbled up from her body. "This is what I want. You, fucking me. Hard. Rough. The way we should have years ago."

His eyes went the deep blue of the Mediterranean Sea. "Yes, ma'am."

She stroked his hair back from his temples. "I know you can make me happy. Because you like to make me happy, right, pet?"

His prick dipped to slide over her wet pussy. "So much."

"Good boy."

She hooked her ankles high over his ass. Knowing she dug her heels into the red marks she'd left there made her crazy. Awesomesauce, dripping-wet *crazy*. She wasn't going to last long.

"Now," she ordered.

He plunged into her in one long, rough push. His thick cock filled her perfectly, opening up the last dark spaces in her soul. He fucked her deep. Hard. Like everything she'd wanted for so long.

God, she'd been right. She was going to fly over in no time. Sharp swells of pleasure made her legs quiver. Made her hands tremble as she scored his pecs. She ground her head into the mattress, almost but not quite frightened of how good it was. *Perfect.* Because all the while, he levered himself over her, wearing an expression of focus like a mask. He was resisting his own needs. Seeking her pleasure first.

Spreading her feet wide, Leah dug her toes into the comforter. Her hands slipped around his back so she could grab his ass. He clenched with every stroke, shook on every withdrawal. So good. So right.

The explosion started in her cunt. Sharp pulses of pleasure nearly verged on pain. White sparks blew behind her lids, but she forced her eyes open.

"Come now," she gasped. Her lungs were still seizing on her climax, but he'd earned his release. "Come for me, Michael."

He needed only a few more strokes. He bit his lip, fucking her. God, really *fucking* her. He folded over and pushed his face against the curve of her neck. His body jerked once, twice, and their hips slammed together in a press that was close to too much, but so right at the same time.

Because it felt like Leah had found herself, just by giving him permission to let go.

Chapter Fourteen

Mike parked his bike next to Leah's, between the hangar and the headquarters. He had more first-day jitters than he would've expected, but that hot pink Ducati was part of the reason. He was schoolboy eager, and not for his first briefing as an Aggressor.

A fucking sweet Aston Martin pulled in across the aisle and braked hard. Out popped a lean, dark-haired man wearing a flight suit that matched Mike's.

He shoved thoughts of Leah away. He still had a job to do, and apparently this man was a colleague.

"Morning," he called.

"Hey, yo. You the new guy?"

"Seems that way."

"Then let me be the first to greet you in anticipation of a good week's worth of hazing." He extended a hand. "I'm Tin Tin. Captain Jon Carlisle."

Ah, so this was the moneybags playboy Leah had mentioned. The two were close, which made the back of Mike's neck prickle. But he shook hands and offered his name in return.

Carlisle arched an eyebrow. "Strap Happy, eh? Maybe I'll stop complaining about Tin Tin."

"I wouldn't. It's a shitty call sign."

"They all are," the younger man said with a chuckle. "C'mon. Briefing room's this way. I hope Fang got laid last night because my head is not up for one of his piss fests."

The austere briefing room was filled with roughly twenty pilots, all suited for flight, all blinking over takeaway cups of coffee under the fluorescent glare. Mike exhaled with a proud sort of relief. This was where he belonged. Among his fellow fliers.

The downtime had been nice, but his overflow of adrenaline demanded that he take to the skies. Soon, and among the people who loved it as much as he did. Whether he flew over enemy territory or flew *as* the enemy didn't really bother him. Not that morning.

Sitting next to Tin Tin, he casually searched for a particular brunette. But Mike's body wasn't at all casual. His muscles locked against a memory from late Sunday evening. He'd stood in the shower with his hands looped around the nozzle overhead. No restraints other than his own will as water coursed down his body.

Leah had leaned against the opposite wall, just out of reach, fingering herself until her eyelids snapped wide. She'd spent the next twenty minutes rewarding him for his control. The best goddamn blow job he could remember.

Then again, he was having a hard time recalling anything before their weekend together.

Tin Tin played the smirking, ungracious host as he introduced Mike to the rest of the squadron. A few names were familiar. He greeted two particular men with firm handshakes and broad smiles. Liam "Dash" Christiansen and Eric "Kisser" Donaghue had both served alongside Mike over Iraq. It always did his soul good to see friends back on home soil, and he was relieved to know his stint in Las Vegas would mean familiar company.

The sexual buzz in his blood dipped back to the shadows, and he was grateful.

Not that it lasted long.

The briefing room's door opened. Major Haverty strode in, clipboard in hand, and Leah followed close behind. She held her wrists loosely behind her back, with her hair wrenched into that regulation bun.

At Caesar's, he'd asked her to leave her hair down. She'd honored him. That's where it had started.

Now they both had work to do.

Mike had learned years earlier that his intimate life was more private than most. Other guys could talk shit about their weekends, but he'd found it easier just to let a joker's smile be his answer. What he needed was too intimate to share, even for hinted half-truths. He'd honed that reflex of privacy until he was almost two separate people.

Seeing Leah in the briefing room was a challenge to that control, but there was no room for error for either of them. Too much depended on discretion.

"Morning, bandits," Major Haverty said. "Hope your weekend resulted in no trips to the hospital for stomach pumps or the removal of foreign bodies. Klingon, I'm looking at you."

Another pilot held up his hands. "Seriously, it was an accident."

Dash Christiansen flashed one of his trademark shark-toothed grins. "That's not what your sister said."

"And that sweet thang wouldn't lie." Eric smirked. "Said I was her best and her only."

"The only one she petitioned for a restraining order," Klingon shot back.

Flanked by Dash and Tin Tin, Mike sat back with a contented smile. This interplay said a lot about the men he'd be flying with.

Only that wasn't exactly right. One woman other than Leah sat in the briefing room too, call sign Brunch. Even as he wondered at the story behind that one, Mike's reflexive unease wormed under his skin. He flew with women. A fact of modern life in the Air Force.

It never got easier to stomach.

Fang cleared his throat. A serious expression shuttered over his smirk. "Enough chitchat, ladies and gents. We have work to do. Our next red flag is scheduled for two weeks, against a contingent of NATO pilots. That means location-centric Aggressor tactics: a smattering of good old Mother

Russia, potentially hostile Eastern European countries, North Africans and a concentration on Middle Eastern forces."

"Damn, I love the Ruskies," Tin Tin said under his breath. "We have so much data on how they fly, I swear I could build a Russian pilot out of pop cans and gum."

Mike only nodded. He'd flown hundreds of sorties over two enemy nations, but the subtleties of the styles Fang mentioned didn't register as anything beyond theory.

As if looking for a touchstone, he flicked his gaze back to Leah. She was all servicewoman now. Face forward. Posture loose but attentive. The fact she stood at the front of the room with the major only reinforced her place in the squadron—one of importance and influence.

Had they been in the bedroom, that would've done gut-crazy things to Mike. In a briefing room, however, it just rankled. She'd not only excelled at all of her early ambitions, she'd zipped right on past him.

Haverty consulted his clipboard. "So, assignments. Group one, Middle East, led by Tin Tin."

"Hell yeah."

For such a cool character, the younger man gave away a great deal about his love for the job. Mike could almost relate, although a slim wedge of envy spiked between his ribs when he thought about the history Tin Tin shared with Leah. He'd been there with her, for the most recent part of it, as she transformed into a strong woman and a toughened officer.

"Group two, standard NATO alpha pattern, led by me," said Haverty. "Hard deck of ten thousand feet. We'll switch it up after an early lunch, then debriefing at fifteen hundred hours. If you're good, you'll be out of here in time to get hammered before supper."

Murmurs of acknowledgment met standard bouts of grousing.

Haverty set his clipboard on the room's lone desk and leaned against it, arms crossed. "And I'm sure you've all met the newest addition to our dysfunctional family. Captain Templeton comes to us from Shaw after four tours over Iraq and the 'Stans. He even has a Silver Star to prove it." Then the major grinned. "But don't let that stop you from being your usual obnoxious selves. I expect a detailed report on the origins of his call sign by quittin' time."

Mike only shrugged. "A guy has to fend off the boredom, Major Haverty, sir."

"Beat it off, you mean," Dash said with a smirk.

"But all jokes aside," Haverty continued, "Strap Happy is off rotation until he crawls his way out of the simulator. Princess here will give him hell until he can keep up with y'all."

The nonchalance Mike struggled to maintain wasn't easy in the face of so many racing images. Him crawling. Leah giving him hell. Not only was his assignment going to test him in ways that didn't appeal, he'd have to do it with Princess Hardass riding him the whole time.

He was damn glad he'd left his cock ring at home. It was friendly fire waiting to happen.

"All right, bandits," the major said, clapping his hands once. "Good hunting and be safe. Strap? Up here, please."

Mike shook hands with Dash and Eric, bidding them good hunting, before working his way to the front of the briefing room. Leah hadn't moved, but her posture locked almost imperceptibly. She watched him out of the corner of her eye. The emotion there was clear to see, even though it scraped at Mike's bones. She actually looked worried.

As if he'd blurt out to their CO something to incriminate them both.

That tightened his jaw.

He kept his eyes on Haverty. "Sir?"

"This is a big op, right? We'll be working closely with the 65th, but I still need you in the air against those arrogant NATO boys." He had the look of a leader searching to see if he could depend on his men. "You gonna be ready?"

"Yes, sir. I'll make sure of it."

"Good. Princess is the best in the simulator, so do what you can to get along, huh, kids?"

With that, he grabbed his clipboard and followed the rest of the squad out toward the main hangar bay. Mike waited. He didn't want to wait—wanted to be the one to speak first. But the odd silence around them made his skin tingle. Three days of obeying her every command was harder to shake off than he'd planned.

"You ready?" she asked.

He hadn't heard her speak since the previous afternoon when they'd said goodbye. Out of condoms and out of food, they'd decided to call it good. Her voice had been soft against his ear. Then she'd been gone in a squeal of tires.

Mike wasn't generally a guy to make plans too far out, but he planned to pick up another box of Trojans that evening when he finally made it back to the store. Just in case.

He grinned. "Sure thing, Princess. Ready and able."

The scowl that firmed her lush lips revealed no hint of their sexual play. "Can it. Let's go."

The no-nonsense tone iced his skin.

Screw this.

He followed her through the hangar where the squad was busy outfitting themselves for flight. Squashing a flare of envy, he kept his eyes on Leah's boot heels. The walk to the simulator was draining in ways he hadn't considered. Maybe in the back of his mind he'd expected a hint of what they'd shared. A little smirk. A private phrase. He wore her bruises and her fingernail scratches like war wounds under his flight suit, but she was a blank wall.

The firm contrast between their weekend and their business selves was hard to reconcile—and this from a guy who'd never had such a problem before.

"All right." She waved a hand toward the simulator, then propped two fists on her hips. "In you go, Strap Happy. You have a lot to prove to me."

Shit, even that did a number on him. She was dead serious, and his pride was smarting, but the primal reaction to please her shimmied up his spine. He buckled in with a rigid back and the makings of a hard-on, pissed as hell that she managed to stay unaffected.

An hour later, the sound of Leah's voice was a knife along his skin. Every critique. Every correction. It wasn't enough that the smell of her was driving him up a wall—that sweet, salty skin layered with something delicately floral.

No, it was how damn good she was at the things that gave him fits.

He was an instinctual pilot. He hadn't even thought about flying when volunteering in the wake of September 11th. But his aptitude scores and physical conditioning had propelled him into the sky. The vagaries and minutiae of prescribed combat styles made him more frustrated than he would've thought possible, not after so many years in a cockpit.

That Leah was the one to see him make mistake after mistake only scraped deeper, shredding his ego. Four hours in the blasted machine dragged on. He was flustered and furious with himself.

Leah checked her watch. "Lunch break, I think."

Glaring, he unhooked his harness before shaking the ground-down tension out of his hands. "You're enjoying this, aren't you?"

"What's that supposed to mean?"

"Pulling rank. You like it. Even here."

"Don't be a baby, Mike."

"No, seriously, admit it."

The tops of her cheeks went pink. "Will you shut up?" she hissed.

Mike unfurled from the simulator, his thighs burning in ways he hadn't felt since he'd traded running for exercises that wouldn't stress his knee—all lactic acid and frustration. "This has nothing to do with your off hours, Princess. This is about you finally getting one over on me with your flying."

She huffed. Her gaze darted to a dozen places before returning to his. "Yeah, it is. If that makes me a bitch, fine. You never thought I'd make it, and now I have. Now you're learning from *me*."

He was, no matter how bad it grated at his nerves. That just meant he'd need to find something to teach her in return. She'd taken to his brand of kink like a natural, but Leah Girardi had no idea how far he wanted to go. Getting there would mean learning from *him*, even if she was the one who wielded the paddle.

With a smile made of one hundred percent anticipation—one she caught, one that made her frown—he climbed back into the simulator.

"Forget lunch. Bring it, Princess."

Chapter Fifteen

By the end of the afternoon, Leah felt like her skin didn't fit over her bones. It pinched across her neck and made her cheeks feel funny—almost numb, as if her tight expression had been duct taped to her face.

Because Jesus Christ, the whole day had been a nut roll of the highest order.

Playing the bitch had never been difficult. Riding someone's ass to make sure they kept their fellow pilots safe in the air? Not a problem.

Until it was Mike's ass. The same ass he'd let her smack until it was streaked pink.

Their weekend had been a different world. This was work.

Because really, did he freaking suck in the simulator or what? He couldn't get it in his head that he needed to fly like a bad guy, or that his usual techniques wouldn't work—might even cause him to crash.

Even worse was his obvious frustration at his suckitude. He kept smiling, but it took on a hard edge that revealed the expression as a lie. The more angry he became, the more his blue eyes paled out. His laid-back, smooth motions became jerkier. Stiffer.

She wanted to pet him, to take him aside and assure him that he'd get it—if only he could center himself enough to take a deep breath. Then maybe she'd see if she could still get a grip on his newly shorn hair.

Leah couldn't indulge those impulses. Not in uniform. Not anywhere they could be seen.

By the time she and Mike left the flight simulator and headed back toward the hangar, she was tied in knots. A fierce protectiveness wired up her muscles, all the worse because she couldn't indulge it. Plus, Mike might chomp her arm off if she even tried. He didn't seem in the mood for coddling.

"Are you going to tell Haverty how badly that went?" he asked with a studied nonchalance. His hand scrubbed over the back of his head, where a pencil-thin line of white showed at the top of his neck. Another reminder of his fresh haircut.

Leah swept her headgear off as they stepped into the dim recesses of the hangar. "I'm going to have to report in."

A tendon snapped in front of his ear. "Of course you are."

"I don't have a choice."

"I know. It's just..." He rubbed a hand down his face. "Yeah. Do what you have to."

She'd thought on Saturday morning that looking herself in the mirror was strange, but that memory had nothing on walking into Ryan's office with Mike at her side. And oh, great, Jon was there to join the party.

Leah had never been less enthusiastic about seeing her two best friends. Their bastion of support was unable to help her now. She wanted nothing more than to stay hidden in Mike's little house, letting him work her up to one hell of an orgasm, or rewarding him for a full-out effort across a tough day.

Ryan looked up as they walked in. "How'd it go?"

Jon leaned back in his seat. "What Fang really means is how many times did you crash?"

Since Jon was sitting in the only chair, Leah and Mike both leaned against the wall of the tiny office. Only after she folded her arms across her chest, did she glance at Mike. He'd taken up an almost identical posture.

Her hands immediately dropped to her hips, but it was too late. Jon spotted the lapse. His dark eyebrows rose, and his mouth curved into a tiny smirk. Leah mentally aimed death threats at him, promising she'd skewer him if he uttered so much as a syllable.

Ryan pointed at the door. "Scram, Tin Tin."

"You steal all my fun. Giving the new guy shit's a time-honored ritual."

Leah rolled her eyes. "Why are you even pretending you want to hang around? Head to Heather's house."

Jon's mouth turned down. He was a whole different person when it came to Heather Morris. "She's working late. Heads to London tomorrow."

"Ah," Ryan said. "That explains indulging me with your presence for the last twenty minutes. But too bad, you're not invited. Go wait outside."

"Aye-aye, sir." Jon offered a tiny, sarcastic salute before ducking out the door.

Only when she caught Mike watching the byplay did Leah realize that she wanted him to like her friends. For ease of relations around the squad, of course. His expression, however, was the same as when he'd finally abandoned the simulator—a man awaiting his execution and doing his best to not give a shit.

Ryan turned his best mean-boss look on Leah then Mike. "So. How many times *did* you crash?"

"A lot." A hard glint shone in Mike's eyes. "I pretty much blew."

Leah jerked her head to look at him. His confession of how badly it had gone was the last thing she expected. "Fang, it's just going to take some more work."

The smile Mike aimed at her was fake. Plastic. It promised that he didn't need anyone to fight his battles with him.

Message received, loud and clear. Eyes forward, she folded her hands behind her back and rolled her nails into her palms.

Mike went on to give a full, unflinchingly honest account of the day's lessons—including many of the failings Leah had pointed out in his technique. Even a few she hadn't.

Ryan nodded. A serious pall pulled his mouth into a frown. "Princess, is he going to be ready for the next Red Flag? Or am I going to have to plan for alternate scenarios?"

Something cold tumbled around in her stomach. A hard knot of discomfort. Had she realized that Ryan was going to put her in this position, she never would've dared Mike to show her his toy collection. But then, she wouldn't have known the absolute perfection of seeing him on his knees. She took a deep breath, doing her damnedest to lock down the memories of their weekend.

"He'll be ready."

Ryan laughed as he stood from his desk and started gathering his belongings—his headgear, keys from a top drawer, and a few folders under one arm. She and Mike took it as their cue to leave. Once upon a time, Ryan had spent hour upon hour at the office. Now he was spitfire eager to get home to Cassandra. He usually took work with him, but the lucky bastard would be there with her.

Yeah, Leah was envious. She didn't know what that crazy weekend with Mike had been, but the answer wasn't the start of something solid. With leather cuffs and spanking on the first night, how the hell could it?

All three stepped into the corridor, where, sure enough, Jon was hanging around. Looked like the poor dude needed a beer. Just not with her.

"So when can I take a few whacks at him?" he asked. "For fun and prizes?"

Mike flipped him off, but the tension seemed to leave his shoulders. His spine uncorked as he leaned against the far wall. "Gimme a week, Tin Tin, and I'll be taking you down daily."

Ryan locked the office door. "Please, please tell me it's possible. Someone needs to take the boy down a peg or two."

Jon only smirked. "You just wish you could do it yourself, Fang."

"That's for damned sure."

Mike jerked a thumb toward Jon. "You guys let him get away with that mouth all the time?" But there was no real menace in the words.

The three men had dropped into the general smart-butt camaraderie of brothers-in-arms. Easily. As if they'd known each other for years. Because they were pilots.

Male pilots.

Leah couldn't help a biting edge of crankiness. She'd needed to work hard to be accepted. Sure, Jon and Ryan were two of the coolest guys she'd met. Otherwise they wouldn't have put up with her shit for so long. They took her for her accomplishments, not her gender. She hadn't needed to be as hard-assed with them.

Yet even that relatively smooth process hadn't been as immediate as their acceptance of Mike.

The situation only got worse when Ryan slapped Mike on the back and grinned. "I tell you what, Strap. You make it through the week in one piece and I'll buy you a drink on Friday. You found Paulie's yet?"

Mike's gaze slid to hers at the same time her spine froze. Her head jerked back a full inch. Her cheeks went ice cold.

Dear God, if he said a word, she was going to hurt him. Not in a way that either of them enjoyed.

"Michael," she said, her voice low.

His full name slipped out automatically, absolutely without thought. She'd needed only three days to train herself. If she wanted something from him, she said his full name. End of story.

She didn't receive the same reaction, not by a long shot. His eyes narrowed and his mouth flattened to a straight line. "Sure, I've heard of it. Stopped by on Friday, even."

That was it. He didn't say another word.

First came relief...then a twinge of guilt. She'd doubted him.

"Great," Jon said. "Then you won't get your ass lost on the way there."

As the men took their leave, Leah followed with heavy steps. Mike slanted her another unreadable look. A tiny tilt of his head encouraged her to step away and talk to him as Ryan and Jon kept bullshitting.

She hooked her thumbs in the loops of her flight suit to avoid reaching for him. "Yes?"

His eyes had iced to that pale, pale blue. She was coming to learn him better now than she had during their long-ago three months. Back then, they hadn't cared enough to get annoyed.

"Don't pull that bullshit on me again," he said, quietly enough that the words stayed close.

She didn't want to talk about it. Not there. Not when she felt so raw at the edges. "Don't know what you mean."

"Don't try to bluff me." He rubbed a hand over the back of his head, as if he missed his shaggy hair also. "It's my ass on the line too."

She bit the inside of her cheek then defensively crossed her arms. "I know. I'm just...tense."

He laughed a little bit, flashing her one of his bright grins. One of the real ones. Laugh lines feathered out from his eyes. "You think you had a shitty day? Try being in my shoes."

"You'll get it." She ran a finger down his forearm where he carried a lot of his stress. When he was really trying to hold back, his tendons stood out in stark relief. "It'll just be a matter of time."

"Trust me, I know." A spark of amusement turned his eyes back to neon. "But if you want to give me some after-hours training, ma'am, I know just the place."

"Behave. We're not in the bedroom."

"Much to my disappointment."

The black coil inside her loosened enough to let her laugh. "I bet. I'll see you tomorrow."

After a mock salute, he swung onto his bike and put his helmet on. When the engine droned its heavy power, he slanted her a wicked smile. She wanted to hop on her own bike and ride alongside him, but she still had crap to deal with.

Instead she watched him peel out of the lot before turning back to Ryan and Jon. Both watched with matching expressions of amusement.

Jon leaned against his Aston, as if the paint job on the expensive machine didn't matter in the least. "What's up with you and Strap Happy?"

Leah choked. A stream of curses wove together in her mind. Trust Jon, the original kink, to figure out that something was up. So damn pervy, he picked up the tiniest little clue like some goddamn sex radar.

She coughed into a loose fist and tried lying. "I don't know what you mean."

"Isn't that the guy you banged forever ago? The one who didn't think you could be a pilot?"

The back of her neck burned. She hadn't realized she'd spilled that much about her old relationship with Mike. At least Jon hadn't caught on to the current strangeness. Besides, he was like Fort Knox when it came to a friend's secrets. Drop into a drunken stupor and confess endless stupidities, and she wouldn't hear a word about it.

Unless he felt like giving her shit.

"Yeah, that's him."

"Dude," Ryan spat, which was about as close as he ever came to cursing unless he was bombed. "That explains what happened when I introduced you two. If I'd realized, I wouldn't have assigned him to you. Or invited him out with us."

She shook her head. "No, it's okay. We're...friends now. It's all good."

She'd be damned if that wasn't more than half the problem. It was *all* good. Everything with him. Even the way he'd called her on her tensed-out bullshit.

Everything...except the way he obviously chafed under her command at work. But they *were* at work and would be for the foreseeable future.

If she could only keep the two halves separate, life would be perfect.

Chapter Sixteen

Paulie's was a helluva lot more crowded than when he'd met Leah there previously. The long weekend must've given everyone time enough to make plans that didn't involve a shady little dive. On a regular Friday night, though? It was packed. As Mike pulled in, freshly showered after another grueling day in the simulator, he could barely find a spot to park his BMW.

A grueling day to top off an absolutely punishing week.

He shook the engine's vibrations out of his thighs and removed his helmet. Now it was time to relax.

Although he hadn't yet flown, he was glad to have come this far with his squad mates. Lunches, briefings, maintenance checks—all provided opportunities to get acquainted with their culture. They were rowdy and slightly cynical, but a righteous sense of purpose permeated every exercise. Their role as Aggressors was to best prepare fellow pilots for combat. The goal was actually positive—building and preparing rather than destroying.

Almost against his better judgment, Mike enjoyed it.

That didn't make his hours in the simulator any easier to stomach, or Leah dogging him for every mistake.

The exterior walls of Paulie's vibrated with a heavy bass beat. Loosening the sour twist of his mouth, he resolved to put all of that aside. He found a casual sort of smile and pushed into the bar.

"Hey, Strap," the major called, waving him over. "Pull up a chair."

The gang, it seemed, was already there.

Mike sidestepped through the milling crowd toward where Fang sat with an adorable redhead nestled under one arm. Tin

Tin was there too, leaning back with his cultured insouciance. Only his eyes gave him away, peering into every dark corner. Frankly, he made Mike nervous, but the guy was also invaluably smart and occasionally hilarious.

Plus he was Leah's friend. There was no getting around the fact that being anywhere near her meant accepting two guys who'd already claimed pieces of her life and loyalty.

A waitress took his drink order as Mike sat, trying not to make it too obvious that he was looking for Leah. Her bike had been outside, but she was nowhere to be seen.

"She's a goddamn star some nights," Tin Tin said.

Mike was about to ask what he meant when the younger man's nod gave it away. At the front of the bar, perched on the little stage and flooded with white light, stood Leah. Eyes closed, she belted out a very convincing take on Garbage's "Only Happy When It Rains". The smoke-yellowed walls rattled as the music continued its rollicking pulse. Rather than be dwarfed by the strong music, Leah fed off its energy and channeled it into her performance.

All Mike could do was watch—as if the entire preceding week, with its shit-ton worth of frustrations, had never happened. He was back in his bedroom, kneeling before her. Only now he suffered the uncomfortable awareness that they were not alone. Every action and reaction would be fodder for her friends, for his new colleagues.

Perhaps that explained the band of sweat along his brow when she finished.

Applause from their table was the loudest, but Leah earned a good number of catcalls and shouts from the rest of the bar. She bowed a few times with a hand pressed against the dip of her V-neck halter. The stretchy black material hugged from her collarbones to the first flare of her hips, where a scant two inches of skin peeked out before dipping into the waistband of her hipster jeans.

"And now that the princess has descended from her throne," Fang said, "I can introduce you. Cassandra Whitman, meet Mike Templeton—our latest whipping boy."

Leah froze mid-motion in the process of taking a chair. Mike did his best to ignore that, as well as the chilling slice of awareness along his forearms.

He shook hands with Cass and forced small talk past numb lips. "The major's a lucky man, I'm sure."

She laughed, tucking a strand of that gold-red hair behind her ear. "Do we have to, Ryan? Really? Tell him rank is off the table around me."

"You heard the lady." Fang tipped his beer in mock salute. "Chill, Strap. After this week, I'm sure you've earned it."

Leah had regained some of her composure, seated on the other side of Tin Tin. Her face was still flushed in the wake of her performance, but Mike noticed the tension around her eyes. Shit, this wasn't going to be easy.

"Princess, you done busting his balls yet, or what?" Tin Tin asked. "I want him in the air and between my sights pronto."

"Nope," she said with a firm shake of her head. "Still more busting to do."

Mike would've thought her too rigid right then to make a joke, but the laughter in her voice was obvious. *Come out and play* was what he heard. For the first time in four days, it almost felt possible. They were off duty now. They were there to have a good time.

Where it wound up was something he'd just have to wait and see.

"Major Fang, sir," Mike said, grinning, "I think you should be advised that you have a sadist in your midst. The woman is *not* natural."

"That's for damn sure," Tin Tin added.

Leah offered a sweet smile. "Aren't you a mite young to be cursing, Jon? Your mommy will be most disappointed."

Mike accepted his beer from the waitress and cooled his throat with a hearty swig. "Yeah, man, what are you, fourteen?"

"Twenty-seven."

"Fuck me," Mike said. "That's obscene."

Tin Tin took a swallow of liquor from a simple tumbler. "Is that why the ladies insist on fixing me a nice cup of cocoa when I'm through making them scream?"

Cass *tsked*. "Jon, does Heather know you talk that way?"

He smirked, hitching an ankle across his knee. "Heather *loves* when I talk that way."

"Wait," Mike said. "You really have a girlfriend? I call bullshit."

As if offended, Tin Tin frowned. "Girlfriend sounds so juvenile."

"Well, that fits, jailbait," Fang said with a laugh. "So she left you for the bright lights of London, eh?"

For the briefest of moments, Tin Tin's nonchalance dropped. Mike detected something almost like...disappointment? Frustration? Or maybe he was imagining it because frustration, as well, had been his constant companion for days.

"Yup, on business for another two weeks. I tell her this stupid 'be a successful director of auditing' shit is really unnecessary now that she has *me*, but the bit of fluff won't listen."

A girlfriend. Who was some big-shot accountant. Mike could almost imagine an adult-video-store clerk or a twenty-year-old art student, but not a mature woman.

Leah rested her chin in her hands, batting her lashes at Tin Tin. "Does she know you sound so...wistful when she's gone? Even though she'd deck you for being so patronizing?"

"Shut up, you. No need to get personal." He paused for a rather menacing heartbeat. "Unless you want me to. Shall I ask how you've been filling your time lately, Miss Dr. Pepper All the Time?"

"You can ask, but you're not getting anything out of me."

Tin Tin waved a hand. "God, you're cranky. What happened to the fun we used to have? Dragging your ass home from bar fights."

"Holding your hair back as you prayed to the porcelain gods," Ryan added.

Leah's hands tightened around her glass. "Will you two can it? You'll give Strap here a bad impression of me."

"My impression can't get any worse, Princess," Mike said. "I already think you're an evil harpy."

"Harpy-hood is one of my many talents."

Mike barely made out the words when Tin Tin said quietly, "You know I'm only teasing, right? You're doing great."

She slugged him on the arm.

Only after the shit-flinging had died down in favor of another karaoke song did Leah glance at Mike, as if testing the waters. *Yes*, he wanted to say. *We can do this. Just loosen up.*

Then her eyes widened as she caught sight of his silver cuff.

Yes, he'd worn it on purpose. Yes, he'd hoped it might set her off. One way or the other. After the bad-as-dysentery time they'd been forced to endure at work, he needed something to grab back power.

The only problem was, Tin Tin caught the direction of her scowl. His eyebrow lifted. He shot a look between them.

Shit.

But much to Mike's surprise, the young man only shrugged and signaled the waitress for another round.

Ryan banged his hand against the table. "All right, flying jackasses. Who's up next? Jon, you set?"

"Nah, man. I was waiting for you to take a sledgehammer to my eardrums again."

"You're under orders now, Dimples. By God, get up there and entertain us."

Cass added a whistle and raised her glass. "You're lucky we're permitting you to pick your own song this time. Just don't screw up or it's Gloria Gaynor next."

"I *will* survive." Tin Tin threw back the rest of his drink and jogged up to the stage.

Mike didn't follow the younger man's preparations for his turn at the mic because Leah had scooted over a seat. She was thigh to thigh with him so quickly that the blood dropped out of his head. Zero G. Just like that.

She clinked her glass against his near-empty beer bottle. "Congrats on surviving this long—in the simulator and in here."

"It's a fine art, isn't it?"

"Sure is." With a flick of her ponytail she nodded toward his cuff. "You're wearing it again."

A sneaky feeling very close to smugness made him smile. "Yeah."

"I took it off you," she said, her voice low and tense.

"Sure. But you didn't put anything in its place." He shrugged. "I'm not going without just because you want me to."

Tin Tin started up on a really decent rendition of "Bang a Gong" by T-Rex, which should've been hilarious. But it wasn't. More like sort of...impressive?

Mike lost interest, however, as soon as Leah's breath touched his cheek. She was that close as she said, "What I want you to do is what you do. Isn't that right, pet?"

A hard shudder closed over his chest. He shut his eyes to soak up the sensation. He wasn't that fucking easy. "Admit it. This thing irks the shit out of you. You don't want it to, but it does."

She leaned back in the chair, arms crossed. Something near to a pout turned down her lush lips. If he thought about those lips on his cock, Mike knew he'd be lost. So he kept his attention on the hot daggers she was throwing with her gaze.

"Who gave it to you?" she asked simply.

"A woman."

"Details, please."

"If this is an information exchange, Princess, then I get some too."

She shrugged as if she had nothing to hide, but her eyes dropped to the scuffed bar table.

"What were Fang and Tin Tin talking about? Do you drink?"

"I did," she said. "I've been good lately."

"Is that what last weekend was, then? Just a fix for your boredom?"

"You're going to pay for this, you know. I can't retaliate now, but—"

"Don't bother," Mike interrupted. "See, because you can make all the threats you want and I won't care." He pressed his thigh against hers, angling his mouth toward her ear for more privacy. "Because worst-case scenario? You drag me home and have your way with me."

"Take it off, Michael," she said, her eyes back on his cuff.

"Hell, no. And have your eagle-eyed fuck buddy take note?"

"My...?" She broke into a full-bellied laugh that dragged Fang and Cass's attention away from the stage. Leah waved them off before returning to Mike, her whisper still mangled by laughter. "You think me and Jon?"

"Why not?"

"Because that's just *ew*. He's an A-number-one control freak who has very particular tastes, none of which go my way." Her breath was nearly a caress against Mike's ear. "I've only slept with one man in the squadron and that was Fang. A long time ago. He was still a captain back then, and it lasted all of three weeks. Now close your damn mouth, Michael, and tell me who gave you that cuff."

He blinked a few times, but her quick confession and tone of voice had done a number on his ability to think. She'd pitched it just right—just husky enough and commanding enough to become part of his blood. He'd resisted throughout the week, when her orders petted his fur backward. At that moment it was more fuel to an already simmering hard-on.

"Her name was Georgia. My first Dom. Divorced. Kids in college. She wanted to show me a good time and I let her. End of story." He pressed his elbows into the table and hunched forward. "Now either quit dickin' around with me or take me home."

Chapter Seventeen

Leah was coming to hate that silver cuff on Michael's wrist. In the low light of the bar, the dully polished surface still managed to gleam. It wasn't as if she had the right to demand he take it off, though that hadn't stopped her. The order had been instinctual. If he was going to flaunt being claimed, as subtle as the cuff might be, she would be the one to do it. Except he was right in pointing out that she hadn't offered anything in return.

"You'll answer one more question," she said.

His mouth curved wide into that smirking grin, the one that made her fingertips itch. "Why should I?"

The way she leaned toward him was a little calculated. The forward shift of her shoulders gave him a prime view down her skimpy halter top. His eyes shifted a whole shade darker.

"You'll answer because you like pleasing me."

He didn't react, unless she counted the jerk of his chest on a fast breath. A glance at Ryan and Cass said they were still fully occupied watching Jon.

She slid her hand under the table, dragging her nails up the inside of his thigh. Such a pity that his jeans would dull the prickling sensation. The side of her palm pushed up against his dick.

"Are you wearing your other piece of jewelry?"

His tongue slicked over his lip before he nodded. Slowly. "Yes."

No *ma'am.*

She bristled. "Aren't you forgetting something?"

"You don't want that," he said with the slightest smile. "Not here."

Goddamn it, he was right—for the second time that night. She crossed her arms over her chest and sat back in her chair, feeling perilously close to pouting. What she really wanted to do was unsnap the woman's damn cuff and leave it spinning on the table as she hauled Mike's ass out of there.

Hello, obvious land. She wouldn't even make it out to her bike before Jon would text her, asking what the fuck was up. Which meant she and Mike had some time to kill. Eventually Ryan was forced onstage, but no matter how much shit they gave him, Mike passed. Vehemently.

Through the whole night, Leah ratcheted tighter and tighter. Her body had flipped the switch between work time, which meant behaving, and playtime—which had her thinking of Michael. The things she could do to him. The things he'd do for her. It wasn't enough that he was sitting next to her and breathing the same air.

For fuck's sake, she practically wanted him to breathe *her* air. The air she gave him.

Sick, much?

Even that didn't stop her. Nor did her second time onstage, singing Puddle of Mudd's "She Hates Me"—the not-safe-for-work version, of course. Her buzzed-high energy kept her restless and so damn horny.

When Mike stepped away to make a run to the bar, her nerves only worsened. In need of a distraction, she narrowed her eyes at Jon, who now sat at the other end of the table. His buzzed head was down-turned, looking at something glowing in his hands.

"Are you texting Heather?"

He flicked a glance up at her before returning to his iPhone. "You gonna make something of it?"

Cass's head swiveled. "If you're dirty texting, you can ask Ryan to give you pointers. He was *very* good at it when I was in Italy."

"Geez, woman," Ryan blustered, wrapping a loose grip over her mouth. "Can't you keep anything to yourself?"

Her eyes sparkled as she tugged his fingers down. "I keep plenty of secrets."

Just like that, they were off to the races again. Nuzzling up against each other. Normal. Happy. *Nothing kinky here, people, move along.*

No sense abusing a pair of cute-ass puppies, so she returned her attention—and her frustration—to Jon. "I never thought I'd see the day when you were whipped."

His eyebrows arched as he tucked the phone away. "I'd be careful of the crap you throw around, Princess. Unless you want me to tell Mike here about the time I picked you up from that bar in the Palms."

"Oh, please," said a deep voice from behind her. "Tell me. I could use something to hang over her head when she's riding me about the simulator." Mike slid into his seat and deposited a round of drinks on the table. Including another Dr. Pepper for her. If she had one more sip of soda, cherries or not, she was going to fizz away.

She shook her head. "Don't you say a freaking word, Tin Tin, or I'll tell Heather about that blonde at the Nellis Air Day."

"Check and mate. Sorry, Strap. You'll have to dig that story out on your own." His mouth slipped into a smirk she'd seen plenty of times before. "Maybe you'll have some luck if you ask her pretty, pretty please."

Cold chills rippled over Leah's skin. Of course if anyone was going to pick up on a strange vibe, it would be Jon. That was just his way, not that he used his kernels of knowledge for anything other than shit-talking his friends.

Beside her, Mike flinched infinitesimally. No one but Leah would have noticed, because no one else was as incredibly attuned to the tiny movements of his body.

Even that realization jacked her higher. More aware. The way his throat bobbed over a hard swallow. The way his laugh lines slipped away. Every observation fed off the last.

She snagged an unclaimed beer without thought. Cold condensation blended with the hotter sweat of her palms.

She'd only taken a swallow before Mike leaned into her space. His mouth brushed over her ear. "You don't get to top me if you're drunk."

"Top?" she echoed.

His voice was as quiet as a kiss stolen in church, and just as forbidden. "Dominate. Tell me what to do. Hurt me."

She shuddered against the visceral reaction that jumped in her stomach. The heavy tumbling. "What makes you think I want to?"

He hiked his arm to the table, deliberately placing that silver cuff in her line of sight. "I think we both know the answer to that."

"Bullshit," she said automatically. But she put the beer down anyway. "I want you to do something for me, then."

He hadn't given her the *yes, ma'am* she was craving. Instead he offered something almost as good, even if he didn't realize it. His eyes immediately shifted to their deep blue. The one that said she'd taken him by surprise. "Name it."

"Meet me in the bathroom. Women's. Ten minutes."

"Done."

She slipped away from the table, making sure to stop by to talk to some women she knew from another unit. They were out for a girls' night, and Leah had to deliver the bad news that yes, Ryan and Jon were both off the market. The questions about Mike were much less deftly handled. She didn't have any claim on him, but she couldn't seem to lie and say he was involved with anyone else.

Instead she popped smoke and headed for the bathroom, nerves making her hands shake the whole way.

Thank God the tiny room was clean. White-tile walls gleamed. Even better, it was private and had a single locking door. Since the night was relatively young, she hoped they wouldn't be interrupted.

Leah managed to keep her guts together until the knock on the door. Then her heartbeat amped to fuck-all overdrive.

Zooming. She plastered a smile on her face, in case it wasn't Mike, and opened the door.

It was him all right. The hot, dark light in his eyes completely belied his casual grin. "You rang?"

She grabbed his T-shirt. Yanked. Hard. He staggered into the bathroom. She slammed the door shut and flipped the lock.

Then she was reaching up and spreading her hands over his head. Spearing through his hair. She could still get something of a grip on him, at least on top. The shaggy, lovely length through the back was all gone.

It didn't matter. She pulled him down to her mouth, took his with a fierce kiss—releasing the energy she'd been riding for the past two hours.

She reared back and gasped. "We won't have long before someone needs it."

"I think we'll manage."

He curled a grip around her hips and lifted her. Fucking *easily*. She'd never been a tiny girl. Not many guys could pick her up as if she were a kitten.

Mike hitched her ass onto the white porcelain sink. "What do you want, ma'am?"

"Make me come. I think you have about five minutes. Can you make it happen, Michael?"

He grinned. "Not a problem."

She grabbed his wrist and cupped his hand against the front of her jeans. Her hips surged up, into his touch. She'd never been much of a skirt kind of girl, not to mention that riding her bike in one was pretty uncomfortable, but she wished she was wearing one then.

Her teeth grazed the thick column of his neck, especially the tendon that said he was holding back on her account. She wanted to bite, but that visible spot would go against his rules.

"Your fingers," she breathed. "In my pussy."

"Yes, ma'am," he said around a smart-assed smile.

He opened the top button of her jeans. Her zipper parted almost as fast. She lifted her hips to let him pull the denim down to her thighs. The porcelain was cold against her ass.

Then his hand was on her. In her. Delving between her lips. Circling her with a single finger. He dipped inside, collecting some of her moisture, before returning to her clit.

God, it was good. *He* was good. He already knew right where to touch, right where to stroke. The amount of pressure she needed to rock up into his moves.

No matter the tension that had been eating her, she didn't want to be caught. Not when she was trying to clean up her name. But she couldn't seem to stay away from him now that it wasn't on-the-job time.

"Kiss me," she ordered in a harsh whisper.

His mouth was on her instantly, as if he'd only been waiting for permission. He kissed her deeply while his fingers kept up their strokes and dips and swirls.

Trembles shook down her legs, even after she hitched them around the backs of his thighs. Her hands felt empty, so she delved under his T-shirt and filled them with his hot, sleek skin. She spread her fingers over thick muscles, then curved them into near hooks—the better to scrape down his flesh in one long, steady stroke. He hissed in a soft breath.

And that was enough.

She came so freaking hard, like her brain shivered into little shards. White flashed where she clenched her eyes shut. Her moan wound free into a soft scream, but Mike kissed it away. Took it into himself.

Just like he took everything else she gave him, then turned it bigger and brighter.

Chapter Eighteen

Mike knew how to drive well, and he knew how to drive fast. Luckily his house wasn't too far away from either Nellis or that dive bar, or he would've needed to sacrifice the former for the latter. Leah was right behind him, but her Ducati couldn't out-throttle his hundred and ninety five horsepower. Just wasn't happening. His competitive streak was at least as wide as hers. He was still the guy. With the bigger bike.

Suck it, Princess.

He was nearly laughing when he pulled off his helmet. Leah had only just drawn her pink nightmare to a stop.

Her ponytail was a gorgeous, sweaty mess, and her delicate features were flushed. Nothing else about her was delicate. "What the hell are you smiling about?"

"Just my mind rambling."

She stalked toward him. No, *prowled*. Her hips swayed like a belly dancer's, although he doubted much of it was conscious. He'd satisfied her. She wanted it again. The strength of her desire shone from her dark eyes, even in those evening shadows.

Whatever she wanted had nothing on Mike. He'd made her come in a few short minutes. The pride he felt in having served her so perfectly edged under his skin. Time for his reward. He knew it, and so did she.

Only, she wasn't going to make it easy on him. The way she met him toe to toe and grabbed his balls, giving them a sharp twist, was proof. He hissed in a breath, doubled a bit. The unexpected bite shot straight to his brain. Pain. And excitement.

Good. It had been so long since he'd been with a woman who had the potential to test his limits.

"Inside, Michael. We have work to do."

"Yes, ma'am."

She gave him one more squeeze and twist before turning on her heel and leading him by his belt loop.

No lights. No prelude. Two hours at Paulie's had been foreplay enough. She walked toward his bedroom as if she'd done so a thousand times. Hell, even he didn't know his new place that well.

A woman on a mission.

"Free rein of your drawer, yes, pet?"

No matter the strong lead she'd taken in this encounter, she still had doubts. One or two. Deep down. A practiced femdom wouldn't have asked. But when beginning a new D/s relationship, he was glad for the concession.

He held her gaze, let his smile unfurl. Those beautiful quirking lips shared his moment of humor. "Anything," he said.

A sharp nod. "Naked. Hands and knees."

The whip crack of her voice meant it was time for a new sort of play. "Where, ma'am?"

"I'm being nice to you tonight," she said. "Sideways on the bed. No cold, hard floor. Generous of me."

Mike had already started on his belt and jeans. "I appreciate it."

She ate him with her gaze. Just...*devoured.* Dark eyes had gone wide, so wide, and her lips were moist as she licked them again and again. She'd shrugged out of her flight jacket. Her respiration was quicker now, with her lush breasts lifting. He would do chin-ups and eat beef jerky for the rest of his life. All she had to do was stare at the results as if he were a living god.

A living god who stood naked before a woman who'd just discovered his English ruler.

"Well, well. I like this." She eyed the toy before turning to gauge his reaction. "Do you like it, Michael?"

"There's nothing in that drawer I don't like."

Her walk was a slinky masterpiece of femininity. She barely reached his chin with the top of her head. Mike took the opportunity to breathe her, absorb her, when that was all she was prepared to give. He was surprised to see her nostrils flare too—the same reaction to their bodies being so near. They stood on opposite sides of a chasm, but they were also on the same page.

Fucking perfect.

"But I saw something," she said. "On your face just now. What was it, pet? You will tell me."

"Apprehension, probably."

"Oh?"

"It's not easy."

"To take?"

"Yes, ma'am."

A cruel, beautiful smile turned her into a picture of all things erotic. Fantasies danced in her fathomless eyes and shivered down her spine. "I said hands and knees. And I also said naked."

She glanced down to his cuff with a severity that was not fake, not exaggerated. She actually hated the thing. Mike *really* needed to hide his smile as he laid the circle of silver on his nightstand. Then he took his position on the bed. Ready.

Or so he thought.

Leah's aim was true, and the strength of her swing choked him on a gulp of shock. No matter how much he enjoyed the rush that came with receiving pain, and the mental challenge of surpassing his Dom's expectations, it still fucking *hurt.* The first strike. No amount of excitement could keep his nerves from doing their job.

Leah took another sharp swing.

Mike grunted, fisted his hands in the comforter. Sweat popped up on his neck. His ass was on fire. The heavy ruler, eighteen inches long, was made of some evil wood from the

Amazon. He'd bought it because it was beautiful, and because he knew what beautiful pain it would cause. It had no give. No remorse. No room for softness.

Apparently, neither did Leah. He wondered if the lack of warm-up was due to her inexperience or some innate streak of meanness.

"That wasn't for fun, Michael. That was punishment. You didn't follow my orders. Instead you were smelling my hair and enjoying it. Deny it."

Oh, fuck yes. A test. And he'd failed. The woman was too good to be true.

"I can't, ma'am. I like how you smell."

"You're lucky I like that compliment."

Leah rubbed her palm over his flaming flesh, almost caressing. She was in a sharp mood, but she eased him through the worst of those initial strikes. Or maybe, on an instinctual level, she knew exactly how to keep him holding on. A little pain. A little reward. Back and forth until he'd gnaw through a two-by-four to earn his release.

He heard the sound of clothes being removed. His dick perked up in a sudden surge of want. She strolled around the bed. "Look at me, Michael."

The sleek, rounded end of the ruler touched beneath his chin. She lifted. His gaze tracked up, up, up her astonishing body. She'd stripped to underwear and a bra, both in matching black. Her trim physique was one part grace, one part muscle. A soft line bisected her abdominals. He wanted to lick his way down to where it softened into the flesh held by the lacy waistband of her panties. To eat her out again...

"All the way up here, pet." Her grin was still on the cruel side, but her amusement was unmistakable. She'd retied her ponytail with regulation precision. Ready for the task at hand. "How much can you take?"

A real question. No joking. So he gave her a real answer.

"As much as you need me to."

She assessed him with a hard look then shrugged. "You had your out."

As if.

What was he going to say? *No more than six, please. My tender little bottom can't take any more.*

She hefted the ruler, smacking it ever so gently against her own palm. The strikes were feather soft, but Mike's muscles tensed every time. She leaned over and kissed him sweetly, as if saying goodbye. He knew why, and his blood surged harder.

Leah rounded to the back of the bed. "Sets of ten, Michael. Count them off."

"Yes, ma'am."

She sank one knee into the mattress with the other leg on the floor. One warm palm settled against his lower back. Comforting, yes. Confining too.

The sudden whoosh of air was his only warning. Left cheek. Fire and shock and release. As calmly as he could manage, knowing how much more awaited him, he began to count off her strokes. She alternated sides. No variation in the timing or strength. Quick, hard and in the exact same fucking spot each time. Mike's "ten" was rougher than he would've liked.

"Again."

The rhythm spiked faster, the swings ever more certain. It wasn't her palm on his back anymore, but a near fist. That sign of tension kept him hanging on, despite the sweat across his shoulder blades. He was in such delicious agony that counting her sets of ten became a mantra. He may as well have been saying her name.

"You do very well at that, Michael. I'm pleased."

"I'm glad, ma'am."

She kissed from his nape to the base of his spine. Licked some. Used her teeth. "You taste delectable. Working so hard for me. More, pet?"

"Please, ma'am."

Her hesitation made him want to turn, to look, to see the reason written across her features. In the end, he didn't need to. She caressed his hot, blistered ass and exhaled long and low. "You have no idea what that does to me."

"You give me a gift like that, Leah, and I can do this forever."

"Good."

No warning. She transformed from lover to Dom so fast that his mind spun. The world slipped out from under him as he sank deeper and deeper into the cadence of their exchanges. Smacks and counting and smooth palms over his aching muscles.

"Nine, ten," he finished.

But he froze. Leah hadn't delivered number ten. He'd been so lost in a spacey haze that his counting had outpaced her whacks. A malicious chuckle bubbled out of her. She was panting. The ruler dropped to the hardwood floor with a clatter.

Like a slinking cat, she crawled onto the bed with him. Her hands were damp when she grabbed his chin. Only, Mike couldn't make eye contact. He was floating.

"Ooh, now that's pretty." She stroked his brow. "Your eyes. Jesus, Michael. Where are you?"

"Don't know." His speech sounded...*off*, even to his own ears. "But it's great here."

"Looks it. So nice. But... You know what you did."

He swallowed. "Yes, ma'am. I miscounted."

"I'm proud you realize your mistake. Yet I'm afraid mistakes deserve punishment. What do you think about that?" Her smile was barely a hint, but it made her beautiful. She was playing with him. Maybe she'd only intended that many strokes, eager now to take him somewhere else.

He'd go with her. Willingly.

"Punishment is just another type of reward, ma'am."

"Very sweet. But that won't change what's coming."

"Me?"

She reached back and grabbed his balls, only this time without the protection of his jeans. "Getting smart with me?"

Mike was awash with the rush of her abuse. He was an adrenaline junkie. Everyone knew that. But his other drug of choice was endorphins. What an amazing thing, the brain. This high would last. That he pushed her, and pushed her again, was testimony. Wherever his mind went when he felt that goddamn good—all he wanted was more. However she wanted to give it to him.

Such was the danger of being a submissive. He needed to trust that his Dom knew limits and stayed in control, that she'd keep him safe when he drifted away.

"Apologies again, ma'am."

She twisted. First gently, testing, turning her wrist. The pain built until Mike flat-out grunted. She must've been waiting for that because she let him go. Relief made him shiver. Then came a shiver of another kind when she stroked his cock.

"Not all the way hard yet? Hm."

"One thing at a time," he said, nearly a gasp.

"What do you mean?"

"Pain first. Like...can't process both."

"But if I told you the pain was done and kept pumping this gorgeous prick? Hard in seconds?"

Mike bowed his head against that fierce pleasure. Such an amazing fucking contrast. His chest heaved. He could hardly hear her words, and his own rattled like stones in his ears. "In seconds, ma'am."

She put that to the test. Up and down, so firm and determined, she jerked him with as little mercy as she'd shown when wielding that wicked ruler.

"You were right," she said, sounding impressed. "Absolutely beautiful, pet."

Through gritted teeth, Mike was barely able to thank her for the compliment. His hard-on was a force of nature now. She was edging him. He knew it. Somewhere in the back of his cloudy, hazy, pleasure-fizzled mind, he knew it.

"Too bad we're not done with testing you," she said. "Because this... It'll be difficult to give this up. I'd like to flip you on your back and ride you. *So* hard."

A growl burned up from his chest. "Want that, ma'am."

Hands off. Just like that. She pulled away.

Mike dropped his head to his forearms and groaned. "Fuck."

"Mmmm. Those honest reactions are gorgeous."

"Honest?"

"When you can't help yourself. Now back up on your hands."

In front of anyone else, Mike would've been embarrassed as hell to realize how his biceps trembled. Leah only watched. She wore a smile of wonder. The crazed light in her eyes seemed to reflect his own need, his own bigger-than-life arousal.

"Very good, pet." Her voice was hypnotic. Just the right timbre to soothe him and stoke his pride. "But we still have the little matter of your inability to count. Seems the Air Force would've made that a requirement somewhere along the way."

He couldn't focus, only heard her rummaging through his drawer. Only rummage wasn't the right word. She was as careful with his things as he was. He liked that. Craved that measure of connection and trust.

Thirty seconds later, he hissed in a breath as cold lube drizzled onto his asshole. "I believe this is called an anal plug," she said, as if giving instruction.

Mike tensed at first, then relaxed as four inches of chilly, unyielding acrylic slid up his ass. He bared his teeth. More fists in the comforter. He was losing it. And maybe she knew that. Her fingers circled the base of his cock and cupped his balls.

"And your cock ring. Can't forget that."

Her voice was ragged, smug and awed at the same time. Barely keeping it together? God, he hoped so.

"Wouldn't want to, ma'am."

"But I changed my mind, Michael. Head back down on your forearms. I love how that pose shows off what I've claimed. This." She pressed her palm against the base of the plug. "And this." Tickling fingers played with his cock and balls. "Mine, aren't they?"

"Yours."

He heard a soft clatter of wood. The ruler. Back again.

"That's right, pet. Just like I still own your ass. Now, sets of ten."

Chapter Nineteen

Leah realized there was something different about her and the way she'd embraced this kink thing. At the same time, she didn't think she could understand women who *wouldn't* find Michael hot. He took so much. Every muscle twitched, and the hazed-out look in his eyes said he'd given up everything.

For her.

That rush went straight to her pussy.

The turn-on, however, wasn't her biggest concern. Yet.

With Mike so far gone, she needed to be the one who set the pace and kept him safe. What a responsibility, but also a thrill.

Another set of ten. Another amazing gift from the man who took all she wanted to dish out. Leah kept her hand on the small of his back, needing that connection. Touch was a mainline, revealing every jump and change in his breathing. She gathered the details of his body even as she layered pain over his ass, always ensuring that the ruler didn't strike the plug. No hurting her pet.

Relentless. She still couldn't believe this was her.

Part of her wanted to stop, wanted to lie down next to him and ask, "Really? We're doing this?"

Then she'd need to relinquish the top-level focus that burned her inside out. She saw everything about him with shattering clarity, because it was all for her.

A leashed beast.

The thing about a leashed beast wasn't just that he was big or had mean teeth—though Mike had the muscles and the brawn to make him intimidating. No, it was the feeling that he could snap at any moment. Flip over. Take out his trainer with a bite at the jugular.

He could, except for Leah's control.

So much. Almost too much. As if the smacks she dropped on his ass weren't enough to spike her brain like heroin.

She liked the long, mean ruler. With the smallest twitch of her wrist, she sent a lovely whistling noise through the air. The hard connection of wood to skin shot up her forearm, followed by a hiss when Michael sucked in through his teeth. Rough counts. His voice hardly faltered now, but the muscles lining his spine still tensed beneath her hand.

She kept on with hyper focus. His moves. His sounds. The way the acrylic butt plug caught tiny gleams of light, which made for entrancing gradations of color between toy and skin. He was tan layered over with red. In the center of each cheek, a white circle bloomed—the places that bore the brunt of her aggression.

She lowered the slender paddle with deliberation and laid it flat over his ass. Rocking it back and forth, she pushed down. Not another strike, but relentless pressure until his breathing jerked when she hit a tender spot.

"There, pet?"

"Ma'am?" His voice was so fuzzy at the edges.

She leaned down, peeked at him. A check-in. His blue eyes were vibrant and gone at the same time.

She suppressed the jolt that choked under her ribs. "That's where it hurts? Is it too much?"

His throat worked on a swallow, then he rocked against the wooden toy. That silent request was enough to make her fall apart with desire. She needed him all the way down to her toes, but she needed to finish this more. There was an undone feeling, as if she still waited for something—something from him.

She caressed his back, but long, smooth strokes turned mean. Like being possessed. Her nails got into the action. She watched her paler hand move across his tan back. Red lines appeared under her fingertips and arrowed toward the cleft of his taut ass.

Becoming more and more focused, she was hit by a pure truth. She loved this. Every moan. Every request his body made. He intensified her senses and hauled her arousal to new heights.

She'd find it fascinating. Later. After they'd finished.

"We're almost done, Michael."

He groaned in response. With a shift of his shoulders, he pushed his head against folded forearms.

The nape of his neck was bare. She scratched her nails against that paler skin. Not hard. No marks that would last past tonight. Across firm shoulders, she dug harder, with deliberate intent to cause pain. Dark red lines puffed. Point and counterpoint. She wondered which he liked more.

Leah certainly knew which she liked.

She reached beneath his body and stroked his thick cock. All the blood in his body had to be charging hard. Just like hers.

"You're going to take ten more strokes, pet. No need to count them off. You might not be able to. I intend to be rough."

He shuddered down to his toes. Beautiful.

She eased off the bed, except for one knee, and bounced the ruler in her hand. She felt herself almost...*elevate*, as if she were two feet above her body and watching intently. She'd never been so overwhelmed and still in control.

Like flying. Halfway between immortal and completely fallible.

She swung her arm. A crack reverberated up her arm. The jolt all but owned her.

She put her whole body into all ten strokes. The red across his ass deepened just beneath the plug. Nine smacks. Her world was Michael. Narrowed down. His tiny grunts became louder, his groans longer.

"Last one, pet." She blew out a quick exhalation. Her lungs burned. She'd been holding her breath for the last two strokes. She owed him her entire self, but that was no hardship. He had it. Every bit. "I'm going to make this one count. You're going to make me happy. Everything goes into this one last hit. Let it go. All of it."

She hardly had the words to explain what reaction she sought or if she had the skills to make it happen.

"Yes, ma'am," he chanted over and over, until it hissed into little whispers of adoration.

She edged her knee toward him until she braced her thigh in front of his. Not that she could stop two hundred pounds of muscle if he went down, but she needed that security. That reassurance for her own nerves.

She let every pushup she'd ever done and every weight she'd ever lifted slam through that final blow.

Michael took it. His groan wound louder and louder, turned into a roar. He cussed like a sailor, although she didn't think it was aimed at her. None of it made sense. Lots of "fucks" and a couple "cocksuckers", with hardly a breath between.

She dropped the ruler from numb fingers and laid both hands on his ass. His hot skin stung beneath her palms. Uneven, already swollen. Sexy as fuck. Her brain hazed out to match his, yet on the other side of the coin.

Rather than gouge with her nails yet again, she made herself ease back. Petting and stroking.

She caressed one more time, then shoved. He landed on his side, with an arm over his face.

"God, you're amazing."

She bent his body and urged him onto his back. He hissed, probably because of the friction of his ass against the sheets, but his smile eased into that place of contentment she was quickly beginning to adore. She soaked up her success at having read what he needed, all the while taking what she wanted—gorgeous.

She softly stroked the hair at his temples. Sweat turned the golden strands darker. A little sticky. Soon she'd get to soothe him and wrap him up and keep him safe. But not quite yet. She still wanted him. "In fact, all of that was amazing. You took it all."

His thick throat worked. "For you."

"That's why it was amazing." She wiggled beside him.

His eyes rolled up toward the ceiling before he looked at her, all lovely side eye and intimate trust. "You could show me how much."

"Right here." She took his hand in both of hers and cupped her pussy.

Jesus, she hadn't realized exactly *how* turned on she was. Her panties were soaked. Drenched. The tiniest twitch of his fingers along her seam was enough to make her whole body jerk.

So concentrated on Michael, she hadn't realized the responses of her own body. Now it came rushing back with angry want. Needy. Violent.

"You see?" She used his hand, pushed her pussy up into his touch. "You see how good you are? Everything you did was for this. My good pet."

She rode his hand. He added a swirl of fingertips and wiggled under the lace. She pulled her panties off and flung them toward a far corner. Her bra quickly followed.

After rocking up on her knees, she straddled him. He hadn't touched her—perhaps because she hadn't given her say-so, or maybe because he was still vacant from his own head. But she needed his touch. Leah took hold of both big, masculine hands and curved them over her breasts. He had the gist of it now, knowing the gentle kneading and pinching that extended her pleasure. Really, it was all about the worshipful look on his face.

She spread one hand wide against his chest and wrapped the other around his throbbing cock. She rubbed his head, over and over. "Good boys get rewards, don't they?"

"Up to you, ma'am."

She felt that one all the way down to her core. "Good answer."

"Truth."

She tilted her head and realized her ponytail had slipped. Long hair shivered over her shoulder. "Oh really? You wouldn't be pent up if I stopped? Frustrated?"

His mouth quirked into something near a smile. "That last hit *was* a kind of release. Not the same as an orgasm, but satisfying. Convince me it wasn't the same for you."

She shook her head. Couldn't even try. At the same time, right between her legs, she enjoyed his gorgeous hard-on. She subtly flexed her hips over it, dragging him between her lips. She shuddered when the cock ring bumped over her clit. "Doesn't mean I'm passing up on this."

He laughed. "No one's asking you to."

After scrambling off to find a condom, she pushed the thin latex over his shaft. She traced the base of his cock and balls with her fingertip along that ring. The metal had warmed to his skin. She licked it. No flavor to the metal, of course, but Mike had a spicy vitality that made her want to take bigger bites.

Crooking her hand around his balls and looping two fingers around his shaft, she mimicked the cock ring. She eased her cunt down his long length. So hard. *Enormous.* She was so goddamn soaked. The way Michael filled her was like returning puzzle pieces to their home.

When she eased her hands back, farther down between his legs, she grazed the butt plug. The laugh she choked down was nearly hysterical. She'd all but forgotten that the man she fucked was riding four inches of acrylic too.

Insane.

Only slightly less insane was when she grabbed the wide base of the plug and rocked her pussy over his cock. She worked his anus with the same rhythm she used while working his prick. He groaned, just as his hands roamed over her body, so restless now. The skin of his ass was hot to the touch. She'd smooth salve over him later and relish every mark and every bit of proof of what they'd achieved.

Just that thought flared pleasure through her chest, melting her insides.

"I'm not going to last long, Michael," she breathed. His eyes lit up and his mouth pulled into a small smile. "You like that, don't you?"

Although she tried to keep her stern face, she laughed again. It grew slowly and bubbled up through her body, only seconds ahead of the orgasm that threatened to undo her.

Why wouldn't he like it? She was *adoring* the whole situation.

Faster. More fierce. She clamped down when he surged up. He was just as hungry for her. Good Christ, the thought alone sent her over so hard that she thought she might come forever. Her whole body tightened. Cunt on his cock. Fingers on his chest. Flat palm on his butt plug. Shoving and hurting and adoring.

Something pushed him over, coming with her, and she'd never know which sensation did the trick. He growled. His eyes burned bright, and he bucked under her. Unforgiving hands clenched her hips with reflexive power. His cock twitched and his eyes rolled closed as he came. He jerked his chin toward the ceiling, which exposed the thick length of his throat.

"Ah, *fuck*, Leah."

Nothing mattered because she was there with him. She'd taken him into the abyss with her, where they floated together.

Chapter Twenty

The excitement of his first Red Flag as an Aggressor crept up on Mike like a slow fever. The days became a countdown as the time remaining for him to prepare dwindled to nothing. Even the weekend he should've spent with Leah in bed was traded for hours on base.

He'd graduated from the simulator to an F-16 on the previous Thursday. Fang, Kisser and Dash had all blown him out of the sky. More hours of practice. More time in the air.

Finally his brain stopped fighting the wrongness of flying as the enemies he'd fought for years. Whether Iraqi or Afghani or any other possible hostile, his reflexes became attuned to those unfamiliar nuances. He'd always flown by gut instinct and, to Mike's surprise, this was no different. Just someone else's guts.

At oh four hundred on the Monday of the Red Flag against the NATO pilots, Mike was called into Fang's office where he soaked in the sight of Leah decked out in her flight gear. She looked as cold and calculating as Mike had ever seen. At that moment, on the verge of taking to the skies, he found nothing but appreciation for her skill. To be honest, he wouldn't be flying so soon without her constant, rapacious prodding.

This was no time to probe deeper. His feelings about Leah—and about women flying—would wait. Everyone had a job to do.

"Princess says you're ready for this, and I've seen real growth," Fang said. "Are we all on the same page here?"

Mike nodded. Leah's approval did uncomfortable things to his body, coalescing in a hard pulse at the pit of his stomach. "Absolutely, sir. I'm ready to be bad."

"Good to hear that, bandit. You're on her wing. Stay cool, keep your eyes open and watch out for that steep learning curve." The major gave him an abrupt nod. "You've done well."

"Thank you, sir," he said with a nod.

"Now, if I'm not mistaken, Princess has something to show you. See you in the air, Strap."

"This way, Captain." She led him into the corridor.

Mike followed her through the offices and toward the darkened airfield. Floodlights illuminated where ghost-on-gray F-16s lined up like huge, menacing toys. His fever of excitement rushed back. When he'd participated in Red Flag training exercises in the past, he'd done so as a member of the allied blue force. Bandit pilots wearing enemy colors had seemed larger than life, full of tricks and skills that repeatedly hammered him down. Each failure on his part had woven into the learning process. He'd become a better pilot every time he flew against those wily, faceless opponents.

Now he was one of them.

Best of the best.

The spring in his step should've been annoying as hell, but he deserved it after so many hours of brain-bending work. That he got to take this walk with Leah was especially satisfying. He couldn't face that emotion, not yet, but it was there anyway— proud excitement right beneath his sternum.

"Here ya go," Leah said.

She stopped before one particular jet, hands propped on her hips.

Mike blinked out of his thoughts. God, she looked amazing. Sleek. Mysterious in the dawn shadows. Somewhere along the way, a woman with a ballerina's build had become a fighter pilot. The combination of soft and feminine, hard and competent, made his blood fizz.

"Show me what?"

She flicked her eyes toward the plane, specifically the seam where the cockpit's glass met the fuselage. "It's yours."

Capt. Mike Templeton.

That pride behind his sternum swelled to something painful but something glorious at the same time.

"Damn," he whispered. "I like the look of that."

Leah's distant expression eased. They hadn't slept together since the round that had started with karaoke and finger-fucking in the women's bathroom. The whole weekend had been theirs to indulge. Each encounter became easier and more pleasurable. The novelty remained—at least, it seemed to for her—just as their roles had become decidedly more confident. They'd mainlined each other for forty-eight hours.

Ages ago, it seemed.

"You've worked hard for this, Mike. I'm proud of you."

"Thank you, ma'am."

Her eyes widened. The courtesy had slipped from his tongue without thought. If Mike pleased her, Leah told him as much. That was how their time as lovers went. God help him, he *really* enjoyed pleasing her. He'd just never reached a point where his professional and sex lives bled so heavily into one another.

Leah glanced around. The menacing Aggressors were emerging from the hangar. Fang led the way, looking all sorts of in charge, with arrogant Tin Tin a half step behind. Dash and Eric followed, both shooting the shit in the early dawn quiet.

Fully twenty pilots in total. Badasses, every one of them.

Mike had been sure Leah would cut off their personal vibe. In the face of her friends and squad mates, why wouldn't she? But she cleared her throat.

"Pet?"

The twitch in his dick had to be from the excitement of their pending objective. Surely. Yet he couldn't find it in himself to pretend.

"Yes, ma'am?"

"Give 'em hell."

She sauntered toward her own jet. Crewmen wheeled out ladders and helped prep the pilots for flight. Mike held his arms out as a flushed-faced Airman First Class double-checked the loops and harnesses.

The young man slapped Mike on the shoulder. "All set, sir. Good hunting."

Mike climbed up the ladder and into his cockpit. He brushed his fingers along the freshly stenciled letters of his name. Fucking A. What a power trip.

Thirty minutes later, his jet was in line for takeoff. The leashed power of the F-16 raced like fire up his forearms. Incendiary. He'd launched in combat sorties more times than he could remember, but this moment held a weight he couldn't ignore. He needed to prove himself. Leah and the others still thought of him, rightly, as the new guy. He refused to be the weak cog in their practiced machine.

The sun had barely tipped up from the flat, desolate Nevada horizon. Somewhere out there were fuzzy-minded tourists and hangovers and fortunes won and lost. That was Vegas.

This was Mike on the verge of a fantastic Monday morning.

Voices clicked and sniped in his radio as pilots checked in with the tower. Leah was next to take off. He watched her jet turn on to the runway. Its nose aligned with the painted guide strips and winking lights. A roar of sound washed back toward him as she screamed down the tarmac. She flew as gracefully as she breathed.

Out across the desert, where they encamped in their temporary Red Flag barracks, the NATO pilots were lining up on their own runways. Nervous as hell. Cocky. Ready to make mistakes that could one day cost their lives.

Time to learn them a thing or two.

"Standby, Strap Happy," came a voice in his ear. "And...go."

He punched the throttle and owned the sky.

The after-flight briefing, Mike decided, was designed to reinforce the fact of solid ground beneath his feet. Pilots on both sides of the exercise had congregated in a darkened lecture room to review video footage, key computer data and expert tactical observers' conclusions. Seated next to Eric on an uncomfortable folding chair, Mike took careful notes, both mentally and on paper. Adrenaline and excitement waned with every passing minute, but not his sense of accomplishment.

Nor his determination to improve.

He'd not only survived his first official day as an Aggressor, he'd taken down two opponents—one just as the NATO hotshot had swooped out of Leah's line of sight. The coordinated punches they'd delivered were nearly as invigorating as sex.

That shouldn't have been the case. Not even close. He'd never flown with a woman on his wing, and certainly not one who evoked such possessive feelings.

Once released from their classroom obligations, pilots streamed back toward the hangar. Congratulatory bullshit followed—the standard trash talk that followed a good day in the air. Mike smiled, oddly at peace to be in such a place in his life.

"Hey, wait up," Leah called. Jogging to catch up with Mike, she wore darker-than-night aviator shades that reflected a goofy-ass picture of his smile.

"Thanks for that, up there." She lifted her face toward the patch of sky they'd just owned. "You saved my butt."

"Not bad for my first day up?"

"Not at all."

Mike rubbed his neck, which was filthy with sweat and desert dust. "Shit, I need a shower."

He hadn't meant it as a come-on. Not really. The quirk of her mouth, however, turned his simple declaration into one. Still, he wasn't going to be the one to push. That wasn't their MO. He wouldn't say no to a Monday night quickie. He wasn't going to ask for it either.

He didn't beg while on base. Period.

"What are you doing tonight?" she asked, taking off her sunglasses.

The fire was brighter there, making her dark irises irresistible. A certain vulnerability waited too.

"Tonight? No plans."

"Want to make some?"

The leap in his blood was a damn fine way to counter hours of debriefing. He'd spent the day zipping through clouds at Mach one. That power roared back at the thought of spending the rest of the night at Leah's command.

Yet he didn't want regrets. Not from either of them. He flicked his gaze around the parking lot. Tin Tin's Aston was nowhere to be seen, and the rest of the vehicles were fast departing for off-duty destinations.

"You sure?"

Leah shrugged. "It's been hard, you know? With you training and me needing to be the one to ride you about it."

Mike grinned, but she only gave him a *bite me* look.

"You know what I mean," she said. "I didn't... I didn't like mixing the two. Does that make sense?"

He nodded. While forced into near-adversarial roles in the simulator, he hadn't felt able to let go of his off-hours resentment of her seniority and skill. He loved the idea of being her colleague in full now. No sticky egos to get in the way.

"Yeah, it makes sense."

He edged closer, trying to keep his body language from spelling out too many obvious truths. That he wanted her. That he wanted her to take control. She smelled of sweat and jet wash, but his cock didn't give a right damn.

"But, Leah?"

"Hm?"

"If we do this, we're going to have to tell people eventually."

She made a sour face. "We don't have to do anything, Mike."

Bristling, he realized how little he liked the short form of his name coming from her. Too casual. It turned him into just another guy she knew.

"I keep enough secrets," he said slowly. "I don't want to be your dirty one."

"Why not?" She glanced around the parking lot. Her eyes were as quick as her reflexes in the sky. "Secrets are fun. For example, tomorrow I'll know that under your flight suit are red stripes from your nape to your fine, tight ass."

Mike's mind fuzzed at the edges. "You know that, do you?"

"Yes, pet. I do."

Shit. She was hardcore. Suddenly he was a hot ball of fire. Whatever she imagined was crystal clear in her mind, although he wouldn't know until it happened. The devious thirst for what they shared was there on her face, curling those crooked lips into a smile made for sin. There in the hangar parking lot, Mike could only lock down the way his flesh washed with hot and cold, all sensation, all anticipation.

"You know best, ma'am."

She tossed her head with a laugh then straddled her bike. She kicked it to life. "Race you, Michael."

Chapter Twenty-One

As Leah stood in line beside Mike, then watched him pay for entry to the Las Vegas car show, she realized she was a little slow—possibly verging on dumb, despite what the US Air Force seemed to believe of her.

Because she'd accidentally ended up on a date.

She knew for sure when Mike turned away from the ticket window and his side-quirked grin made her stomach flutter.

Damn it. A car show shouldn't have been a big deal. She and Jon had gone the year before. He'd zipped around the venue with surprisingly unchecked enthusiasm. Instead of feigning the bored playboy, he'd spouted car facts and engineering numbers like a Class-A gearhead. A great time, overall.

So when Leah had spotted the full-page ad in the paper, she hadn't thought it a huge deal to turn to Mike and suggest they go. After all, a drizzly rain meant no bike rides for entertainment. They'd come to enjoy sharing long, aggressive rides along endless desert highways.

Now it sank in that she'd been wearing only a tank top and a pair of panties while sitting at Mike's counter, trying to swig down a cup of his atrocious coffee. After yet another night of smokin' hot sex, that sure sounded like the best way to arrange a date.

Whoops.

That wasn't to say she was *opposed* to the idea of dating Mike. It was the next logical step after how much time they'd been spending together. Leah was so one of the guys that no one would think it strange if she went to look at fancy cars with a squad mate.

Only, she would've liked to know if Mike thought it was a date too.

If so, she would've put on something fancier than a Wonder Woman T-shirt over jeans, or do something other than skim her hair into yet another ponytail.

Stepping inside the giant convention center, they paused and gazed upon the labyrinth of booths, vehicles and brightly covered banners. Mike snagged a brochure with a map. He twisted it around to orient the front entrance.

"Where to first?"

"We don't need that. Just wander. That's the fun part."

He lifted attitude-laden eyebrows. "I think the fun part was this morning."

That quickly, she flushed hot. Because that quickly, she remembered the tension of his hands on her ass. She'd bent over in front of him, demanding that he lick every inch of skin he could reach.

"Shush," she said.

"No dirty talk? You normally like it."

"Not here." Being in public was something else entirely. She just wanted to...be. She liked who she was when she was alone with Michael, but it was just that. Alone together. This, now, was unfamiliar ground. "C'mon. I think the performance section is that way."

"You? Heading for the sports cars? This is me being decidedly unsurprised."

They wandered through the cars without any real sense of purpose. The reboot of the Porsche 911 was Leah's favorite—same sleek, distinctive lines but with boosted performance.

"Whaddaya think?" She rested one hand on the low roof and bent over the hot-as-hell machine. "And you better not give me your opinion on my ass."

"I already did that. Repeatedly." He bracketed her against the roof. "I was looking at the car. Totally."

"Can you believe that transmission?"

"Do you have a hidden collection of speeding tickets shoved under your bed?"

She pushed him back and tossed her ponytail in affront. "I've only had three. That's not so bad."

"How many of them were for reckless driving?"

"None, thank you very much. But in this bad boy, maybe I could fix that."

"Zero to sixty in less than five seconds is pretty cool."

Maybe she should do it. She had a little cash stashed away, and not so oddly, it racked up faster now that she wasn't drinking. Turned out alcohol was expensive. However, she wasn't really in the mood for a new car. For the moment, Michael was giving her enough hardcore thrills.

They drifted away from the Porsche and wandered down a new aisle.

"Check it out," Mike said, pointing over her head. "Simulator."

She grinned. "Don't you get enough of that at work?"

"Yeah, but look. They have an arcade bank too. I could so kick your ass in a race game."

He looked damn good, even under the harsh fluorescent lights of the convention center. It was unfair. Or it would be if the warm feeling spreading through her body didn't remind Leah how she could have him whenever she wanted. She had full rights.

"Says you. I could outfly, outdrive and outrace you on any vehicle. Any time. Any stakes."

"Do it."

They waited a few minutes for their turn in the head-to-head racing game. Then they were strapped into tiny boxes, each with its own screen. They chose the hardest route, of course.

Game on.

Except no matter how hard Leah smashed the pedal, she couldn't get around his flashy neon-green digital car. She pushed the steering wheel to its limit when she spotted an oncoming telephone pole. Her red car lost traction. The seat shook under her in an approximation of a crash.

She didn't just fail to beat Mike. She'd flamed out in spectacular fashion.

A few curses. Sure. Unavoidable. She sank in the seat. "Best two out of three."

"People are waiting their turn." Mike hauled her out of the game and slung his arm around her shoulder. "Let's go."

"Damn it, that wasn't fair."

He dragged her away, that arm still around her. Warm. Heavy. She ought to pull away. It was one thing to be seen hanging out. It was another to get busted being more intimate.

Geez. Paranoid much? The chances of being recognized in that massive convention hall were almost nil.

So she didn't make herself give him up. Her skin tingled with want, which would have to wait until later. Right then, it was nice to have him demonstrate his possessiveness. Man and woman in a way that made her insides watery. He smelled of his subtly intriguing cologne. On some guys the scent would have been too much, but Michael pulled it off. So much goddamn confidence.

"We could go to the back of the line," she said. "Go again."

He looked down at her. "Are you serious?"

"Why not?"

"You're really, truly, insanely competitive."

"I resent the word *insanely*." She ducked her gaze away. People streamed around them, ranging the full spectrum. Only in Vegas would a car show attract a gaggle of chicks in miniskirts on platform heels, along with Asian businessmen in full business-suit regalia.

"Look," she said. "It's not unreasonable to be disappointed in myself when I lose over a stupid mistake."

"Crashing?"

"I could have won if I'd known the course better."

He pulled them into a less traveled walkway. The main product in the booths seemed to be wrenches. A balding salesman perked up when he saw them, only to have his shoulders droop when Michael waved him off.

"What would it take?"

"To put me in a good mood?"

"Yes, ma'am." His voice curled around them, keeping them apart from the crowds.

She shivered on the chilly burst of need that turned her veins to live wires. Two words were all she needed to become wrapped up in him.

What she needed was a drink. Damn it. She would breathe then. That slow unfurling of tension would let her ease up. Car shows meant beer in plastic cups, just like going to bike races. She'd grown up in the motocross world. Her dad and brothers had all but lived at dirt tracks, with Leah right there too. That fun had always been doused in ice-cold beer from red Solo cups.

Because of the rain, Michael had even driven them to the convention center in his beat-up Bronco. She could keep it to one or two, and he'd be able to get her home.

The way he was looking at her, and the quiet "ma'am" he'd used... He was offering her something else. Something irrevocably separated from alcohol.

She shook off the high-strung buzz then reached for Michael. His hair was so soft, the strands barely long enough to wrap around her fingertips. She pinched and tugged. "This, pet? You'd offer yourself over a silly game?"

His eyes drifted half-shut. The corners of his mouth quirked. "That's always an option."

She leaned up on her toes, took his mouth. The shape of his lips was just right to fit hers. They slipped together, each taking a little at a time. She could get lost in him if she let herself—forget where she was, forget how everything would be different on Monday when they went back to work.

She nibbled his bottom lip once for good measure. "You taste like crappy coffee."

"Gonna offer me something tastier to lick?"

"Is that what you want?" Unable to resist any longer, she snuck her fingers under the hem of his snug T-shirt. He was all thin skin over strong muscle. Lovely. "You want me to ride your face like the toy you are?"

Now he grinned with infectious humor, no matter the sex blazing between them. "If it would help your cranky-ass mood."

With a grin she said, "So noble and sacrificing."

Looping a finger through his belt, she tugged him back into the main stream of foot traffic. The touch of leather against her skin was changing her in irrevocable ways.

"You're going to buy me cotton candy instead."

"One does what one must," he said with a put-upon air.

However, he didn't let her drag him along. He needed only two strides with his long legs to eat up the distance between them. He walked at her side then took the lead.

That was hot. He really did mean "only in the bedroom". Thank God. She wouldn't have enjoyed their play *at all* had he been some sniveling sub who begged mommy to give him a spanking. Mike was one hundred percent man. He was strong, sexy and marvelously self-assured. Those qualities meant that when he gave over to her whims, he satisfied them both with explosive results.

A few minutes later, with his corndog already gobbled down, he presented her with a pink-and-blue cloud of cotton candy.

"Thank you." She smiled as she pulled off a piece. Like being a teenager again.

After that first sugary bite, she offered a piece to Michael. He took it right from her fingers, which stopped her pulse. His eyes never wavered even as his lips grazed her fingertips and his tongue swirled sugar crystals off her skin. Prickling heat climbed her arm. Her nipples beaded. Instantly.

This accidental date needed to be no big deal. Nothing special. She had too much riding on toeing the line. All she needed to do was keep her nose clean and she'd make major soon. She *needed* that rank—a tasty carrot to reward this being-good-ness. Otherwise she might completely lose her shit. Fall apart again.

So she ignored an unexpected want for more. More of Michael, on every level. She was already addicted to speed, thought too highly of booze and was probably way too high-strung. She didn't need to get addicted to Michael too.

She coughed and looked away from his distinctive neon-blue eyes. "Sorry about that back there. To say I get competitive is probably an understatement."

"Because of your brothers?"

"Yeah. It was kind of hard to be seen next to them, unless I beat them at their own games."

He took her wrist and dragged more pink fluff to his mouth. His tongue arched gently over her fingers, in the seam between, tasting her and the candy.

"*I* see you, ma'am."

Fuck. Just *fuck*. Her heart took a stupid free-fall tumble. He knew too much, understood too much. And hell if he wasn't too easygoing and accepting. Could he accept her, faults and all?

Something in his eyes said yes. Yes, he could.

She was in so much trouble.

Chapter Twenty-Two

Mike's grin felt permanently stitched to his mouth. He really *liked* Leah. Forget the sex for a minute—although that was nearly impossible. She was just cool. Her little pink Ducati darted past his BMW, all sleek lines and exuberant flash. She bent low over the handlebar with her elbows folded against her ribs. It was a textbook sport-racing posture, with the bonus of jeans wrapped taut across her perfect ass.

Yup, his grin wasn't going anywhere.

He gunned the throttle and passed her when the next light flashed green. Lucky thing it seemed that the entire LVPD parked on the Strip, especially on a Saturday night. Otherwise he and Leah would've risked getting smashed with speeding tickets. The fuel of their unspoken competition was just too high. She'd been so pissed at losing that stupid race game, though his victory was a balm for the bitch-ass weeks he'd endured after arriving at Nellis.

Now he was winning their race too. The traffic thinned. The roads became more normal, stripped of all things Vegas, except for a rearview of the glittering skyline. He swerved up an on-ramp and took off. Full speed. He loved the rumble in his chest and the hard pulse of the bike *he* controlled. The thrill and danger rivaled ripping past Mach two. Here, he was closer to the ground. The wrong patch of asphalt would mean the end.

Not that the idea would stop him.

Adrenaline junkie. He knew it. He rather liked endorphins. He couldn't imagine a sub who didn't. There wouldn't be any surviving the delicious pain without that floating, peaceful reward. Adrenaline, however, had thrilled him since well before he'd discovered his proclivities.

He must've backed off while letting his mind wander down to his cock because Leah rushed past him in a sizzle of color. She flipped him the bird and darted ahead.

Oh no you don't.

She owned his ass in bed, and she outranked him on base. Fuck losing now.

And they'd been having such a polite time...

Not thirty seconds later, he pulled alongside her and returned her one-fingered gesture. He took off like a shot and put a quarter mile between them without even pushing his bike to its limit. The ride sucked away any sound other than engine and wind, but he could imagine Leah cussing like the Aggressor she was. Frustrating the hell out of her was becoming one of his favorite hobbies—again, if he forgot about the sex.

Which was fucking impossible.

Deciding to be merciful, he pulled off at the next ramp and turned back toward Vegas. Eric had told him about a little dive nearby. He'd called it the best, corniest Mexican restaurant in the city. Good enough. Mike wanted a bit of corny. Leah dealt with the hard stuff well enough, from her badassery on base to her domination in the bedroom, but he'd been intrigued by her behavior at the car show. Hesitant. *Really* unsure of herself. That had surprised him almost as much as finding out how well their desires aligned.

Leah Girardi. Uncertain. It didn't scan.

The only thing that made sense was, well, she didn't usually come across as a chick. He was beginning to realize how hard she worked to be accepted. Now that she wasn't drinking, she pushed that line even harder. Eyes on target. Goal in sight. Keep the boys from drooling over her absolutely amazing bod.

So, he'd tagged along to a car show. That meant absolutely nothing in the scheme of what they'd already shared. Yet she'd been as flustered as a girl on her first date.

Time to keep that up. He needed to know what manner of female waited under the flight suit and hot pink helmet.

Matching black underwear, that's what.
Goddamn. Forget the sex.
Maybe for a minute.

He signaled to turn into the restaurant's parking lot. *La Hacienda Grande*. How very original, and very in keeping with Las Vegas. A neon sign in the shape of a curvy woman wearing only a sombrero perched on the roof. No wonder Eric had recommended the place.

He killed the engine and pulled off his helmet. Leah did the same. For a moment, their gazes caught. They were both breathless, sweaty, and riled with an indescribable buzz of energy. Her eyes were wide. Her lips parted and quirked in that way he could relish for an eternity. He couldn't recall another woman who so effortlessly combined cute, sexy and daredevil into one irresistible package.

Then again, when staring at her, Mike couldn't think about much of anything. Just her. He was always curious where they'd go next, but leaving the sexual direction up to her freed his mind. He'd come to appreciate his easygoing response to most things, which was decidedly more peaceful than white-knuckling his way through tours of duty.

"I got you once," she said.

"When I let you."

"*Let* me?"

"Give it up, Princess. You're never gonna beat my machine."

She looked him up and down, her smirk just this side of voracious. He wasn't beyond admitting that he dressed for her when they were together. Form-fitting black T-shirt? Worn-in jeans and black biker boots? Flight jacket? Check, check, check. He knew what drove her crazy. The power didn't go one way. Her frank appreciation, followed by a flash of unchecked hunger, proved as much.

Yes, it was good to be a sub. That didn't mean he was completely without desires and intentions. He only needed to go about them in a different way. He'd cultivated a certain set of skills to keep things interesting and satisfying—for them both, he hoped.

Only they weren't in bed yet. His smirk felt good. Let her chew on a loss for a while.

But damn, the girl was relentless. "Gimme that beast on the way home and I'll beat you," she said. "Hands down."

He laughed outright. "If you think I'm letting you on my BMW other than plastered across my back, you're insane."

Leaving her to whatever competitive protest she needed to mumble, Mike walked toward the restaurant's front door. Mariachi music. The scents of cayenne pepper and cumin and fry oil. Awesome.

He waited, holding the door, until she met him there. "After you, Princess."

Another middle finger as she flounced past.

He laughed again. "Is that the theme of the evening?"

"Fuck you? Yup, sounds about right."

"Excellent."

He needed a minute to admire Leah as she shed her flight jacket. Same squad patches. Same blood chits sewn in the lining. They were comrades. That still sent a weird jerk of discomfort down his spine, but it wasn't as strange as before. Flying was probably more intrinsic to her identity than it was to his. He'd just about lucked onto his path. She'd barreled there with that same determination, surpassing his accomplishments along the way.

Target. Goal. Win.

In any man, he would've admired her ambition, but he couldn't get it through his head when it came to her, or any woman pilot. How could he still be so opposed in the face of one obvious fact?

He respected her.

A short, portly man with a giant black mustache ushered them into the main dining area. It wasn't hard to follow him in the packed joint. His sombrero was *massive*. The walls were painted in classical Mexican pastels and geometric shapes, but those shapes vaguely resembled six dancing girls.

"I didn't know Picasso did restaurants," he said near Leah's ear.

"I didn't know you had such questionable taste. It's making me reconsider our whole relationship."

"Relationship, eh? That sounds serious, Princess."

"Shut up. All I'm saying is that I took you to one of the most spectacular car shows in the world. In return, I get Rorschach nudes."

"Seems a fair trade to me."

Her grin let loose. "Let's just hope the food is good. One star for atmosphere."

The sombrero deposited their menus on the table of a back booth. Black pleather crackled beneath Mike's ass as he sat down. Leah shot him a wicked eyebrow when her seat made the noise. *"Really?"*

"Yes, really," he said.

The man took out a small notepad. "Drinks?"

"Coke," Leah said.

"Same."

Mike watched his departure. "That has to be the most intimidating sombrero-to-head ratio I've ever seen."

This time she laughed so hard that she snorted. She clapped both hands over her mouth and smothered the sound. For a moment, he could only stare. He'd never heard her laugh like that. No smirking or husky anticipation. Just...*free.*

"You ass," she finally said, gasping. "Now the whole restaurant's staring at me."

"You think a lot of yourself. Naturally they're still dumbfounded by that UFO on his head."

"I'm gonna buy one for you and make you wear it." Her brows wiggled suggestively.

"Red light."

"Wuss."

A different man—perhaps their real waiter rather than the maître d'—brought their Cokes and took their orders.

Mike ran a finger along the top of the red plastic tumbler. "I would've been disappointed with real glasses."

"Now all we need are plastic plates."

"And so much cheese that it won't matter what the hell we ordered." He sipped out of a straw and leaned back. Leah's eyes followed the movement of his chest. Yes, very nice. "Anybody can do fancy in Vegas and anybody can do gaudy. It takes real skill to find genuinely inadvertent tacky."

Her eyes shimmered with humor—almost as nice as her appreciation of his body. He liked knowing they had some spark of connection outside of work and sex.

"How did you find this place, anyway?"

"Eric," he said.

"Figures."

"He's not as bad as your tone implies."

"He's absolutely that bad and you know it."

"Yeah." He grinned. "Yeah, he is."

Leah didn't like Eric, although she seemed okay with Dash. Hell, if Mike were a chick, he wouldn't have been Eric's biggest fan either. The guy was positively Neanderthal when it came to women. Sex, yes. Equals, never. That attitude used to align perfectly, back when he and Eric first met in Afghanistan. Not so much anymore.

Hoping to scramble back from a topic that wasn't laughing or bullshitting, he spied a mariachi band as they emerged from the kitchen.

Leah turned to stare then dropped her head into her hands. "It just keeps getting worse."

"No, *better.*"

"You make me doubt the sanity of the Air Force recruiters. Seriously." No matter her protests, she hadn't stopped smiling since sitting down on the creaky black upholstery. "I mean, there had to have been a section on humor, right? Did I forget?

Maybe because 'funny' and 'not funny' should be damn obvious."

Mike dug his wallet out of his back pocket. He pulled out five dollars. "Well, lookie here. It's a mariachi magnet."

He hadn't known Leah's eyes could get that wide. "You wouldn't dare."

"No?"

"Absolutely not. Mike, put that away."

"See, here's the thing." He tried to take her hand, all fake suave, but she slapped his knuckles. That only made him chuckle harder. "If I lure them over here and that pisses you off, I get tons out of it."

"How do you figure?" Her mouth had scrunched into something like a pout—probably the closest she could manage.

"I get to see you blush, and probably laugh. Then I get to enjoy how you'll exact your revenge when we get home."

"You assume you're going home with me, Michael."

Her tone was so perfectly modulated that he did a double take. She held her dominatrix expression for about three heartbeats, which stopped him cold. Only a sparkle of play across her top lip gave her away. In the spirit of fairness, it was his turn to give her the finger.

"It's gonna become tradition," she said wistfully. She placed her chin on interlaced fingers and fluttered her lashes. "I'll never think of being flipped off the same way."

When Mike reached out again to take her hand, she let him. He kissed her knuckles, whereas she'd slapped his. Sounded about right. He looked into her eyes. Dead on. No games. Just the weight of all he could bring to bear as a man. The effect registered across her features: dilated pupils, an intake of breath, lips parted so slightly.

Against her skin he whispered, "I *am* going home with you, ma'am."

"Yes." Her voice was a rasp. She took a quick drink of Coke. "Yes, Michael. You are."

He released her completely—hand and eyes. "But not before a song."

Leah tried to catch his forearm while he waved the fiver toward the trio of mariachis. "Don't! Mike!"

He was way bigger, in every sense. Holding the bill out of reach was no trick. He chuckled at her attempts, particularly enjoying how her struggles bounced her breasts. That filmy double-layer tank top wasn't doing a very good job of containing her eagerness. Her nipples were hard points beneath the lace. He liked to think it wasn't because of the air conditioning. The fire snapping in her eyes laid that doubt to rest.

"We're just supporting independent artists," he said. "It's the philanthropist in me."

The food arrived just before the mariachis surrounded their table. Huge guitars. Huge hats. A huge grin on Mike's face. His cheeks were going to bust open. He paid the men and pretended to take their musical skills *very* seriously while snatching glimpses of Leah's expression. She doggedly ate whatever she'd ordered. It definitely had cheese. If he didn't know better of her courage, he would've sworn she was trying to hide her face with her hand. She kicked him beneath the table. Repeatedly.

The singers crooned until Leah couldn't hold back anymore. She hid her mouth behind a couple paper napkins and leaned back in the booth. Laughter danced in her eyes and shook her shoulders. Maybe she was hiding proof of Mike's victory, or maybe she tried to keep from hurting the musicians' feelings. Either way, they shared that moment from across the table.

He licked his lower lip. On purpose. Like some sort of club slimeball. She gasped for breath and swatted the air, as if that would make him lay off. Not a chance.

Just when his tolerance for his own game was wearing thin—*damn* they were loud at such close range—the mariachis bowed and moved on.

A young woman followed them. In her arms was an oblong basket bearing roses. This time Mike didn't show off while retrieving money from his wallet. Leah was still chuckling to herself, eating in earnest rather than as a means of defense.

His own food would be stone cold by the time he got around to it. Didn't matter. Different hungers stirred his body, and he couldn't claim they were entirely sexual. He liked her competitive streak and her one-of-the-boys ability to shit talk, but he adored being able to make her laugh.

"*Señorita?*"

The young woman veered toward their table. The exchange of dollar for rose took place so quickly that Leah had no time to protest. The flower girl was gone in a whisk of colorful fabric and dark hair.

He caught Leah's hand again and reclaimed the entirety of her attention. Again, that balance of power. He would deny her few things in the bedroom, but out in the world? He was the man. That meant giving his date a flower.

"For you, Leah."

She shook her head, as if by reflex, and then with more force. He almost believed she would refuse it, which would put a whole other spin on their future.

A dead end on more quasi-dates.

Enjoy the sex while it lasted.

Then back to colleagues.

Slowly, however... So slowly, she lowered her eyes to gaze at the single red rose. She closed her fingers over the stem and swallowed. "Thank you, Michael."

Chapter Twenty-Three

Almost a week later, Leah pushed a different plate away with a groan. Her hands folded over her stomach as she leaned back in her seat. "God, I feel so naughty."

Cass Whitman smiled and licked chocolate sauce off her spoon. "I'm pretty sure this qualifies me as brilliant."

"I agree." Leah couldn't resist another forkful of triple-chocolate cake. "Are you going to tell Ryan on me? He'll make me run ten miles if he finds out we went straight to dessert."

"I'm not telling him anything." Cass's big blue eyes sparkled with a constant sense of good humor that never seemed to leave.

When Cass had called out of the blue, inviting Leah out for the night, she'd almost said no. Almost. Even though Ryan and Cass had been dating for something like seven months, the two women hadn't gone out without the guys. If Leah had a free night lately, she spent it with Mike.

So she'd gone. It would be something different that didn't involve getting blitzed on alcohol or getting blitzed on Michael. She'd begun to wonder if she was verging on addicted to the man.

When Cass had suggested they skip real food and order the dessert mini-sampler, Leah could've kissed the woman. She'd needed some chocolate. Stat.

Until even the dark chocolate puddle cake had managed to remind her of Mike. The raspberry sauce in the middle had been hot enough to prick her lips with heat. She'd wondered what Mike would do if she drizzled it over tender skin.

She shifted in her seat.

At the same time, it was way easier to think of deliberately applying heat and pain than to remember the perfect rose he'd offered. She'd actually dried it in an attempt to keep it beautiful forever. How very unlike her.

Cass put down her fork and leaned her chin on a fist. "So, what's wrong?"

Leah laughed. "Nothing's wrong. That's half the problem."

"Trouble in paradise?"

Something about the way she asked—probably the knowing look on her features—sent a chill down Leah's spine. She picked up her water glass in an attempt to look...cool. Christ, she was a dork.

"I'm not tracking."

Cass waved her fork. "You and Mike. Getting so good you're scared?"

The water turned into chunks in her throat. She sputtered. "How the hell did you know?"

"Oh, please." Cass rolled her eyes. "When you guys disappeared at Paulie's? And you came back with that pink flush in your cheeks? How could I miss it?"

Leah rubbed the base of her thumb over her sternum, which still burned from the coughing spasm. "Does Ryan know?"

"Nope." Cass seemed blissfully unaware of the relief loosening Leah's joints. "He *never* has a clue about things like that, unless Jon gives him one. Which he didn't, by the way. I figure it's not my business to point it out if he doesn't ask."

"Thanks," Leah said quietly. "I don't think he'd mind, but...I just like keeping my business to myself."

Cass pointed the fork at her again. "That's because you don't have enough girls for friends. Lucky for you, I intend to fix that."

The laugh that burbled out of Leah was the aural embodiment of more relief. "I'm sure I couldn't live without you."

"You will be sure. Just you wait and see." Cass pushed her chair back from the table. "When you see where I'm taking us next, you'll be completely and totally convinced of my brilliance."

"Just so long as it's not the *Thunder from Down Under* show. I see enough sweaty, posturing males at work."

Had Leah possessed any idea of where Cass was going to take them, she'd have volunteered to buy the show's tickets. They pulled into a tiny asphalt-topped parking lot and went through an unremarkable door.

That opened into a sex shop.

The place had weird washed-red lighting and a sound system that blared heavy rock. Shelves and rows and racks were filled with plastic wrapped...implements. Vibrators, costumes and almost anything a girl could think of—including a full row of black leather and silver buckles.

The back of her neck burned fire hot. It was one thing that Cass had guessed she and Mike were sleeping together. If by some devilish trick she'd guessed the things they got up to, Leah might die.

Well, maybe. On the other hand, she hadn't been able to talk about it with anyone. Not even with Mike, really, since he already knew what he was doing. She kept trying to hold up an unbreakable front—show no vulnerability. Yet the secrets were nibbling at her from the inside. She was Michael's ma'am, and she didn't have a clue what she was doing.

Her fingers trailed over a feather-topped tickler. She could do interesting things to Michael with that.

A quick cough cleared the flush of lust from her chest. "Are we here for anything in particular?"

"Nope," Cass said blithely. "I just think this place is great. I didn't have the guts to come in here for a long time, so now I make sure to stop in on occasion. See if there's anything new and tasty." She picked up a tiny white outfit and held it out at arm's length. "What do you think?"

Leah peered closely. "Naughty nurse?"

"Yep." She smiled then put it back on the rack. "How about you? Anything strike your fancy?"

God, Cass was too easygoing. Relaxed about everything. Leah could tell the other woman that she liked stripping naked and doing cartwheels, and it would be fine.

"Kink," she blurted.

Cass's eyebrows wrinkled with confusion. "Honey, everything in here is kinky. Except maybe the lube. That can just be a necessity."

Leah turned on a heel and slipped down the aisle, then turned left to the BDSM section. She'd only glimpsed it when they'd entered, but she felt drawn there. The expanse of leather was almost dizzying. The scent. The variety. All the possibilities.

She picked up a three-strap slapper—the one tool she knew best. She'd used Mike's several times since their first weekend. Even as her cheeks burned with what she was about to admit, the weight of the implement fit just right in her palm. The familiar tingle spread between her shoulders.

She held the slapper up. "Kink."

Cass's eyes went wider before she grinned. "No way."

The petite redhead's good humor was infectious. Leah smiled and even laughed a little. "Way."

"I gotta say, there's something about some bad-girl action. If you're lucky, there's a spanking afterward."

Leah started to put her hands over her ears, only to remember she still held the slapper. She tucked it back on the rack. Mike already had that. "Swear to God, I'll go wait outside and never speak to you again if you bring Ryan into this."

Cass shook her head, but her smile never dimmed. "Mum's the word, I promise. I have to say, I never expected you'd be into getting that kind of dirty on. Flat-out honest? I cannot picture you on your knees. At all."

Leah swallowed around the knot in her throat. This was surprisingly hard. It had been a long time since she'd had a female friend. If anyone would keep her secrets, it would be Cass. "I'm not."

"What?"

Words about Michael stuck in her throat. Well now, there was a surprise. Apparently she didn't want to give away the lovely, private things he did for her. She couldn't bring herself to directly say that he was the one who knelt for her.

"I'm... I'm the one holding the slapper."

"No way," Cass squealed again.

"Way."

Cass clapped her hands twice. "You go, girl." She blinked. "Wait, does that mean Mike...?"

Leah turned away, the better to hide the blush that was eating her alive. At the same time, Cass's unhesitating acceptance was nice—a balm to her frayed nerves. She and Mike had been hiding and ducking for more than six weeks.

"Let's not go there, okay?" Her fingers trailed over a row of leather cuffs.

"No problem." Cass shrugged. "So I guess the whole sex-shop thing isn't as novel for you?"

The grin came easier with the blush abating. "Actually, not so much. I'm fairly new to the game."

Cass's eyes lit up. "Ooh. Then we definitely need to get you something special. Something that will blow his mind." Her brows drew together. "But lordy, I have no idea what that would be."

As if against her will, Leah found herself standing before a row of canes. Lots of lengths and colors, all of them slender. Black or white or red, made of various different materials. One had a long shaft of pale wood. The blue nylon around the handle reminded her of Mike's eyes.

"I think I know."

She took it in hand. The slender rattan was so light in her palm, but she knew it was anything but gentle. If wielded improperly, a cane could inflict significant injuries. The internet had proven to be a wealth of knowledge, including information about methods and how long she'd need to train.

Buying the damn thing would be a commitment. There'd be no running over to Michael's house and saying *Gee, look what I came across.* She'd have to practice and admit, if only to herself, that this was what she wanted. Not what she'd happened into. Not what she was doing just to get her hands on Mike's amazing body—though it certainly had its own appeal.

The payoff would be worth it. Mind-blowing, probably. Michael's eyes would go dark as soon as he saw it in her hand. He'd grin, as if he didn't think she had it in her. Until she had him bent over the end of his bed, taking her strokes. Testing them both.

She wouldn't bind him for their first time. If she wanted to know the full extent of what he could handle—and what she could dish out—she'd leave him unstrapped. To see every delicious twitch. To see if he pulled away.

Her mouth went dry. Between her legs a deep heat beat steadily with her pulse. Her heart was making dips and loops that any trick pilot would envy.

"That's pretty." Cass tweaked the price tag and tilted her head to look at it. "And they're awful proud of it, aren't they?"

Leah jumped an inch. So lost in her head, she'd forgotten the other woman was there. "Proud?"

"It's kinda pricey."

Bouncing the very tip across the inside of her forearm, Leah smiled to herself. Touching even that tap against her skin caused a flash of pain. A sting resonated inside her flesh. If she did it right, she'd leave striped welts across Michael's ass and legs, all with a mere flick of her wrists. And damn if he wouldn't beg for more. She hadn't yet found his limit.

Though if she screwed up, she could hurt her pet. Badly.

A cold chill went through her. She forced a smile, so Cass wouldn't see how deeply she was affected. It was one thing to admit she got into a little of the dirty. It was something else entirely to let slip that she yearned for it.

"I suppose it takes a lot of work to make a good cane. The price isn't that bad." She bit her lip. "I think I'm going to get it."

"Good. I'm glad you're not all weirded out that I brought you here."

Leah's laugh was involuntary, and it felt good. More relief to steady her arousal. "I'm glad you're not weirded out too."

"So, chocolate desserts and sex-toy shopping." Cass grinned. "I win at making friends."

Leah remained giddy as they walked to the counter where a purple-haired clerk waited. But a sudden choke of nerves made her stomach clench. "Wait. You're not planning on telling Fang, are you?"

"Oh, heck no." Cass laced her arm through Leah's and bumped their hips together. "A girl's got to have some secrets, or her guy might start thinking he's got her all figured out. Then where would the poor dears be, with their egos that huge?"

"Screwed. We definitely can't let that happen."

"See? It's for his own benefit."

Leah flourished the cane in the air and snapped it gently against her jeans. His own benefit. That was cute.

Because she was starting to feel like everything was for her.

Chapter Twenty-Four

Mike wasn't a stranger to strip clubs. What serviceman could claim otherwise? He didn't know any who'd try to with a straight face. So when Eric invited him and Dash to head to the Playful Pussycat, he didn't hesitate and he didn't clear it with Leah.

Why would he? They were weekend types. All business at work—just easier that way—and sex that friggin' blew his mind once Friday night rolled around. They'd taken to stocking food and condoms to last until Sunday night. Afterward, she returned to her place or he rode back to his. He awoke in his own bed, alone, on Monday morning.

He'd be fine with it if he wasn't falling for her.

He hadn't been a saint since he and Georgia parted ways. There were always places where a male sub could get his rocks off with a paid femdom, but that was it—coming hard when a regular hook-up wouldn't do. He'd tried it once or twice, although it always smacked of hiring a prostitute. The danger, too, made him uneasy. Instant trust? A Dom's instant understanding of what he needed? He hadn't ever felt that with a two-hour session.

Now he couldn't imagine such a scenario. Leah was beginning to know him inside out. What he could take. What he *wanted* to take. It was hard to keep barriers in place when that give and take became so vital. At least it hit him that way. Maybe other subs, male or female, could stick their needs into a box at the end of the night.

He wasn't built that way—not that he wanted to be. It got complicated quickly. His growing attachment to Georgia had precipitated their breakup. She'd wanted a fun time, and he'd wanted more. Hence staying away from the whole damn thing for so long.

Now there was Leah.

He served her. Happily. Eagerly, even. Her approval and satisfaction had come to dominate a hefty part of his daily life. Waking. Sleeping. Didn't matter. She set the pace, and he submitted. The switch to making an emotional connection was a half-step away, and he knew it.

So, ta-da. Strip club. Something to clear his mind and remind himself that he was a red-blooded male who could sport a raging hard-on while watching nubile, goddamn flexible women writhe onstage.

"Man, where's your fucking head?" Eric slapped him on the back.

"Right here, Kisser. Don't dodge the fact it's your round. Jack and Coke."

Dash was the designated driver, pretty much as always. "Near beer." He said it with a scowl, which was really unlike his generally devil-may-care personality. Mike exchanged looks with Eric, who only shrugged and headed off to the bar.

Mike settled back into the oversized red leather booth. He crossed his ankles where they stuck out into the aisle. Dash was even taller. They needed room. Hell if a dude wanted too little space between himself and his buddies when there was *any* possibility of a stiffie.

He ignored Dash's scowl, focusing instead on a dancer whose red hair was like something out of a *Star Trek* episode about an exotic space chick Captain Kirk would eventually bang. Yeah, she was hella hot. Curvy in the right places. Dark eyes, with wide, exotic cheekbones and a golden complexion. Mike had been stationed around the world. He'd put money that underneath that neon dye job, she was something near to Filipina.

She wiggled out of her sexy librarian costume and proceeded to dry hump the pole midway down a little catwalk.

"Look over there," Dash said, his scowl gone. A definite plus. Instead he wore his trademark shark-tooth grin. It took up his whole face when he smiled. Their resident jester. "Kisser is such an asshole sometimes."

If Dash was the jester, then Eric was the ladies' man. From deep in the slums of Detroit, he'd beat his way free. Boxing. UFC matches. Of all the men in the squadron Mike wouldn't want to tangle with, it was built-like-a-Mack-truck Kisser, named for how many times he'd been smacked in the mouth.

Only, he wasn't fighting right then. Mike snickered along with Dash as Eric waved dollars at the redhead. She was bare save a tiny garter belt. She slunk over on hands and knees. Her sultry smile almost looked genuine. She arched like a cat and flipped her hair back. Then, with flexibility that must be a job requirement, she gracefully slid one leg off the stage. The garter was right there for Eric to feed with bills. One at a time.

"If he touches her any more, he'll be in trouble," Dash said.

"Cuz of the bouncers?"

"Nah, cuz he'll knock them out. You remember that time in Tucson when he took out two guys with one blow? That's all he'd need with Fang watching him like a hawk." Dash shook his head. "And then there's the potential for an arrest, which would end our evening real quick. You feel like posting bail?"

"Not on the best of nights, man. He's such an asshole sometimes," Mike echoed.

"But of course he'd say we're just green with envy."

"Someone envy you?" Mike swallowed the last of his drink. "Fuck, Dash. Sunny's hot as hell." He smirked. "If you don't mind my saying."

"Sure she is. Sweetest piece I've ever had. And to be married to her? I'm a lucky guy."

Something about the way he said it meant just the opposite, as if he recited by rote words that had once been heartfelt. Whenever Sunny was out of town, Dash became a wrecked bastard. Fun times.

"Spit it out," Mike said. "What's going on? I don't wanna psychoanalyze you all night like Oprah or some shit."

Dash only waved him off. "Forget it. Kisser! Get the hell off that chick and get our drinks!"

Eric whispered something in the maybe-Filipina's ear. This time her smile was genuine. She shook her head and waved him off—but without any real grit. The way she crawled away with her primetime ass in the air was a thing of beauty. Eric just stood there, arms crossed, and brazenly watched every sinuous move. She used the pole to climb back to her feet, gave him a toodle-oo and strutted toward stage right.

How the hell did he manage that shit? The man had balls of solid rock when it came to women. A confirmed poon hound. If Mike didn't admire the innate skill so much, he'd have dredged up some moral compunction. But why bother? Kisser was a rock star.

That he and Jon, one of Leah's best friends, got along like a cat and a dog tied in burlap wouldn't ever be easy to navigate. Mike always felt caught in the middle of the pilots' feud—one that had started before Mike's arrival on base. But he wasn't there to think about Tin Tin, or even Leah.

"Give it up, Dash," he said. "Before Eric brings our drinks and gets all up in your shit."

Sometimes he was just so *Dash* that Mike forgot the man's real name. Captain Liam Christiansen. It just didn't fit. His call sign was a short form of "dumb as shit", and he certainly played up that moniker.

That evening was a glaring exception. His smile drooped. He raked his hands through his buzzed hair before cracking four knuckles. "Sunny's in DC again. I fucking hate when she leaves. It's getting...strained."

Mike frowned. "Like, *bad* strained?"

A terse nod. "We haven't said anything about dick. Doesn't mean everything's smooth sailing. I'm supposed to support her choices. Hell, she made it through my overseas tours, and we got through her years at law school. You'd think... Ah, fuck it."

He shook his head and went back to cracking knuckles. Conversation over. Not that Mike needed more. *Shit.* Eight years together and this was what a marriage could look like? His skin went cold. Focusing—intently, purposefully—on the next dancer didn't help. Her sizeable tits looked real. Sometimes a beautiful expanse of female flesh was enough.

Not this time.

Yeah, he might be falling for Leah. What the hell did that matter? She was going to make major. Unless she mustered out before him, she'd always outrank him. The traditional side of him still rankled and didn't take kindly to the fact. He liked his mom and dad's relationship. She'd raised Mike and his brother and sister. Dad had worked in a shitty steel-mill job. Their example was the only way Mike knew how a marriage should go.

New worries from Dash only reinforced his admittedly caveman point of view. Sunny's decision to take a high-profile job in DC meant she was gone almost as much as she was home. No wonder Dash looked out of sorts.

"You limp dicks enjoying yourselves?" Eric plunked a triangle of drinks onto the table.

Mike didn't budge to make room, so Eric slid into the opposite side of the booth.

"What's not to enjoy?" Dash's terse confession seemed to unburden him. "Shall I list out amusements so we can choose a favorite? Is it how you made a slavering shithead of yourself? Or how you *actually* looked hopeful? Don't tell me. That pretty young thang promised she'd blow you after her shift."

Eric crossed his arms with a smirk. "Exactly what she promised."

"Suuuure," Dash said, chuckling. "Quite the smart business decision. Did you know that's why strippers are notorious for their fat investment portfolios? It's true. I read it in *The Wall Street Journal.*"

"You mock. In the morning, I'll let you know how it went."

Dash took a swig of his O'Doul's then held it up to a light. "I'm gazing into my crystal...bottle. Unfortunately I see a very different scenario. You lurk around outside her dressing room. She says, meet me in the alley behind the club. You will, cuz you're a sorry little man, and you'll wait until about three o'clock. Then your poor, disappointed dick will have to admit the truth."

"That strippers give awesome head?" Eric grinned, smug as hell. He did up the necessities of a tequila and downed the shot. "Oh, wait. I forgot. You got married at age twelve. Wouldn't know a damn thing. When *I* was twelve, I popped a girl's cherry."

"Horseshit," Mike said on a laugh.

"I didn't know you have a sister, Kisser. You love her long time?" Dash made a kissy face. "That's the only scenario I can imagine where you'd get laid before your voice changed. At least tell me sister dearest was good."

"As good as a hummer from a stripper," Mike added.

That shark smile of Dash's was out in full force. "But didn't your daddy get pissed? I'd have thought he had dibs."

Eric only shook his head. "Jealous bastards. You two have the most piss-awful sex lives at Nellis. Deny it. Dare ya. I'll force your flight suits down your lying throats."

Dash didn't answer, which Mike caught in a heartbeat. Brotherhood to the rescue. "Hell, man, there's a reason for my call sign. That girl, for example." He nodded to another dancer—slim, brunette, ballerina's body. *Aw, damn.* Too much like Leah. He forced himself to say, "She's just begging for a good spank."

"Wank, you mean," Eric said. "Exactly what you'll go home to."

"While you're getting blown by that redhead," Mike replied. "Yup. That's exactly how it'll go tonight." After finishing the last of his drink, he unfurled from the booth. "My round. What'll it be?"

Eric stood too. "Change for a twenty."

They made their way through the club. All done up in red, dingy white and gold, it looked exactly how an off-Strip club should look. Somewhat rundown. The music was giving Mike a headache—always the same thumping beat that guaranteed gyrations.

His need to look back at the girl onstage was annoying. Although the dancer's body resembled Leah's, never in a thousand goddamn years could he imagine his ma'am on her knees. This woman's pout was all wrong too. Where was the keen, hard-eyed lust he'd come to expect when he and Leah were deep into a hard session? She owned him with those eyes.

Shit. Just...*shit.*

He ordered the drinks—a double Jack for himself this time. No fooling around. He wanted to get blitzed. Eric, holding a rolled-up wad of dollar bills, joined him. "So what's with sharkface? He's a grenade with no pin. Three, two, one...bam."

"No clue."

"Liar."

"If you wanna know, you ask him. I'm not a girl at recess."

"Ass."

Mike shrugged. "Some trouble with Sunny. That's the best I could manage."

"Shit, man."

"Yup."

Mike watched Eric shake off the unnerving news and return to the catwalk. A blonde this time. Pretty one. Nearly innocent. She wiggled in a way that suggested this was her first dance. She was nervous. Virginal. That hit Mike in a way he wouldn't have guessed, but not along the lines of debauching a barely eighteen-year-old.

No, it was the thought of what Leah would do to her.

He was all manner of screwed up. After swallowing the Jack in three gulps, he signaled for another. Thinking better of returning to Dash's funk, he joined Eric by the catwalk.

"Gimme five of those bills," he said.

Eric grinned. "About goddamn time you joined in. She's good."

"Sure is." Mike waved the dancer over, but he glanced toward Eric. The man's smile was pure honey. No wonder chicks flocked to him. "You do know the difference, right? She's not *really* a wide-eyed innocent with eyes for you alone."

"Of course I do. What fun would that be?"

The blonde squatted before them, her knees wide. Physics didn't seem to mind how she balanced in clear five-inch stiletto boots. Mike didn't seem to mind the G-string that proved she was a fan of Brazilian waxing. Gorgeous tits with rosy nipples. That innocent smile.

For the first time that night, he was hard. The hit of arousal was still a surprise. He wanted to wrap the girl in a bow and throw her over his shoulder. Give her to Leah. Watch what she'd do to a submissive girl. Breathing became way too difficult.

The dancer pulled the elastic of her G-string away from her smooth hip. Mike's hand wasn't steady as he tucked all five dollar bills inside. He'd pay hundreds to play out the scenario whipping through his head and pounding down to his cock.

Only Eric was going to spoil the illusion. He crooked his finger, and the girl's nearly innocent expression slipped a notch. Pure, mercenary interest flared in her blue eyes. Mike turned away before he lost his fantasy.

He needed Leah. Now.

He slapped Eric on the back. "Have a blast, man. Good luck with the blow jobs."

Kisser offered a sloppy salute. "Will do." Then he was back to his games and his unbelievable rough-edged charm.

Mike grabbed his flight jacket from the booth. "Hey, I'm gonna turn in," he said to Dash. "If I'm gonna be hungover tomorrow, I might as well get it over with."

"Dude, don't leave me with Casanova."

"Sorry, bro. Next time everyone gets a taxi. Then you won't be the designated driver he cries to."

Dash flashed his sharpest grin. "He's *such* an asshole sometimes."

Mike smiled, but his mind was already two steps ahead. He was in the cab. He was in her bedroom and hissing as she raked those talons she called nails down his back. Not soon enough, he stood in front of her apartment's security door.

He *was* falling for her. Damn it all.

Forcing his eyes to focus, he found the name he needed. Girardi.

Buzz. Wait. Buzz again.

"What?" came her sleep-groggy voice.

He closed his eyes. "It's Michael."

Chapter Twenty-Five

With her thumb on the intercom button, Leah couldn't mistake the hot jolt that scrambled under her ribs and flipped her insides. Heat pinged down to warm her guts.

Michael. Not Mike.

"Come up." She released the downstairs door then cracked her entryway door too.

She waited for him in the living room.

Of course he knew his way around her place. He'd been there enough over the past few weeks. They preferred Michael's tidy house for noise control and easy access to his collection, but sometimes a girl needed her own territory.

Plus she was dog-tired. She sprawled back on the couch. The book she'd fallen asleep reading flopped to the floor. She'd lost her bookmark. Twisted half under the couch, searching, she realized she was nervous.

Nerves, or maybe anticipation. It was hard to tell the difference with Michael. She thumbed the TV remote to switch from a true-crime show to a music channel. She didn't want gruesome to get in the way of fun.

When Michael appeared in the arched entryway of her small living room, she packed away a certain range of her expectations. He leaned a shoulder against the wall and teetered. His goofy, slightly boyish grin told her plain as day.

"You're drunk."

He held up two fingers a small distance apart. "Lil' bit." His eyes narrowed on such a wide, wide smile. She felt that smile all the way down to her lungs. She was so sunk.

"You mad?"

"Nope," she said. "C'mere."

He shuffled the long way around her couch. Drunk logistics?

Yet more lurked in the way he watched her. He spun and sat in one move, landing with his head in her lap and his feet on the padded arm of the couch. "Miss me?"

"Tonight?" More than she wanted to admit. "Nope."

"Wha'd you do?"

"Went for a run once the sun went down. Made some dinner. Read."

"Boring," he said, but the way he smiled soothed away any unkindness.

"And you?" She traced his brow and stroked his hair. Gold and brown blended perfectly. "Where have you been that has you so obviously looking for what you can't have?"

His eyes were mock sad and still muddled by drink. "Can't have?"

The agreement coiled in her throat felt a little wry. "If I can't smack on you when I've been drinking, you can't take smacks when you smell like a distillery. Now spill. Where'd you go?"

"Don't tell my ma'am," he said in a fake whisper. "I went to a strip club."

Her laughter was sudden and genuine. "You think she'd be mad?"

"I hope she would be." His grin was so unbearably cheeky. "She's fucking hot when she gets mad."

Her hands kept moving, stroking down his chest, beneath his snug T-shirt. The skin of his stomach was warm and thin over sleek muscles. She slid the tip of her fingernails to the line of ligaments that veed above his jeans.

"Only when she gets mad?"

"Nope. All the time."

Said with so much sincerity, she thought she might dissolve like the wicked witch under a bucket of water. So much trust was better placed in steadier hands, but Michael sprawled in *her* lap.

"Tell me more about the strip club."

"There were girls. They were naked. Dash and Eric were there too, but they weren't naked." He squeezed one hand between the couch and her back. "Thank God."

"Any of the girls hot?"

He stretched then and pushed, turning over to bury his face between her legs. His mouth rested where her thighs were bared by pajama shorts, not the ten inches higher where she wanted. He mumbled against her flesh.

"What was that?" She found purchase in his hair and tugged his face up. The Caribbean blue of his eyes... She couldn't get enough, even when they were hazy on booze.

"Maybe one blonde."

"Maybe one?" She chuckled. "You don't have to pretend, pet. I know strippers. It's their job to be hot. Tits and tight asses. Legs up to their ears."

His fingers snuck under her thighs. Played with the hem of her cotton shorts. "None of them were as sexy as you. Not even the blonde. She was young and sweet looking. Maybe sort of naive. I wanted to bring her home to you."

She continued to chuckle, until she realized he was serious.

"Would you, really?" That didn't seem like a fair question to expect answered when he was all but pickled. Didn't mean she could contain her curiosity. "I don't know about that one, Michael. Girls aren't really my thing."

"Not even to boss her around? Order us both around?" His voice dropped. Something way sexy was getting to him. "Together?"

The idea of another woman...not so much. Leah hadn't ever swung that way. But the idea of having both Michael and some fresh-faced innocent kneeling in front of her sent a sizzling coil of want through her chest. Her pussy responded with a flash of heat and dampness.

"What would you want to do to her, pet?"

His answer was immediate. Instant. "Whatever you told me to."

"And that's it? Even if I never let you lay a finger on her flesh?"

"Even then." He nuzzled between her legs, then nudged them apart and licked the inside of her knee. "Especially then."

"What if I told you to fuck her? However you wanted, whatever you wanted to do." She scratched over his scalp and down his back.

"I mean it, ma'am. Whatever you told me to."

Aroused in an instant, she tugged his shirt and he sat up, letting her strip it off. It took only the smallest want on her part—and he fulfilled it. Obedience was a gift she hadn't known she craved.

Maybe they couldn't play with pain. That didn't meant she had to behave herself.

She stretched her arms along the back of the couch, shifting to center her ass on the cushions. Spreading her knees, she invited him with more room to play.

"Kneel."

He didn't even stop to say yes. Just moved.

His jeans dipped low on his hips. Masculine hands rested on her knees. Softly. Waiting.

"Show me."

The boyish, foolish grin never changed. "Ma'am?"

"Show me exactly what you'd do to her. Pretend I'm sitting over there, on that chair in the corner. I'm watching you both. I want to know how you'd touch her, how you'd make her feel. She'd be so young and innocent and good, until you got hold of her with that giant cock."

His shoulders shuddered. Dark, hot desire strained his features. Though he moved slowly at first, he framed her face the way he used to, so long ago, when everything between them had been frustrating tenderness. She was swallowed up, reminded that she really was so much smaller than him.

The heat of his mouth burned everything away. Sharp whiskey was a taste she remembered well, but underneath was Michael. Her Michael, all the way through.

She sank into the couch—more like he drove her against the cushions. Absolutely overwhelming. Just this once. He took her mouth, bit her bottom lip, palmed her breast through the thin material of her tank top. Unleashed sexuality.

She writhed beneath his rough touch, focusing on their game rather than the control he seemed to be stealing. Michael was still hers to command, even when he stripped her panties with ruthless precision, belying his drunken state. Still kneeling, he hitched her knee over his shoulder and ducked. His mouth surged against her wet pussy. He licked. He feasted.

"Oh, fuck. Right there." She couldn't help but pull his hair, although she knew some tiny stripper wouldn't know shit about what her pet needed.

Not like she knew, either—totally making it all up as she went along. Someday all the threads would unravel. She'd lose her career and perfect roses and lovely, mean sex. Either Michael would realize what a fool he was for putting so much in her fallible hands, or their cover would be busted. She'd be forced to choose between being disastrously public or losing him.

No. Not now.

"Did you see her tits, Michael? Or her cunt?"

"Tits, yes." He smeared his mouth over her stomach and sucked his fingers clean. His low voice was slurred, adding to his boyish sex appeal. "Not her snatch. Well, not all of it."

"Did you want to?"

"Fuck yes." He dug a condom out of his back pocket and rolled it down without asking. Perhaps out of habit, he held the blunt head of his dick at her entrance. "Still like I would that girl?"

"Yes," she hissed. "Fuck me like you would her. The anonymous stripper you brought me as a present."

Michael let go.

His cock stretched her. The slight burn reminded Leah of his delicious size and the way they fit together. He wedged his wrist under her knee, wrenching her open.

He fucked her so hard that white stars bloomed behind her eyes. She crossed her forearms behind his head and joined their mouths. It was no kiss, but a hard clash of lips and teeth. He scraped his teeth across her bottom lip, heralding a shock of pain. Normally she'd pull away. He didn't get to hurt her.

Yet she took it all. She reveled in the game, fascinated as she watched him through narrowed eyes. His were nearly shut. His flawless rhythm faltered once or twice, probably because of the booze. Didn't matter. She ratcheted up so high, so damn fast.

His cruel strokes sparked pleasure through her bones and loosened her muscles. She stretched up to graze his earlobe with her teeth.

"Fuck me, stud. That woman you brought me home to? She's watching us. Her eyes are on your ass. She keeps clutching the arms of the chair." Her words broke off on a grunt when he hit a sweet spot, a place that made her cunt clench on his solid length.

"You little blonde bitch. Do you think she'll make me pay for fucking you?" His voice was a rumble that rolled from his chest to hers. Leah's nipples tingled.

"Depends. Do you enjoy that crop in her hand?"

He wedged her knee up so high she could have kissed it. He rammed into her like a desperate man. Short, hot jolts took over her brain. His eyes rolled when he came on a long, tense groan. Beneath the pleasure was so much emotion. She wanted to shy away, without any faith she could handle it.

She snatched one of his hands and joined their fingers against her pussy. His cock was just hard enough to ride.

"Your duties aren't over yet. Now you're *my* fuck toy."

A full-body shiver said he liked that. She did too. Pleasure fizzed through her blood as she came. The explosion was as powerful as any they'd shared. Round and round they went. There was no such thing as being *less* together.

If she didn't know better, she'd think she was completely lost in the magic they made.

Chapter Twenty-Six

Mike ducked out of the BX on a mission. He had about ten minutes before his carefully constructed timetable would go to shit. Tin Tin had mentioned grabbing a quick lunch before his thirteen hundred safety briefing. Leah was still in a meeting with the major. No telling how long that would last. Eric and Dash would spot Mike soon enough, both of them sniffing around for grub. For either of them to find him talking to Jon Carlisle would raise eyebrows.

If Tin Tin really meant a quick lunch, he'd be in the food court.

As Mike scanned the cavernous array of tables and purveyors of fine junk food, he smiled. He never would've imagined as a teenager how much the military felt like high school. Same cliques. Same petty shit. An even more rigid hierarchy. That meant the food-court tables were invisibly reserved at different times. Desk jockeys sat with desk jockeys, and on down the line.

Perhaps because Leah and Major Haverty were still in that meeting, Tin Tin sat by himself. It looked really odd, probably because the arrogant kid was usually the center of attention— good or bad. Silence and solitude didn't seem his style.

Neither did Cheetos, a Slim Jim and a Slurpee.

"That's quite the lunch, Tin Tin."

Dark, quirking eyebrows lifted, as if charting the way for the rest of his face. "To fuel the temple that is my body. We can do tradesies if you have Twinkies. But I don't do generic."

"Wouldn't think of it."

The kid had really unnerving eyes. Dark on dark. Narrowed almost perpetually. Like some sort of magician, he had this...*way* about him. He sure as hell recognized that Mike's friendly bit of banter had a purpose.

"Take a seat, Strap." He nudged a chair out with his toe.

Mike glanced at the phone in Jon's palm. "How's your imaginary girlfriend?"

"Think what you will, hater." He set the phone facedown on the plastic table and leaned back. The pose was all business—until he noshed a Cheeto. "What's up?"

Shit, this was going to be tricky. The timing had been hard enough to fudge. Now Mike didn't know what to say. Jon meant a lot to Leah. Although he didn't harbor any sexual jealousy, Mike really would've liked the insight two years of friendship gave Jon.

"I'm asking you to be discreet. For Leah's sake."

Jon didn't reply with some snarky remark. No salacious gleam appeared in his eyes. He still tried to pry inside Mike's brain, even harder now, but that seemed to be his default mode. "Done," he said simply.

"No questions asked?"

"That would damage the whole 'discreet' thing. Spill it, Strap."

"I want to take her out. Do something she'd like. But..." He shrugged. "Hell if I know what that might be."

Jon nodded sagely. "Sometimes it's hard to talk when fucking."

Mike tensed. No, he was beyond tense. "Forget it."

He stood to go, but Jon grabbed his arm. Damn if the kid wasn't a helluva lot stronger than he looked. "Relax, man. I said no questions, but this is Leah we're talking about. I'm trying to keep it light so I don't grill you."

"Throwing out random barbs to see which ones stick?"

Jon smiled, showing off the dimples he hated to be reminded of. He sucked down Slurpee. "Something like that. Now, you feel like hearing me out or not? I have..." He checked the time on his iPhone. "Four minutes."

"The safety briefing, yeah."

"Oh, no. Ditching that. Turned in my report yesterday. My imaginary girlfriend and I have lunch plans."

"What about this magnificent feast?"

"Let me rephrase. We have plans to enact over her lunch hour." Before Mike could smack the kid's nose into the back of his brain, Jon sobered. "Look, you probably already know enough about her to guess. She's a chick, but she's a throttle jockey like the rest of us. So what does she like? Things that go fast. Things that are dangerous and stupid. That used to mean drinking herself into a bar fight and the possibility of a public-nudity charge, but thank fuck, those days are gone."

His words hit hard. The relief in Jon's voice was impossible to miss. Whatever edginess Mike had been carrying since thinking up this stupid plan suddenly eased. Sure, Jon was a filthy-minded punk, but he really was one of Leah's best friends. If Mike wanted anything to do with the woman, he'd need to do more than put up with that fact.

Jon sat up, snapped his fingers. "I got it." He started gathering his stuff. Slim Jim and phone in the pocket of his flight jacket. Slurpee in hand. "Rock climbing."

"Seriously?"

"Yup. When she was just crawling onto the wagon, she mentioned it to me. I was a dick because Heather and I were in the middle of some tough shit." Again, that hint of sincerity. Mike could hardly believe his ears. "Anyway, I never took her up on it. Would've been fun. But lunch dates are fun too."

He turned to go, but Mike couldn't risk a damn thing. "Tin Tin? Not even to Leah. Got it?"

"Oh, believe me, I know." He offered a half-assed salute. "Good luck, Strap."

He'd left his Cheetos. Mike only noticed when, scant minutes later, Eric and Dash slumped like rag dolls into chairs at the same table.

"Right on time," Eric said.

Dash laughed. "Through no credit to you, ass face. I dragged you away from that hot brunette sergeant so Mikey here wouldn't be lonely."

Mike let their usual asshole banter become part of the food court's white noise. He'd deal with those two bozos in a minute.

Rock climbing. Made sense. The only trick would be convincing Leah he'd thought of it himself. In the meantime, he had to believe Tin Tin was as good as his word.

"And you promise it doesn't involve *any* mariachis?"

"None," Mike said with a grin.

Full of bubbling anticipation, he gripped the wheel of his beat-up old Bronco. He was a pussy for being so pent-up eager, but this was important. Something he'd planned. Something he hoped she liked. It was a helluva lot riskier than waiting for her next command. With their sex life, the payoff was guaranteed.

The wind whipping through the cab played with her dark hair. She tucked loose strands behind her ears. "No musicians of any kind?"

"*Negativo.* That's Spanish, by the way."

"*Chinga te, pendejo.*"

"Anytime, Princess."

"Deal."

She laughed, then glanced back to where he'd put a tarp over the rock-climbing gear. He hadn't gone so far as to pack a picnic. Planning an outing didn't mean it had to be all Martha Stewart perfect. Protein bars and Gatorade—that was just practical. The ingredients for roasting s'mores—that was a seduction in the making.

"And you promise we're not driving into the desert to dispose of the body you've stashed back there?"

"If I told you, I'd have to kill you." He smiled like an innocent. "But I like you too much. So no body disposal."

"C'mon, pet. Fess up."

"Nuh-uh. Put it away, ma'am. You know that doesn't work out here in the real world."

"Yet."

Shooting her some serious side eye, he thought about protesting. Nothing came.

Yet.

Part promise, part utterly fucking terrifying threat. And not the kind that could get him off. The kind that kept him single.

However, he couldn't deny the decision he'd made that morning. While dressing for the day, he'd looked down at his right wrist. The gleam of silver no longer suited him. Memories of Georgia seemed like a distant planet. Removing the cuff and sticking it in his medicine cabinet had been as liberating as it was nerve-racking.

A choice made. An expectation forged.

He returned his full attention to the road because it was a lot safer. The city was about forty-five minutes behind them, with only the barest highway traffic on that clear Saturday morning.

"Not even a hint?" She'd put away her bedroom voice in favor of the playfulness he wanted. "A teeny one?"

"Is this you being a girl? Like, *really* trying? If so, you need more time with Cass."

"You dragged me out of your nice, warm, cozy bed and made me drink Drano coffee, and for what?" She threw up her hands. "The desert. Gee, something new!"

"You're as impatient as you are competitive."

"Known, quantifiable fact."

"How about you just chill out and trust me?"

She inhaled and looked out the passenger-side window. "It's not you," she said quietly. He barely caught the words over the sound of cool wind.

"What was that?"

"It's not you, okay?" Louder this time. Almost...angry? Although he didn't think it was directed at him. "I could trust the hell out of you, but that doesn't mean surprises are any easier. I just don't like them."

"*Could* trust me? Does that mean you don't?"

"Never mind." Her forced cheer was not what he'd wanted to hear. "I'm sure it's gonna be great."

Damn it.

If she'd unclench for half a second, she might have a good time. Maybe years of trying to prove herself had created some two-headed monster. She was either frayed at the edges, like Jon had hinted about her days of drinking and partying, or she was crushed down into some complete control freak. Did she really distrust herself so much?

Again, it didn't scan. She was one of the coolest, most in-command chicks he'd ever met. She wasn't supposed to hesitate, but he'd seen it at the car show. She wasn't supposed to white-knuckle her way through surprise outings, but she was doing that right now.

"Rock climbing, Leah. Does that help?"

He glanced toward her, and sure enough—relief. She actually exhaled, as if a thousand unpleasant scenarios had been beaten back by two words. A stay of execution.

What was he supposed to do with that?

"Cool." This time the enthusiasm was genuine. She practically bounced on her side of the bench seat, craning her neck out the forward window. "Ooh, it's Red Rocks, isn't it? Nice! We're not that far then. Maybe ten minutes?"

Mike forced himself to calm down. She was who she was. That didn't mean speaking her language was easy, mostly because she sure as hell wasn't the kind of woman to open up and ramble on.

"Wait."

He frowned. "What?"

"How did you know I like rock climbing?"

He couldn't get into her head, but she was dug tight as a tick into his. "You're athletic and a daredevil. Seemed perfect."

The laser beam of her gaze was unmistakable. Mike kept his eyes on the road and tried to loosen his shoulders. Saturday morning. Fun drive. Nice day planned. Why was this feeling so stiff?

"And you just...guessed? Don't lie to me, Mike."

He blew out a breath. Indulging in a temper hadn't been his style for years. "I asked Tin Tin."

"Oh, for fuck's sake. Thanks for sharing our sex life with the world's biggest pervert."

"*You're* the one always talking about how he's such a good guy. It's not like I pulled down my shorts and showed him my bruised ass. I wanted to *surprise* you, which is apparently a no-go. And I wanted it to be something you'd like. Other than planes, bikes and flogging me, I don't have a clue what that is." He took another deep breath and let it go. Anger was easier to ditch than disappointment. "So forgive me for needing to ask *your* friend. It wasn't my favorite conversation."

To his surprise, she chuckled. "How'd that go, exactly?"

"He was eating lunch in the food court."

"Cheetos?"

"Yup."

"And texting Heather?"

"If that's the name of the phone-sex worker he calls his girlfriend."

Her smile widened briefly. She slid to the center of the bench and fastened the lap belt. Mike put his arm around her when she nuzzled his shoulder. They were close to the park's entrance, but he planned on holding her until the last possible moment.

"Jon will keep his mouth shut," she said. "I'm not worried about that."

"Back to this being about you?"

She only nodded.

"So..." He nodded too as more pieces of Leah came together. "Another surprise you weren't ready for."

This time it wasn't a question. Impatience and a competitive streak the size of Nebraska had nothing on her need for control. In and out of the cockpit. In and out of the bedroom. He'd been a bigger stickler for control during their first affair—probably a huge part of the problem back then. In the years since, he'd learned to let go.

Just the opposite for the woman he held.

"I'm sorry, Mike."

She lifted her head and kissed his neck. Peppering kisses. After edging those little apologies to his mouth and back down his throat, she snuggled along his side once again.

"I mean it," she said against his upper arm. "I didn't mean to fuck it up and get so jumpy."

Mike shook his head softly. Did many people come close to understanding how complicated Leah Girardi really was? Why did realizing he was one of them make him feel proud rather than scared as hell?

"Apology accepted, okay? We'll just enjoy the day."

"Out of the city? Risking life and limb? I can do that." God, her smile was back. Her dark eyes were brighter. Excitement sizzled from her body into his. "I promise."

He kissed the top of her head, trying to ignore the tightness in his chest. "But you had every right to be jumpy. There *is* a dead body in the back. I hope you're good with a shovel."

"Just tell me it's a dearly departed mariachi singer, and I'll do whatever the moment requires."

Chapter Twenty-Seven

Leah was no rock-climbing superstar, but neither was Michael. As they unpacked the gear from the back of his ancient SUV, she quizzed him on his level of experience. They'd both had rappelling through the Air Force. He dabbled in his off time, which didn't sit well with her. That need to win, yet again. Most of the equipment was his personal stuff.

Still, this was going to be a blast.

She hopped from one foot to the other as they ran through the checks and lined up ropes. Her fingers flew through knots and felt for frayed pieces.

Within minutes they were on the rock, with Michael on belay below her. Holding the end of Leah's rope, he literally held her life in his hands. That she could relinquish her trust so easily...

Maybe they had a real shot after all.

Yeah. A damn good day.

The rough sandstone scrubbed her fingertips as she reached for handhold after handhold. Balancing on the outside edge of one foot, her thighs began to burn. The sun was bright and provided just enough warmth on her back to keep her blood going. A rare but welcome spring breeze reached out to wick the sweat from her skin.

She slid to the side before she found a way up, using her thumb to dig into a tiny dip of rock. Her breathing wanted to blow fierce. She pushed it all down, made herself still, even while adrenaline snapped in her veins.

She looked down.

Only twenty feet—a relatively short drop in the scheme of Red Rocks. This was only an overnight trip, and they wanted to hit as many different opportunities as possible. At the same time, saying she was *only* twenty feet above hard-packed canyon sand was like saying she'd only jumped off a roof. The drop could kill her. She owned the fucking world in the balance of one foot and three fingers.

Perfect day.

She dipped her free hand into the chalk bag at the small of her back then shook off the excess.

"You feel like moving any time soon?" Michael called.

Shading her eyes, she squinted down at him. His golden hair glinted in the sun. "I thought you were supposed to be the Zen king. What the hell are you complaining about?"

"I'd like to be Zen *after* I get my turn."

"Who says you get a turn?"

"You really wanna shit talk the man who's holding your safety rope?"

"I'm pretty sure I can say anything I want when I'm up here. If you go home without me, you'll have to answer to Jon and Fang. You wouldn't like Fang when he's angry."

His laugh rolled up to her. Hell, it rolled all the way *into* her. She grinned like a schoolgirl.

"He can look like The Hulk when he's pissed." He flicked out the tail end of the rope, which slithered across the ground. "But don't worry, I kinda like you. I feel like keeping you around for a while yet."

"Oh gee." Dry deadpan didn't have the same impact when she was trying to make her voice carry. "I'm so very relieved."

She was. Because she couldn't help thinking he meant it. Awesome, really. Up on the rock, on such a beautiful day, she could admit that.

"But for strictly nefarious purposes, though," he added with a chuckle.

"That's my line, pet. Now shut up so I can clobber this thing."

They climbed for hours, taking turns. The only thing better than being on the rock herself was standing at the pitch point and watching Mike move. He wore a slim gray T-shirt that showed off the breadth of his shoulders. Every reach. Every hard pull as he hauled his body up the sheer rock face. Sweat slicked down his spine, darkening the gray to sleek charcoal. The harness cupped his ass with flat black straps. Tasty.

But there was more. More she'd need to process.

Just before taking his first grip on the stone, he'd stripped out of his jacket.

His wrist had been bare. Still was.

The silver cuff that always niggled at her, the one he'd been given by his first mistress... Gone. The thick muscles of his forearm and the tendons of his wrist were bare, revealing tan skin and the finest dusting of blond hairs. No fanfare. No big demonstration. All quiet and still, which was exactly like Michael.

Yeah, she was happy he'd ditched the damn thing, but now what? She shivered despite the day's heat.

They'd tackled a couple different routes by the time the sun dipped toward the horizon. Leah was half dead from exhaustion. Jesus, did it feel good—from her sweaty ponytail to the weakness at the backs of her ankles.

Michael crested the top where she sat at the edge of a cliff. They'd intentionally left this route for last. It rated only a 5.7, but the view was amazing. After unstrapping his harness, he eased onto the sand beside her. Their toes dangled over the thirty-foot drop.

Leah didn't say anything, not for a long time. The peace was utterly beautiful.

Miles of long terrain stretched out. Golds and reds, covered with the slightest brushes of dark sage. The dipping sun extended the reds into the sky and added royal purple. The blue at their backs disappeared, and even the air held the crisp promise of the oncoming night. Far away was the magnetic glow of Vegas, but they ignored it in favor of the sunset.

She breathed. Deeply.

The only thing better than the clean smell of juniper and creosote was Michael. His sun-warmed vitality eased her more deeply into the moment.

Hairs like tiny butterflies prickled her senses as she slipped her fingers over his wrist. Bare skin beneath her touch. No longer the barrier of another woman's silver.

"You going to tell me about this?"

Apparently it was impossible to keep her mouth shut.

"I was ready to take it off." His expression was placid, but she knew him. Deeper emotion always waited beneath his easy calm.

She wanted to ask. Make him face her. Her questions, however, would give away her insecurities. *Why, Michael? Why me?* How could he know she was worth giving up a token that had been a part of him for so long?

Folding her hands around his bare wrist, she simply...enjoyed. Their peace and perfection were enough for now. The rest of the world would shake out later.

She slid closer. Michael hooked his arm around her shoulders in the way that always made her feel small and sheltered. *So* ridiculous. They were sticky with drying sweat and gritty with sand. She only nestled closer.

"This was a great idea. I'll have to thank Jon."

He pinched her shoulder in his big grip. "Hey, now. I'm the one who did all the work. I take the risk, I get all the praise."

"Is that how it works?"

"Damn straight."

"Thank you." She stretched up and kissed first his cheek, then the hollow behind his sharp jaw. "Thank you, Michael. This has been fantastic."

"I wonder what kind of reward I'll get tonight when I break out the marshmallows and chocolate."

"I could replace your cuff with a new one."

She went rigid. They both did, as if dipped in carbonite like Han Solo.

Had she really just said that?

"You could," he said quietly. The breeze tried to snatch his words away, but she heard them.

Those two words filled an ache in her soul. She wanted that. She wanted to buy him a beautiful cuff that would accentuate his male power and stake her claim. Both.

Doubts tried to creep in. She couldn't handle it. She'd screw it up. She could only keep so much rolling at once. Her career as a pilot—the yardstick she'd used for a decade to demonstrate her worth—would tank if she fell so deeply into Michael's orbit. Not because of anything he'd do, but because she'd never experienced this kind of obsession. Not for flying or even winning, but for Michael.

It was already hard as hell to keep her jumbled impulses in lockdown. She didn't have any extra resources.

Except... This wasn't the time or the place for that fear. Staring into the sunset while nestled against Michael's big body was a moment outside of time. A moment so much kinder than she was to herself.

She breathed in the desert perfume. Michael's tranquility seeped beneath her skin, into her soul. To help herself along, she spread one hand flat over his stomach. Calm, warm and so strong.

"How long have you been rock climbing?"

Ugh. Avoidance, much?

Trust Michael to call her on her shit. He tugged on her ponytail. "We just tripped over your comfort level."

She made a sharp gesture with one hand. "Swan dive."

"Got it."

He cupped her face. She never, ever flinched from his size. He was so much bigger, so vital. He possessed more power in his hands than she did while wielding a flogger. That was part of the amazing rush she got when he handed it into her keeping.

A small frown drew his brows together. "Will you let me say one thing though?"

When she swallowed, it was past a solid lump in her throat. Her tongue slicked over dry lips. She always got these cold shots of fear whenever anything serious reared up. The cast to his features said serious with a capital S.

She made herself nod.

"If you gave me a cuff, I'd take it. But the fact that I'm not wearing my old one... It doesn't have to mean anything more than it does."

"Which is?"

He brushed his knuckles over her bottom lip. "That when I'm around you, I can't think about any other woman."

Leah's smile bloomed so slowly, coming from the warm kernel deep inside her. She was happy. Completely and fully happy.

She touched her mouth to his. From roses to such perfect declarations—how was a girl to resist?

"You're too good to be true."

"I am." He kissed her back just as softly—the slightest sip and caress. "Just wait 'til later. I'm going to stuff you with s'mores and sit you under the stars. Then I'm going to have my wicked way with you."

She snorted with laughter. "Oh, you will?"

"You see, I have a plan. Cuz then I'm going to feed you coffee. My crappy, nasty coffee." He grinned. So much mischievousness. "You'll end up dropping your panties and jumping me just to end the horror."

"Oh, my God. You are a mad genius."

"Truly devious."

"Shut up and kiss me."

"Yes, ma'am."

He gave every order his full attention. This was no exception. He swept his mouth over hers, delving his tongue between her lips. She framed his face and held him steady. Held them both steady. The kiss swirled her brains and turned her body warmer, softer. The day's hard-charging activities bled away.

She was tempted, so tempted, to revel in Michael's kiss forever.

Chapter Twenty-Eight

As Mike watched dawn sunshine halo around his blankets-for-curtains, he couldn't deny it anymore.

He loved waking up with her.

He loved *her.*

Goddamn it.

Half of Leah's body sprawled across his. She slept on her stomach, which meant a knee across his abs and an elbow dangerously close to his eyeball. What made it awesome rather than annoying was how, even in sleep, she held him. Maybe that was why waking with her in his bed, or he in hers, was such a thing of beauty. Even waking with her in a tent two weeks ago had been fun—proof they could laugh, lounge, chill the hell out.

With a sigh, he pillowed his head on his free arm. The sting across his back made him smile. She'd become very proficient with the flogger, with last night the best yet. He knew it took practice. The idea of Leah working at home to get it just right, for him, was almost more than he could take. Sometimes she kept him at arm's length. He suspected her issues about control held her back, but that didn't make the effect easier to take. Yet she cared for him and took their physical trust very seriously.

He'd felt it coming for weeks, like a wave that wouldn't be held back forever. That morning just happened to be the morning when his heart smacked him in the head. No more denials. He tucked his nose against the top of her head and breathed deeply. She had come to mean the world to him. Would he wait for her to feel the same way? *Could* he? Even the easygoing nature he'd worked to cultivate—for him, a necessary means of coping with the unknowns of the military—wasn't going to see him through this mess. She'd blown on through that barrier. He wanted her too much to keep cool.

Slowly, she began to rouse. He'd learned to catch her small, telling movements. Grumbles first. A clenching of her limbs, possessing him even before she opened her eyes. She wiped the loose hair from across her face and turned to look at him.

"Morning," he said.

"Time?"

"Eight thirty."

"Hell."

He grinned. "What happened to Miss Runs-a-Lot?"

Her hands slid to his pecs. She scratched across skin striped by the distinctive bowtie marks left by rows of clothespins. He rolled his eyes closed on a long, contented sigh.

"I had my workout last night," she said with a devilish smile. "You did so well, pet."

Shit. Damn. Fuck.

He was screwed.

"Thank you, ma'am." He pulled her closer until their bodies were plastered together. Morning wood was unavoidable with her breasts pressed against his ribs and her knee inching suspiciously up toward his cock.

"I want a repeat," she whispered against his neck. Teeth on his earlobe. Expected, but no less powerful. "Well, after you heal up."

A chuckle shook out of his chest. "A couple days, then."

"Mmm, sounds about right. In the meantime, Michael..." Her hand trailed across his stomach and took sudden possession of his growing hard-on. "Come here. Now."

Quick and fast and straight vanilla. Mostly. She still instructed the pace, scraped every inch of skin she could reach, and granted permission for him to come. Maybe they'd never escape that gorgeous play. Why would he want to?

In the sweaty aftermath of their passion, Mike cleared his throat. He had plans again, this time all for him. At least he'd learned not to keep it a surprise. Lord knew how she would be able to handle trading presents on their upcoming birthdays— only three days apart. They'd already discussed a joint celebration, complete with a gift exchange. Civilized. Nearly a full-fledged couple, even if she still insisted on keeping them a secret.

Her mention of replacing Georgia's cuff had raised his expectations to a level he really shouldn't risk—that she'd finally trust herself enough to trust him.

"I'm having a sod-laying party Thursday after work. You want to come by?"

She sat up on her elbows. She looked like a totally fucked-up mess, and damn he loved that. *He* did that to her, made her vulnerable after blowing her mind. "What the hell is a sod-laying party? I think that's even a made-up word. *Sod-laying?*"

"When I'm not flying exceptionally fast airplanes, scaling mountains like a goddamn pro or racing a crazy woman on a pink Ducati, I *do* have other hobbies."

"Don't forget the masochism." She nodded in that deadpan way of hers.

He answered with a wide grin and a hand on her ass. "How could I?"

"So, these hobbies? Gimme."

"I play guitar, for a start."

"Seriously?"

"Yup."

"Wow, that's explains your brotherhood of the mariachis."

"I'm *good*, Princess Leah. But I don't sing. Not in a million years."

She frowned slightly, as if trying to solve some logistical mathematics problem. Was he really that hard to figure out? He didn't think so. Open book, except for his bedroom preferences. Or was she really that unobservant? Didn't make sense when compared to how acutely she read him during their sessions. Then, she was hyper-focused to the point of mind reading.

"But back to sod-laying," she said, apparently shaking it off. Her ability to compartmentalize was impressive.

"I've been prepping the backyard for the summer. Getting the topsoil ready, all the right nutrients and water levels. The rolls of sod are being delivered Wednesday. Thought I'd make a party of it since Dash and Eric volunteered to help." He paused, met her eyes. Although he tried to keep his posture and expression casual, he was anything but. "Sunny's going to be there too. Thought you might want to join us."

A host of thoughts jumbled in her eyes. Those quirking lips scrunched into what he was beginning to regard as her thinking face.

"See? I'm learning. No surprises."

She nodded. Her mind was still spinning. He saw it in the unfocused distance of her gaze.

He didn't like the next part, but he knew it was a necessity if he wanted her to show up. "You could come by on your own. I don't expect you to be here when the others show up. If that's what you need."

The real Leah returned from whatever place she'd traveled to. He just wanted to shake her. *I'm here. I'm not going to fuck this up.*

She wouldn't believe him, might not even hear him. Head in the sand. For such a ballsy woman, her ability to face up to the hard shit was surprisingly lacking.

"Sure," she said with a shrug. "You're insane for trying to grow grass in a damn desert."

"I like it. My mom did it too. Her hobby—gardening and the lawn. Not easy where they live in Kansas, either. Dad put up with it, even if he thought it was a waste of time."

Inwardly, he cringed. *Duh.* Clue smack. That was why he'd taken it up himself. His dad's snide remarks about what his mother did in her housewife spare time had never seemed fair. She offered Mike advice now, which kept them closer than mere updates on very different lives. He enjoyed having that in common with her.

"Then I won't tease. Don't wanna be a dick about whatever you like." Leah kissed him gently on the mouth. "Sod-laying party it is. What should I bring?"

He smiled and rolled her onto her back. Greedy. Happy. "Bring dessert."

"Moron. You had to pick the hottest day so far."

Mike stood up and rubbed the ache from his lower back. "Shut up, Kisser. This is not the time to turn chatty. You've done way less work."

Dash hauled another roll of sod over his shoulder, from where dozens had been stacked on the patio. "And all you've done is the fruit roll-up part. Do some lifting, you big bastard."

With a shrug, Eric met him at the pile of sod. "Sure. Must be a trial being so scrawny."

"I'd go all physics teacher and point out the power ratio of longer limbs relative to muscle mass. Alas, big words bounce off your dented skull." Dash grinned. "So bite me."

Eric smirked. "Isn't that Sunny's job?"

As if tugged by a string, Dash turned to where his wife sat beneath a shade umbrella. She'd already laid out the food in Mike's kitchen. Now she was reading a fashion magazine.

"I heard that," she said, not looking up from *Vogue*.

"Doesn't mean it isn't true," Dash replied.

He was a whole other man when she returned from DC. The dark clouds from that night at the strip joint were gone. The notorious smile had returned, with no sharp edges. He still looked like a bird of prey, but his mile-a-minute sense of fun was a welcome relief.

While Dash hauled his roll to the next row—they were about a quarter done—Mike met Eric at sod central command.

"Hey, Leah said she'd come by too. Can you do me a favor?"

Eric lifted his brows but didn't answer.

"Keep your damn mouth shut. I don't want to play referee between you two."

"Quite the request, Mikey. Anything you're not saying? Or you gonna stick to ordering me around?"

"It's my party and I'll make rules if I want to."

"Whatever. She seems cool." He leaned in with a vicious smile. "And I won't hit on her."

"Fuck off."

Eric offered a pissant salute. "Yes, sir, Strap Happy, sir."

"Get back to work or no beer."

From across the lawn, Dash perked up. He was on his knees with his hands deep in the roll of grass and soil. "No beer? I was promised beer. What sort of thieving racket have you got going on here? Sunny, it's time to head home."

"No." She wet her index finger and turned a glossy page. "I still haven't seen buff fighter pilots take their shirts off."

"Well, shit," Dash said. "Now I have to first. Otherwise it'll be painfully obvious these vultures are making a play for your attention."

A teasing smile was his reward. "Do it then, butt munch."

Sunny's parents were Indian, and she was a lawyer, so the foul mouth she let loose among friends was still a surprise. Mike and Eric grinned and, because they were dudes, returned to their work while Dash stripped. It wasn't five minutes later before Eric was shirtless too.

Mike knew he was waiting for Leah. He was a goddamn showoff when it came to pleasing her. He checked his watch and squelched a tickle of unease. She said she'd show. That meant she would.

So it was back to the sun-drenched chore of laying his lawn. He loved the smell of the warm dirt. Bermuda grass was unheard of outside of casino golf courses, but here it was because of his doing. Small accomplishment. Big reward in his head.

"Sunny, you're not pulling your weight," Eric called. "Get dirty with us."

Still not looking up from her magazine, she grinned. "Piss off, meathead. Besides, I ordered the pizza. Wouldn't want to get too worn out."

In an exaggerated whisper to Eric, Dash said, "We have plans, you see. Nighttime plans. The kind *you* have to pay for, Kisser."

"She put out, by the way. That redheaded stripper."

Mike rolled his eyes. "You should've been a writer for *Hustler*. Flying jets neglects your talent for dirty fiction."

"First the BJ she promised." Eric shrugged. "Then doggie style."

"Bullshit!" Dash said, rising to a kneeling position. "See, it's the Kisser-gets-it-up-twice-in-one-night part that's most unbelievable."

"I should've known it'd be all trash talking today," came a welcome voice. "Though it'll be worthwhile if it means three men on their knees doing women's work."

Mike looked at the bright green grass beneath his knees and smiled. An exhalation slipped out of his nose.

He turned to see Leah standing on his porch, one hand on her hip, smirking. She wore the world's tightest jeans, which did mind-bending things for her slim, toned physique. Usual holy Christ tank top. Usual ponytail. And she hefted a grocery-store cake.

The other pilots greeted her with customary insults and bickering. Mike only stood and walked to face her. Two feet separated them. She'd worn perfume—a touch of floral that seemed more like making an effort. He liked that.

"Glad you could make it, Princess. Nice cake."

"Where do you want it?" A sparkle lit her eyes, suggesting a whole manner of subtext.

"Anywhere you want. Indoors probably." Just as he'd planned, he ran a hand through his hair and found his nastiest grin. "Damn it's hot out here."

Leah's dark eyes flared with hunger. She gave the smallest nod.

He grabbed the T-shirt's hem and pulled it over his head, tossed it aside. The knocked-dumb expression on her face was worth every moment he'd spent working with the sun on his back, magnified by a layer of sweaty cotton.

"Don't suppose you'll join us?"

She wet her lips. Blinked. "In the grass or shirtless?"

"Either."

"Nope. I think this beautiful lady has the right idea. It's been a long week, Strap. I'm gonna put my feet up and just...watch."

Chapter Twenty-Nine

Leah stashed the cake in Michael's kitchen before making her way back outside. Unlike most dudes she knew, his patio furniture wasn't plastic. Instead it was classic wrought iron, with a glass-topped table and an umbrella. The woman sitting in the shade was beyond elegant. She wore what looked like silk, which Leah had always taken for one of those after-sunset sorts of things. The blouse was distinctly Indian, wrapped almost like a sari, but paired with trim black slacks.

The woman looked up with a small yet friendly smile. "Sunny Christiansen." She held out her hand. "It's nice to finally meet you."

She returned the sentiment before dropping into one of the cushioned chairs. "Leah Girardi."

"Captain Leah Girardi, yes?"

"My reputation precedes me."

Dash's wife fanned shut the fashion magazine. "You say that like you assume it's a bad thing."

Leah chuckled, but the cold burn in her lungs didn't bear any resemblance to humor. "I know my reputation."

Sunny's hands were elegant, with a French manicure and pampered skin. She watched Leah with dark doe eyes that were clear and steady. "Let's see... You used to be known as a party girl, but those days are apparently behind you. No one's witnessed you with bruised knuckles or smelling like booze for at least six months. Shall I go on?"

Leah gulped. She nodded, almost against her own will.

"Dash says you're an excellent pilot. You're conscientious of the aircrews that take care of your plane. You're Fang's right-hand girl. Plus Dash is really, really impressed with your motorcycle, though he thinks your ovaries were showing when you picked pink."

Leah shifted. Twisted again. She leaned back in her seat. She ran a thumbnail through the fringe along the side of a placemat. "Maybe I was wrong."

She'd thought herself marked. Once somebody hooked up with a particular reputation, it was hard to shake within the small community of the military. That led her to wonder what else she was wrong about.

She avoided Sunny's way-too-astute gaze and turned toward the yard. Half done now. The three men's bare chests covered the spectrum of masculine appeal. Dash with his slim, precisely cut torso. Kisser was made of hefty curves, with shoulders that sloped down from a thick neck. He looked like he'd been artfully swirled in a vat of black ink, with a distinctive abstract tattoo spreading across his chest.

They caught her attention, but Michael kept it. He was her golden boy—the perfect balance, with his lean hips and an upper chest thick enough for a girl to hang on to. His hair gleamed like sunshine, and his smile made her insides tumble. She liked him so damn much.

Hearts and flowers and puppy dogs sort of liking.

"You know, Princess," Mike said with a grin. "It's better you're not trying this."

She lifted her brows. "Is that right?"

"Not up your alley. Too tedious."

Dash nodded along with him. Right. They were both so damn subtle. Except not. "Really, you just stay up there with Sunny. This is man's work. Best not to trouble your pretty little heads about it."

"You're assuming that I'll get my nose out of joint and prove myself by mucking around in the dirt." She folded her hands behind her head in the most arrogantly relaxed pose she could manage. "You'd be wrong."

"How about you, Sunny my lovely angel?"

216

The woman blew Dash a kiss and returned to her magazine. "Fuck off, darling."

"You see how she sweet talks me?" He punched Kisser in the shoulder as he stood. "Means she loves me."

"If that's love, count me out." Kisser rocked back on his heels, looking something like a hunk of meat on the hoof. His hands dangled between his knees. "I'll stick to pulling tail."

Dash flashed his wide grin. "Pulling your own pud."

"Classy, dude," Michael replied. His eyes cut toward Leah. His smile...changed. The smallest shift of his lips made her brain melt. Was he going soft on her?

Christ's angels, would she even mind if he did?

She couldn't bring herself to think the L word. They weren't there yet. She knew that much. Her heart seized in fear every time her head started down that road. That had to be a big sign, right? If she were actually in love, she wouldn't be so afraid. End of story.

Didn't mean she was blind to the possibilities. She was thinking of buying him a cuff, for God's sake. All the research she'd done about D/s taught her what a big deal that was—not to mention the pressure she felt to get it right, to find the perfect one.

She'd been looking—officially—for over a week. She couldn't find anything to match her specifications, and that didn't count the unofficial, wistful looking she'd done before admitting how much she wanted this. Wanted Michael as hers.

The cuff couldn't be silver because that color on her pet's wrist would always remind her of another woman. Unacceptable. She also needed it to be rough and masculine. No girly shit for her Michael.

Absolutely nothing had hit her standards. Time was ticking down. Less than two weeks until they were going to celebrate their nearly joint birthdays. She wanted to give it to him then, but the fact that she wasn't finding the right one...

Maybe it was another sign.

Or maybe she couldn't think anymore. So tumbled around.

217

The guys hit a stopping point. Eric grabbed a six-pack and slumped onto his ass, shaded by the umbrella. Dash leaned a hip against Sunny's chair. His long fingers casually draped on her shoulder. He leaned down and whispered something in her ear, kissed her there. The woman's answering smile was so private that Leah looked away.

Michael approached her, but he didn't stand close enough.

She wanted to tuck her fingers in the pockets of his loose shorts and pull him near. They dipped dangerously low on his hips. Combined with his bare chest, she was treated to a lovely display of skin. Unmarked, but Michael wouldn't have taken off his T-shirt had he been bruised.

Eric took a bottle by the neck and reached across the table. "Beer?" he asked Leah.

It was the first thing he'd said directly to her. Ironic that it had to do with booze. Everyone knew she and Jon were close, while Jon and Kisser were *definitely* not. No skin off her nose if they wanted to play measure-the-dicks. The beer he held almost seemed like a peace offering. Too bad she couldn't take it.

"Nah, save it for your second round."

After a moment's assessment, he nodded and leaned back in his chair. Dash snatched the beer instead.

"There's soda inside," Michael offered.

Sunny reached up to pat Dash's cheek. "Hop inside and get me one of those?"

Another kiss from Dash, this time aimed at her temple. She turned and looked up at the last minute, just in time to meet mouth to mouth, both smiling.

"Regular?"

"Diet today."

He laughed. "As if you need it."

Holy Christ they were painful to watch. Leah had never felt so unbelievably hungry for affection, for that easy ebb and flow of acceptance and trust. She dug nails into her palms, when she wanted to be driving them into Michael's back. The fact that he stood so close and so very exposed was almost too much.

Technically, all she had to do was reach out. If she slipped her fingers in his, she knew without asking that he'd accept them. Accept her. That'd be tantamount to declaring their relationship to the entire squadron.

Apparently she'd shaken the last dregs of her shitty reputation. She couldn't throw another sordid layer on top—one that said she slept with squadron mates. To assume people thought of her as a fuck-up had become standard. To know they admired her recovery, only to watch her fall back into old patterns...? She couldn't think of anything more humiliating.

So she all but sat on her hands. Mike shrugged and dropped into a chair just as Dash returned through the sliding glass door. He deposited a can of soda and a glass with ice next to Sunny's magazine.

"Ice too. Very considerate." With a cute little smile, she pinched low on his abdomen before pouring her drink. "But you can go away now. I'm done with you."

"You'll need me tonight."

"If you're lucky," she said on a giant grin.

Eric knocked back a healthy swallow of beer and scrubbed a hand across his forehead. "If you lovebirds are done, can we get on with it?"

Mike stretched, cracking his back. "I appreciate everything you guys are doing."

"No problem." Leah hitched one leg over the other, crossing them. "I'm working my tail off up here. All this ogling is hard work."

Eric didn't smile so much as give a little twitch of his lips. He looked out from under his heavy brow. "I'll give you something to ogle, sweet cheeks."

"I'm pretty sure it still counts as sexual harassment even if we're not on base," Michael said.

"You haven't given her a chance to respond." Kisser waved his beer bottle. "Maybe she wants harassment. Some women are into that."

Sunny maintained a beautifully ruthless smile. "I feel an overwhelming urge to give you my business card, but I don't specialize in personal injury."

The big bruiser gave a good impression of affronted, his full lips parting. "Why do I need personal injury? Hale and whole."

Mike chuckled. "I worry about you, Eric. She totally meant for when some woman loses her mind on you and ends up breaking your head."

"Kisser can live with a broken head." Dash shook his head. "He just can't live without *getting* head."

Sunny cringed. "Worst pun of the day. Do you really have to break them out? Ever?"

He was absolutely unrepentant. "Of course I do. How else would I amuse you so thoroughly? But don't make snap decisions about your *absolute* favorite. There's hours yet until I rest."

Eric stood, putting the beer on the table. He wiped his face with the T-shirt draped over the back of his chair. "I don't care if someone breaks my head. Just leave my pretty face alone. It keeps the ladies rolling in."

"C'mon," Dash said. "We've got some layin' to do. And there's also sod to put down." He mimed a rim shot in the air.

"Ugh," Sunny said. "Please. No more."

"But, honey, it's why you love me."

She answered by rolling her eyes. The guys went back to work. They'd be done in no time, with pizza on the agenda. Sunny offered Leah one of the magazines, but she declined.

Too much normal. Too much tempting.

She hopped up and made her way into the kitchen. On autopilot, she pulled a glass down from the cabinet, ice from the freezer and a soda from the bottom shelf. She stood behind the sliding glass door, watching. If anything, she knew Mike's house better than her apartment. She'd certainly spent more time there than in her own bed, where she'd placed the dried rose in a vase on her nightstand.

Outside, Mike paused while bent over. His wrists were deep in a pile of dirt. He used the back of his forearm to push hair back from his forehead, then looked around. For her, maybe?

She really liked that. She wanted to be the one he looked for when he had a spare moment, when he wanted that quick connection. When he needed her.

So many maybes in her head. It actually hurt to look at him. It hurt to want something she didn't believe she could have. As always, she pushed it all away. The sun was shining, an intelligent woman was there to chat with, and three half-naked men paraded around a lawn of green.

What else was a girl going to do but enjoy the view?

Chapter Thirty

Mike didn't think he should be so nervous, but hell if his heart rate wasn't way up. He sat at the bar, trying his hardest to sip his whiskey rather than slam it back.

It had seemed such a harmless idea earlier in the month. Now he was in the midst of it and having second thoughts. A birthday dinner together. What had he been thinking?

Probably that it wouldn't hurt. That the coincidence of their so-very-close birthdays ought to mean something.

They'd agreed to go out. A private celebration. They'd do it up right too, which meant dressing to the nines, high-end reservations at Puccini's, and a present exchange that was wearing a hole in his brain. The tenuous nature of their relationship meant shopping for Leah had been torture.

"Hey, Captain," came a slinky voice.

He turned...and forced himself to shut his mouth.

"Damn."

Leah was wearing a dress.

Not just any dress, but a spaghetti-strap number in fire-engine red. The shimmery material draped across her cleavage and fell in ripples that hugged her small waist and trim hips. The hem tickled just above her knees. Sexy red stilettos and elegant unbound hair made her seem even taller, more graceful.

Mike stood from the bar. He took one hand in his and kissed her knuckles. "You look amazing."

An almost girlish smile tipped her scarlet lips. "Thanks. You don't look too shabby yourself." The frank appreciation in her dark honey eyes shot fissures of awareness through his muscles.

"Quit looking at me that way or we won't eat."

"Oh, but *I'd* eat, pet. You're a feast."

With a low groan, he tucked her hand through his arm and led her to the maître d's stand. "Two for Templeton, please."

"This way, sir."

The man led them through the restaurant, which was thick with the smells of luscious Italian cooking. Mike's stomach rumbled so loudly that he thought Leah must've heard. But she was too busy soaking in the sights. The intimate bistro created a sense of privacy for each table. Tin Tin had suggested the place, which meant it was both elegant and astoundingly expensive. One special meal with Leah? That was worth any price.

He grinned. Sure, he was nervous, but happy as hell too.

Only when they went to sit did he realize she carried her hot pink helmet. "You didn't ride your bike in that dress, did you?"

Driving in from different ends of the city meant meeting up made more sense. To be honest, he'd liked the surprise of seeing her there in the bar. The awe of it.

Leah laughed, accepting a menu from the waiter. "Nah, took a cab. But you rode, yeah?"

"You asked me to, didn't you?"

Pure satisfaction and a hefty dose of heat softened her expression. "Yes, I did. And you did while wearing that suit?"

"Sure."

"Nice. Okay, I need a minute with that image."

Mike grinned and touched his tongue to his lower lip— knowing it drove her crazy. "Take all the time you need, ma'am. I'll be here."

"You can take me for a ride later. That's why I brought my helmet."

"Dress and all?"

"Hitched around my thighs? Straddling that big beast of yours, my breasts pressed against your back? I'll manage." She slid him a saucy smile. "And now you have something to think about too."

The energy between them quickened, deepening again. Mike tried to swallow, but it took a time or two. Shifting in his seat, he indulged in the feel of his cock swelling slightly and the delicate bite of the ring he wore.

They ordered antipasti, salads and a main course—the full Italian works. He kept flicking his gaze toward Leah and that astounding dress. He wanted her in it and he wanted to strip her out of it. Both. On his BMW and in a decadent hotel room bed. All of the above. She was far more of a challenge than deciding on the menu selections. So many possibilities.

Part of the fun of their sex life was not having to choose. He could ruminate on the many options—and happily would as the night progressed. When it came time to act, however, her whims dictated the play.

His thrill was the wait. Anticipating. Knowing whatever she chose would blow his mind.

Maybe other guys wanted control. Craved it. That didn't appeal, which was something he'd decided long ago not to stress about. Whatever got people off in a safe and consensual way was fair game. Who wouldn't want to be at the tender mercies of such a beautiful, deviant woman?

In deference to Leah's valiant effort at going straight, and what seemed to be her request that he drive them to their room at Caesar's, he switched to water. The condensation on the glass helped cool his palm. She'd used ice on him once, when he was strapped spread-eagle to his bed. On his chest. On his stomach. In her mouth as she'd gone down on him.

"You're staring too, Michael. And risking an early departure."

"Caught me."

"It's not like you were trying to hide it. When you get it in your head to stare at me, not even a statue could compete."

He swigged a hefty gulp of water.

"I can tell, you know," she said, her eyes heavy-lidded and soft. "When you're wearing it."

"Oh?"

"Don't play innocent, Michael." She leaned nearer, affording him the slightest glimpse of shadowy cleavage. "You're thinking incredibly delicious thoughts. I can see them in your eyes. You're wearing your ring, aren't you?"

"Yes, ma'am." He shot her a grin. "Felt right for the special occasion."

"Must be rather tight right now."

"Getting there."

"Such a good boy," she said, leaning back. Her gaze walked down his throat, as intense as a caress. "Now, what did you get me?"

Mike chuckled. She always played him just right. Part tease. Part friend. "You're not the most subtle person on the planet, are you?"

"Why bother? I want what you have to give, pet."

The food arrived first, and Mike used the opportunity to realign his frantic heartbeat. He wasn't going to last long if she kept winding him into knots. He loved it, but he wanted to put up a token resistance at a minimum.

Only after the waiter cleared away the plates from the first course did Mike dare to hand over the gift. Make or break time. "Have you waited long enough, ma'am?"

"I think so," she said with a grin. "Give it here."

He handed her a small package, wrapped inexpertly with dark red paper. He'd needed to buy tape to wrap it, and even that small chore—running up to the shoppette after hours—had made him smile. When had he fallen so head over heels for her? Looking it in the face made his chest pinch.

"I like small presents." Her red nails flashed as she tore into the paper like a kid. Her motions slowed, however, as she lifted the hinged lid. "Oh, Michael."

She drew out the gold chain—a box chain, he'd been told, which was sturdier. A pendant shone in the candlelight of their private table. The artist had done a remarkable job with that lush metal. Its folds and creases were slightly irregular, not perfectly aligned, which made it look even more realistic.

A little paper airplane made of gold.

Leah's expression had softened beyond anything he'd ever seen. The sparkle in her eyes had amped, but she blinked it back. "Michael, it's just...it's beautiful."

Her appreciation loosened the knots under his sternum. He breathed again. "It was either that or a new set of tires for your bike."

A tremulous smile edged her mouth. "Will you put it on me?"

With a nod, he pushed back from the table and laid his napkin on the seat. He unhooked the tiny spring clasp while Leah swished the hair away from her nape. After carefully securing the clasp, he smoothed a caress down the delicate bumps of her spine. He bent low and kissed her there. His lips skimmed over gold and skin.

"Beautiful," he whispered.

Before he got caught there, wanting only to taste and drag her soft floral scent into his lungs, he returned to his chair. Leah was holding the tiny airplane, with her chin tucked low to admire it.

"It's..." She took a quick sip of water. The color was high on her cheeks. "It's perfect, Michael. Thank you."

"You're welcome."

Another course arrived, but the conversation between them slowed. Mike couldn't explain it for the life of him. She liked the pendant. That much was obvious by how often she touched it. Feathery caresses. Something about it had changed the atmosphere.

He tucked into the main course, enjoying the fare as much as any he'd had in years, but his gusto was gone. He set his fork and knife aside.

"Leah, what's wrong?"

She shrugged. "Nothing. Sorry. Your present was too large for riding on your bike, so I had it sent to the hotel. It'll be waiting for us."

The voice she used was standard-issue Princess. A little clipped. A little try-too-hard. It slid a chill along the inside of his clothes.

His present wasn't a cuff.

The disappointment he felt was way out of proportion with any sense of reality, but he couldn't help it. He wanted more. From her.

That didn't look like it was happening.

"Great," he said, trying to find that easy smile of his. It didn't feel right. "Can't wait."

The waiter cleared away the plates and brought desert. Leah picked at hers, even though he knew her weakness for all things chocolate. Any other time he would've made some allusion to the choice application of chocolate sauce, but his appetite for innuendo had shriveled up.

He suppressed a sigh and gently shoved his plate aside. "You said you want to ride my bike, yeah?"

A glimmer of the Leah he wanted perked up. She rubbed her toe along the inside of his trouser leg. "Sure do."

"Then how about now?"

Whatever cloud had slunk over her mood dissipated some. She stood from the table, retrieving her helmet. That little gold paper airplane glittered where it sat in the hollow between her collarbones. "Now sounds perfect."

Chapter Thirty-One

The weight of the necklace was entirely too slight to feel beyond the occasional shift of the chain around her neck. That didn't mean Leah was in any way capable of forgetting about it. Her fingers kept drifting to the tiny gold airplane while she watched Michael pay the check.

He'd found her the perfect present. Absolutely perfect. There was no other word for it.

While she'd bought him a cop-out gift.

She'd *looked* for a cuff. The ones she'd seen in the store had been so sexy, so beautiful. Her gut reaction had been hot. Possessive. Eventually she'd backed right the hell up. The cuffs weren't quite right. They'd only been together awhile. A couple months. She could barely even call it dating. They fucked like minxes any chance they got.

That didn't mean she had a right to claim him. If she ever did, she'd make sure everything was perfect. Michael deserved one hundred percent right, and she'd never quite found that.

Her hand drifted up to the fine chain. The gold had already warmed from her skin.

Outside, he tipped the valet. The noise of street traffic and a little honking was the only thing spinning between them.

So many things Leah could say—if she could make her mouth work. She laced her fingers through his instead, hoping that might settle her. If she was going to go through with what she'd planned for the rest of the night, she needed to have all her ducks in a row. Be crystal clear on her purpose.

Mike seemed so damned self-assured as he patiently waited for his bike. As he had when he'd given her the gift.

She was supposed to be the one in charge. What a joke.

The valet brought the BMW around with a grin. He revved the engine a few more times upon parking it. Who could resist?

Mike popped his helmet on then swung a leg over the bike. He grinned at her. "You coming?"

"Gimme a second." She licked her lip. "This is too pretty to pass up."

Whoa and damn, but was it ever. Michael looked good enough to eat. The sleek black suit he wore over an open-necked black shirt combined with the sexy S1000RR to make an image worth photographing. Instead she'd keep a copy in her mind rather than in her nightstand drawer. Definitely worth spending some private time with.

He laughed, but there was something uncomfortable about the sound, as if he were abashed at being so obviously ogled.

So, naturally, Leah dragged out her appreciation. She took in the long length of his legs and the way the trousers pulled over his thighs. The dark suit did nothing to conceal his wide shoulders. Freaking *hot.*

Finally, she put her own helmet on before looking around. The act of getting on a motorcycle in a dress was a little exposing. The valet had obviously realized that and was subtly watching to see if she slipped up. She twirled a finger. He turned away, giving a shrug as if to say it had been worth a shot.

She tucked her skirt down between her legs, grazing her already-warmed pussy. The vibrations of the bike shook up through her body. Every single one of her cells woke up and took notice. She wrapped her arms around Michael's lean waist, sneaking her hands under the edge of his jacket.

"Straight to the room?" he asked, twisting to see her.

She shook her head. "Just drive for a while. I'll tell you when to stop."

Captain Leah Girardi, fighter pilot and chickenshit extraordinaire.

She needed some time to gather herself. Put together the pieces she'd thought she had under control.

There was no better way than on the back of Mike's bike, plastered against him. He drove fast, pushing the speed limit further and further as they left the bright lights of the center of town behind them. She got all the best parts of riding—the speed revving her blood and the wind whipping at her—while the chill helped clear her head.

They had what they had. Did what they wanted to. There were no real expectations on either of them.

Basically she needed to stop freaking out.

Right, like it was that easy. She was the one getting all the prime benefits out of their relationship. The wickedly depraved things he let her do... The rough orders he always followed without question...

Then he'd gone and given her the most perfect birthday present ever, even better than the rose he'd offered with so much sincerity at the Mexican restaurant. What woman was worth the trust he placed so easily in her hands?

It sure wasn't her.

Eventually she tugged on his shirt then pointed back toward the glaring streak that made up the Strip. Time to get the show on the road.

Caesar's Palace was gaudy, all bright lights and fake-gold accents. Despite that, Mike looked damn good walking through the lobby. Leah felt almost as good walking at his side.

He held his arm out to her, letting her hook a hand around his biceps. "Do we need to check in?"

She shook her head. "Nope. I came by earlier. Had to drop off some stuff."

That made his eyes darken in the way she loved so much. It probably wouldn't last once he saw her present. She forced a smile as she led the way to the banks of elevators.

Three stumbling frat boys spilled out of brass doors but then, Lord-a-mercy, no one else got on with Mike and Leah. As the doors shut behind them, the air went thick. Heavy. She punched the button for their floor with a trembling finger.

His bright, shiny grin was back. "I think it counts as a minor miracle to get an elevator all to yourself on a Friday night in Vegas."

"That it does." She leaned against the wall and crooked her finger at him. "Come here and help me celebrate. Kiss me, pet."

"Your wish is my command," he said, with only a hint of that smart-ass tone she loved to hate.

He edged into her space. Pushed his body up against hers, then grasped her hips. She wrapped her hands around his face, spearing her fingers up through his hair, scratching her nails over his scalp. His mouth tasted like deep, rich chocolate. Tantalizing. She couldn't get enough of him.

Their lips slid together, taking and teasing in turn. She lifted a foot, bracing a stiletto to wedge into his hold. She'd probably scuff the wall but couldn't give a damn, not when she had Michael in her arms again—where she felt more assured of them both.

She rode higher on the wave of want, finally settling into her own skin. This, she knew. This part of them, together, made sense.

The elevator doors dinged open. Michael drew his head back. His lovely mouth was slicked wet. She loved marking him any way she could.

The door started to close again, but he whipped out a hand and held it. "Shall we?"

Her grin felt devious even to her. Or maybe that was the sudden, dirty bend of her thoughts. The sharp reminder of what she hoped for the night. "Oh, definitely. We shall."

Swishing more and more swing into her hips, she walked ahead of him down the hallway. She reached up to sweep a thick chunk of her hair forward over her shoulder—and brushed the chain of her new necklace.

Renewed anxiety pinched her spine. There was nothing she could do about the disparity now, except try to make the rest of the night perfect for him.

Mike whistled softly as the door swung open. "Nice digs."

They certainly were. Leah had gone big, choosing a one-bedroom suite for their night. The living area was spacious, with a huge flat-screen TV and dark brown couches, but it had nothing on the bedroom.

When stopping by earlier to drop off her stuff, she'd taken a second to jump on the huge king-sized bed in her bare feet. Doing so with Mike present would get him laughing at her rather than looking at her with such dark heat.

She pointed at the breakfast table, or more specifically, the silver-wrapped present on it. "For you."

He drifted closer. "May I open it, ma'am?"

"Of course," she said, but she had to swallow twice.

Long-fingered hands moved efficiently over the paper. When he had it unwrapped, he paused for half a second. She noticed. She noticed everything about him.

He threw her a grin over his shoulder. "A primo coffee maker? What are you implying?"

She made herself laugh. "That I've been a saint for drinking gallons of jet fuel. No longer."

"So," he said, dragging the word out into a tease. "Does this mean you'll be around to drink more of it?"

It was the least she could admit, especially after he'd put so much out there for her. "Yes. Lots more, I hope."

She slipped up to his side, running a hand under the not-quite-proper suit jacket. He looked entirely too badass to be a businessman. Even in the spike heels, she had to reach up to kiss him. Having to push onto her toes didn't make her feel any weaker, not when he shuddered under the scrape of her nails. She brushed her mouth over his, more of a promise than anything else.

"I got something else too, pet," she breathed across his lips. "Something for both of us."

"Did you?" His answer was a deep rumble.

She eased her body up his in a deliberate provocation. Maybe she could help him ignore the obvious difference in their birthday presents. Maybe she could ditch her own lingering doubts.

"I did. You'd make me very, very happy if you let me use it."

The skin across his high cheekbones went taut. He licked his bottom lip. "What is it?"

"That, you'll have to see." She grabbed his belt buckle. Putting on the best bitch-mode act she had, she sauntered into the bedroom, dragging him along behind her. He certainly followed willingly enough.

Leah stopped when he stood in the doorway.

They both looked at what she'd so carefully placed in the center of the pure-white bedspread.

The cane she'd bought. The one she'd practiced with for hours, determined to get it right.

Heat swept up from her pussy, up into her stomach. Her heartbeat went into triple time, just from having Michael and the slender cane in the same room. The moisture dried in her mouth—pure anticipation of how he'd groan and jump under each stroke, of how he'd moan in her ear when she made him fuck her afterward.

She risked a glance out of the corner of her eye. He seemed almost as affected as her. His chest jerked on harsh breaths. His mouth had fallen slightly open.

Deliberately she stepped between him and the bed. Her hands slipped slowly up his wide chest and spread across his shoulders to push the jacket away. She pinched his nipples through the fine material of his dress shirt. Setting her teeth to the thick column of his throat, she bit down. Harder than she'd ever bit him there before—just shy of leaving marks.

"What do you say, pet?" She licked his salt-tinged skin. "Will you make me very happy tonight?"

Chapter Thirty-Two

Mike let his eyes slide shut. A heavy shudder worked across his shoulders. His nerves still popped in the wake of Leah's bite.

But her question...

After four active tours of duty, he would've thought his sense of self-preservation a little better developed. A *lot* better, actually. Using a cane was serious business, but there he stood in the sumptuous suite, reveling in the possibilities.

He hadn't been on the receiving end of a cruel caning since his few months spent under Georgia's tutelage. Frankly, he hadn't trusted anyone else that deeply. A woman's commitment to his safety and care needed to be extraordinary. His desire to please needed to be hypnotic—an anesthetic and an aphrodisiac all at once.

Leah possessed that sort of hold over him.

Despite the throb in his cock, which threatened to numb conscious thought, he wasn't entirely insensate. There were limits to what he'd do. Limits to what pain he could endure. Forcing anything defeated the point of having a good time.

He met her eyes, which were dark. So dark. He saw every delicious fantasy in those depths, just waiting to be brought out into the suite's soft white light.

After a tense swallow he asked, "You've been practicing?"

He sounded hopeful. There was no denying the heady, thousand-mile-an-hour blast that came from imagining what sort of night they could share. She'd picked it out, waiting for this opportunity. Planning. Working to get the aim and the heft just right. He imagined her frustrated but still persisting—as she had with the flogger, as she did when faced with any challenge. All the while she'd have been racked with excitement, fantasizing about him.

To be wanted that badly made his stomach weak.

Leah backed out of his arms. Two steps took her to the bed where she traced an index finger along the rattan tip. Gracefully, her motions smooth, she placed a decorative throw pillow in the center of the bed before grasping the cane's handle. The red of her nails shone in the hotel room's gentle lighting.

She smiled at him, as if sharing a secret. Those beautifully quirky lips, shiny and scarlet, tipped up at the corner.

With a quick flick of her arm and wrist, working in a perfectly timed movement, she struck the cane across the small square pillow. Dead center. Perfectly balanced, so as not to gouge or pierce too sharply. Her follow-through was graceful as well as she angled the toy's natural bounce up toward the ceiling.

Another time. And again. With uniform results.

She turned to face him, hands on hips. The pale length of rattan was framed by the swoops and swags of her killer red dress. "Well, pet?"

Mike rubbed a hand over his mouth. The whistling sound as the cane flew through the air had sent shock waves of pure craving up his spine. His hands shook with a fine trembling he didn't bother to conceal. Nothing could disguise the jerking cadence of his breath or the hard ridge of his erection.

"We'll warm up, ma'am?"

"Absolutely." Something dark—maybe even hesitant—swished across her expression. She laid the cane aside and returned to his arms. Two slender hands framed his face. "But only if you're sure."

"Ma'am?"

"Yeah?"

"I'm sure."

The moment of hesitation vanished. She was his ice princess again, with her mouth set in a seductive smirk. "Do you know how much I want you, Michael?"

God, he loved hearing his name when her voice went sweet and husky. "Will you tell me, ma'am?"

Able fingers began to unfasten his buttons. One at a time. A slow torture. When the shirt gaped open from throat to navel, Leah raked one red nail down his skin. She repeated the long, sharp caress, harder the second time. Mike could only watch, transfixed, as pale pink streaks marked her path.

"I want you," she said calmly, as if she'd found the same place of peace that he always did when she took control. "I want you shaking and tense and needy. I want you as strung into knots as I am for you."

"You've been imagining this night for some time, haven't you?"

"Yes, I have."

He wet his lower lip, relishing the way her eyes followed every subtle movement. The attention made him ache for more. "For how long?"

"Does that matter?"

"I'd like to know."

"About five weeks." She pushed the shirt from his shoulders then yanked the tails out of his waistband. Leaning close, she flicked her tongue over one nipple. Her fingertips dug deeply into skin along his ribs. He might've laughed, just a little ticklish, had her grip been any more hesitant. "I practiced almost every night. Sometimes it was too much."

"Too much?"

"Wanting you. Imagining you. I'd hold the handle in one hand and touch myself with the other."

Mike's pulse picked up speed. "That's a lovely image, ma'am."

"*You're* lovely. Now off with these slacks. I want you on the bed."

The game had begun in earnest. Mike's rational brain took a back seat to the sharp thrill of pleasing her. Anticipation stretched each nerve taut, waiting, waiting for the next sweet sting and the way she'd make it last.

He retrieved a string of condoms from his pocket then shucked his trousers.

"The nightstand for those, please," she said. "I want you on your knees in the center of the bed."

Obeying, silent now, he eased into the quiet moments before the storm.

"Arms up, Michael. Hands behind your head."

Leah watched silently as he got into position. With her steps sultry and swaying, she slowly circled. The intensity of her gaze, studying him from front to back to front again, burned hot over his naked skin.

Jesus, he was hard. Completely vulnerable and exposed. Leah's sensual appreciation of his body made him strong. Chest high, back straight, he kept his elbows out to the side and his fingers laced at the base of his skull. The grace of her palms along the backs of his calves made him twitch.

"Easy, pet."

"I love when you touch me."

"I know you do. Believe me, you give me quite the thrill too."

It was so easy. So easy to be what she wanted, when she gave him those reassurances. More than that, he couldn't wait to prove, again and again, what sort of man he was. Man enough for anything she desired. The challenge of the pain awaiting him was a fierce dare. A test. Just how much could he take?

Leah crawled onto the bed. Her breasts brushed along his back. "So strong, Michael."

He swallowed, eyes to the ceiling. Every touch felt like it was just the beginning, even though she pressed harder and sharper each time.

"Say what I want to hear," she whispered against his spine.

237

"All for you, ma'am. Only you."

She trailed soft kisses down his backbone then edged her teeth against the top curve of one buttock. Mike exhaled as she bit down. He groaned. Almost as soon as she began, she released the deep bite and swiped her tongue over that sensitized skin. Again, then again, she bit and licked high across his ass. He only knelt there, elbows wide, as he soaked up every ache.

"Very good." She straightened again, running her hands up his sides, around to his chest. Rubbing, scratching, pinching, she broke down his defenses and reached past his reflexive need to draw away. Instead he melted into each new caress. "Now bend over, pet. On your hands and knees."

Mike obeyed, chancing a glance to the side. The stilettos were gone. She'd hiked her hem up, kneeling on the bed in her sexy red dress.

With her right hand, she smoothed a sweeping stroke over his ass. More friction. More speed. He knew what was coming. His cock strained, heavy and erect between his thighs. His triceps tensed, just waiting. A low moan built in his chest, but he held it back. She liked when he was silent in these maddening moments before the first strike.

Crack.

He grunted, with his body shaking around the hot snap of her flesh against his. Slowly, with ever more force, she warmed his ass with smack after smack. Sweat beaded between his shoulder blades and at his hairline. Leah established a maddening pattern. Strike and soothe. Again, on the other side. He would just grow accustomed to the rhythm and intensity when she'd switch it up. A stronger hit. A series of softer blows with no soothing between. A long, lingering caress.

"Oh, Michael."

He smiled to himself at her breathless whisper. Giving over to her care was so much more gratifying when he heard the little tells—how his submission affected her. How it gave her the same intense pleasure. Their needs dovetailed in the purest way.

"What would you like, Michael? If you could have anything at all right now, what would it be?"

This was new. He almost blinked at the surprise. But he didn't tell her the truth. He wanted to be hers. *Entirely* hers. He wanted to be claimed in daylight and at night, with her cuff around his wrist. Maybe his physical vulnerability and abject need kept his request silent. If Leah were going to be his, and if she were going to claim him, he wanted it when they were both stone-cold sober—not high on the rush of their roles.

Still she waited.

"I'd ask that you take off your dress, ma'am."

"You don't like my dress?"

"Your dress is incredible."

"But?"

"But when you hurt me, I love to see your body move."

Eyelids heavy, she took a deep breath, which lifted the gentle swells of her breasts. She wasted no time. Off the bed, she positioned her body in the perfect spot for him to watch. The dress was up, over and off in a graceful sweep. She wore a matched red bra and panties. No stockings. Just her cream-colored skin.

"Like this, pet?"

"Yes." He breathed, but the air wasn't getting to his brain. "Just like that, ma'am."

"Then come here. On the edge of the bed."

Mike shifted, turning until his feet were flat on the floor, slightly wide. He leaned at the waist, giving the weight of his torso to his forearms and elbows. He clasped his hands together, fingers laced. Anticipation tensed in his belly. The ring beneath the head of his cock was tight, as if Leah squeezed him there.

She wasn't touching him. Just watching in that ravenous way. She laid the cane on the mattress, right next to his tensed forearms. The leather handle brushed his skin, covering him with goose bumps.

Leah took her position on his left side, which freed her right hand. She began anew, slapping his lower back, his upper thighs, his ass. Each new hit was sharper than the last, no teasing now. Mike braced against the gathering burn. The blaze in his brain was bright and hot now, needing more. Aching and waiting. His nerves had taken on a delicious tingle—just numb enough to crave something harder and deeper.

She was breathing quickly. Her breasts bounced with the strikes of palm against tensed muscle. Her abs contracted with each reverberation. The long, unbound hair that had been so neat at the start of dinner was damp now. Erotic strands clung to her cheeks and neck.

She stopped unexpectedly, just when he'd been sinking into that soft, peaceful place of warmth and stinging pain. Mike flashed her a glance. She'd leaned close. Her eyes gleamed and her crooked lips perched in a delicious half-smile. Leah kissed his shoulder. Tenderly. Reverently.

When she straightened, she curled her right hand around the handle of the cane.

Chapter Thirty-Three

Through all the long hours of practice, Leah had kept this moment in the back of her head. The moment when Michael and the cane would come together under her touch.

It was everything she'd imagined. More.

Her palm still stung from the blows she'd landed over and over. Long stretches of his skin carried a pink wash.

He was beautiful. The hard-edged, restrained beauty of a male warrior. A sheen of sweat made his muscles gleam. His thick, strong chest jerked on harsh breaths.

So good.

She trailed the sharp tip of the cane over his skin. Slowly. Gently. After cuddling the touch up to his back, his spine, she let a single touch drop along the crack of his ass. The backs of his thighs twitched under his restraint.

"You're such a good boy," she breathed. Her hand followed in the wake of the leather-wrapped handle. "The things you let me do, Michael... They please me so much."

He turned his head to watch her. His eyes had gone glassy and such a deep blue that they appeared almost as dark as her own. "Not let."

Her hand stilled. The cane was a pale punctuation across the small of his back. "Pet? Explain?"

"I don't *let* you. I want it too. Crave it." He said it so quietly, with his voice a rumble of acceptance, as if it was the most normal thing in the world.

Maybe, deep down, it was. For them.

She certainly felt normal when she was with him like this. Poured-on energy flowed down to her cunt. She was so wet that her tiny red panties clung like a second skin. Her mind was finally of one path. Michael. Making him jump and groan and taking the responses he gave her.

"Thank you for that, pet." She brushed a reverent kiss over his back, along the vulnerable, exposed line of his spine. "You give me everything I need."

His eyes closed slowly. A peaceful smile curved his mouth.

She edged his feet farther away from the bed, closer together, briefly touching along his shins. He eased his torso down to the flat of the bed. He was so tall that he didn't kneel so much as drape from mattress to floor, but that was good. She wanted his thick muscles.

Drawing out each caress, she dragged the bamboo against his skin. Saying she started softly with a cane sounded absurd, but she did. Short, soft bounces barely kissed his lower ass. She flicked her wrist with the steady moves she'd practiced.

Smooth. Even.

Each gathering stroke was a continuation of her heavy breathing. Her chest clenched at the sight of neat red streaks lining up under her ministrations, right across his skin.

Through it all, Michael gathered his usual mix of calm and excitement. His groans spun out like pretty, pretty music as his thighs jerked and played beneath her harsh treatment. His neck bent as he melted into her attention.

Leah hit harder. She flicked her hand so that the cane landed in rhythmic whacks. The fierce instrument swished through the air. The sound of rattan hitting his skin was surprisingly quiet—quieter than that distinctive whistle.

The effect, however, was devastating. He twitched, flinched, hissed. Although her Michael never truly pulled away, she could see how his body seemed to hunch in defense. That he fought his natural reactions, no matter how hard she hit, created the most powerful arousal of her life.

His groans dragged louder. Harsher. And more thoroughly aroused. It was as if he felt no pain at all. Only pleasure.

Red stripes laid out exactly where she'd meant to place them—parallel across his ass and down across his thighs. She even tapped a few lighter strokes along his flanks, ribs and soles of his feet. His hands remained splayed on the pure white bedspread. She became nothing more than his responses. Everything ratcheted together like feedback.

So she wasn't sure what went wrong.

A false twist of her wrist maybe.

The blow she'd meant to land flat on the back of his right thigh hit at a sharp angle. The tip gouged his skin and bounced to slash at the back of his calf.

Michael hissed in a breath. "Red light," he grunted. "Fuck."

The cane dropped from her numb fingers. *Shit.* Her blood simply stopped pumping.

But *she* moved. Leah was by his side in an instant. Nonsense comfort words spilled from her mouth as she touched him. She eased him fully onto the bed, then crawled beside him and petted the damp hair back from his forehead. "God, Michael. Are you okay?"

"Will be. Give me a second."

"Here, let me see." She bent low, inspecting every inch she'd stroked and lashed. And yeah, she left the worst for last, because sometimes she was such a goddamned coward.

Across his ass and the tops of his thighs, his skin was flushed and streaked with perfect crimson lines. At first his muscles and tendons twitched beneath her gentle caresses, then eased along with his harsh breathing.

She twisted to see the side of his leg. A bright red bump had popped up on his calf. The really scary part was the gouged weal on his thigh, with a slender line of blood in the center. She'd broken the skin.

"Jesus. I'm so sorry. I didn't mean—"

He shook his head against the mattress. "It's okay. You stopped. It's how these things work."

She hadn't wanted to be the one to mess it up. To break the trust he'd handed her. But she'd known all along that was how it would be.

"Stay right there." Slipping off the bed, she caught her balance on the nightstand. Her knees almost gave out with the sudden rush of blood to her head.

At the other end of the room, she dug through the combat medic kit she'd converted into an aftercare kit when their sessions kept intensifying. She smeared numbing antiseptic cream on two sterile cotton squares and took a deep breath, fighting for calm. She'd thought for just a moment that she had everything under control, that she could at least give him this much when he'd been so absolutely perfect.

Nope.

Michael hadn't moved an inch. His breathing continued to even out. He was always so calm in the way she couldn't find, because even as fear turned her guts into a roiling mess, one truth remained.

She was still turned on, even at the sight of his wound. *So very wrong.* Her body rode high on the adrenaline of watching his body absorb everything she'd given him.

To tend his angry skin, she pushed that reaction down. She pressed the cotton square against the welt. He hissed again. Every muscle in his lower body jumped. She held it against his thigh until he eased when the numbing cream had time to work. Then she taped the second one with surgical tape that glowed white against his tan skin.

Guiding him up on the bed with her, she leaned against the pile of pillows and gathered him close. Her hands kept stroking. Heat burned up from his skin, nestling in her fingers.

"I'm so sorry," she said again. "I didn't mean to."

"I know." He pressed his face into her stomach. His shoulders loosened on a long, slow breath. "It was...good. Until then. So good, ma'am."

She pushed the hair back from his forehead. "I'm glad, pet."

"We'll try again some other time."

No way could she contain a shudder. His easy acceptance of another try was too overwhelming. Her fingers trembled as she rubbed the back of his neck.

She was tearing in two. The part of her that cringed at doling out unintentional pain crashed against the part of her that reveled in the idea of being allowed to try again. Another try at taking him higher. She wanted to see how far she could push before he crumbled to beautiful, satisfied pieces—pieces she'd be trusted to put back together again.

"We'll see," she said quietly.

He slid a hand around her hip, delving beneath the band of her panties. His fingertips grazed the top of her ass as he brushed a kiss along the bottom arch of her ribs.

They stayed curled together for a long time. How long, she had no idea, since the curtains were drawn—like they'd gone to ground together. Hiding from the world.

They couldn't stay wrapped around each other for long before Leah's blood started churning again. Michael dropped soft kisses along her skin, tracing his tongue around her navel. She tilted his face with a hand under his sharp jaw.

The kiss she pressed over his lips was all silent apologies. She hoped like hell he could hear them since she couldn't push words out through her clenched throat. Maybe he did because he kissed her more deeply. His tongue dipped between her teeth.

He eased up her body. Bare masculine skin slipped along hers in a tantalizing promise. The sweat had cooled between them, but that didn't mean Leah was any less excited. Any less wet. His cock dug into her hip as he trailed slow touches over her stomach, her thighs and the lace front of her panties, pushing against her soaking pussy.

She indulged in exploring his sleek, strong back before drifting down to the still-hot skin stretched over his ass. He shuddered and pressed into her touch.

No orders this time. No permission. Just a slow swan dive into the depths they'd always been able to reach. He drew her panties down before dropping them over the side of the bed. His fingers teased her lips and circled her clit. Leah spread her knees because of that tingling pleasure, to better enjoy those sharp waves of enjoyment.

Mike nestled between her legs, making room for himself. Her inner thighs brushed over the smooth skin at his waist. The thick heft of his cock slid through her wetness. She gasped when his ring thumped gently over her clit.

Making herself reach for the condom was harder than she'd expected. Excitement, nerves and a strange, sensual lassitude made her hands tremble as she smoothed it over his length.

Christ, the way he looked at her. Watched her. His eyes glittered despite that unbelievably deep blue. A soft smile curved his wide mouth.

She wrapped her arms around his upper ribs and pulled him down, enjoying the way he pressed her flat into the bed. She was solidified and grounded by his weight. When Mike fitted his prick against her, she tucked her forehead to the thick bow of his shoulder. She let her eyes drift shut as he thrust, so slowly, as if his tenderness would sew her together again. Even in this, she was taking—using him to make her whole, when she ought to be tending to him.

She opened her mouth over his chest. Hot licks of his salty skin. No teeth. Not this time. She didn't trust herself. Her fingers spread wide over his back, which shifted with every dragging push. Still she wanted to mark him, to drag her nails over his skin, to know she claimed every inch of this incredible man.

She denied the urge and banded her legs around him. Intentionally, she hitched her ankles high enough that they locked over the small of his back—not his ass or his thighs.

The sweetness building between them made her eyes prickle. Leah closed her eyes so tightly that the skin above her cheeks pinched. She kept her face hidden against his flesh.

Michael never increased his speed. He dragged out slow, dripping pleasure. Time spilled wide as they pushed into each other. She could almost believe they had the whole world at their disposal. Almost.

Her orgasm crept up like a lazy river of sensation. Her nipples prickled from the rub of his chest hair. Her cunt clenched down on his cock. She stretched up, up so that her mouth hovered over his ear.

"Now, pet," she said, unable to keep the orders at bay. The need to command had sunk claws into a deep part of her—the same part that was ready to break apart under his slow patient body. "I'm coming now. Go with me."

Mike's back jerked under her grip. His hips pulsed, driving that beautiful cock into her, grinding, sending a burst of white-hot pleasure out from her center. A low, quiet groan spilled over both of them as they came. Together. Like she'd asked for.

Like she both needed and dreaded.

Chapter Thirty-Four

Mike lounged on the couch in his younger brother's living room in Tampa. His six-year-old niece, Olivia, sat on the floor eating Pringles and watching *Max and Ruby*. She had a sport bottle of juice with a Hello Kitty topper while he nursed a lukewarm Coke.

A week had passed since his birthday celebration with Leah. Nothing had clicked after that. He didn't get it. Sex with an edge of D/s was risky, let alone the full-blown kink they'd indulged in.

Her sudden withdrawal left him confused. Safe words were there for a reason. She'd stopped, he'd been fine with no serious damage done, and they'd enjoyed a fucking fantastic vanilla time of things afterward. It'd been reassuring, actually, to know they were capable of something so good. How they *could* be. The trust and the compromise. Even the improvisation and sweetness.

It hadn't been that way for Leah. Complete shutdown.

Needing a break from that tension, he'd asked Fang for a few days to visit his brother's family. Tom and his wife, Shelly, had insisted—in part, he knew, because Olivia's spring break would devastate their schedules. Tom was in marketing, and Shelly sold real estate. That meant Mike had a nice niche as "uncle who occasionally stays for a week to help out".

That he stuffed Olivia with chocolate and took her to a go-kart track was her parents' cross to bear. Uncle privileges trumped all.

He would've been enjoying himself and the time off, had Leah called. Or texted. Email would've worked. Or smoke signals. Pretty much anything.

His phone was in his pocket, as always. Sometimes he willed it to ring. Long minutes passed when he didn't think about her, content to cloak himself in the simplicity of a six-year-old's world. Then something would click. A word that had made Leah laugh. A song that dragged him right back to her arms. He'd been sleeping piss poorly. No matter that he was technically on vacation, he hadn't been so fatigued since his last tour.

No amount of wishing or waiting changed the fact that she hadn't reached out.

He'd thought they were stronger than one mistake.

Tom and Shelly arrived home within five minutes of one another. The flourish of a family's routine was disorienting. Mike nodded to both as they hustled in, carrying empty travel mugs, computer bags and stacks of mail. They greeted him in return as Olivia darted in between their bodies, chattering about her day at the go-kart track.

They did this every night? No, most nights would be even more hectic, with picking up Olivia from school.

Only, it wasn't the one-sided relationship Mike had grown up watching, with his mom in the kitchen and his dad on the couch with a beer in hand. Instead, Tom retrieved defrosted hamburger patties from the fridge while Shelly switched out a load of laundry. They both worked their asses off. They were successful. From what Mike had seen after five days in their home, they were a unit. A true partnership.

And by that fifth day, he was damn envious.

After a dinner of burgers, chips and potato salad, Shelly went to give Olivia a bath.

"Beer?" Tom extended a longneck from where he stood by the fridge. He'd just finished loading the dishwasher.

"Yup." Mike followed his younger brother to the back patio where the balmy heat of Florida in early May crawled into his lungs. "Damn, how can you stand it here in the summer?"

"How can you? Vegas? C'mon."

They grinned and clinked beer bottles.

"You've really got something here, Tom. It's amazing."

"Don't I know it," his brother said with a grin. Looking at him when he smiled was like looking in a mirror—if that mirror were younger and thinner. Tom took a hefty swig. "Couldn't do it without Shelly. You see that now, right?"

Mike found himself taking offense when he didn't even know the reason. "See what?"

"How screwy Mom and Dad were."

"There's nothing wrong with them," Mike said, but the protest felt hollow. "I talk to Mom all the time. Her gardening and stuff."

"Tinkering with a hobby because it's all she has is a lot different than a life of her own. Shit, Mike, did you know that Shelly makes more than me? About twenty percent more. In what lifetime would Dad have been able to stomach that?"

"Never."

"Do you remember how you used to argue with me? I was in college and you'd just got back from Iraq."

"That first tour? Yeah." He exhaled heavily. "Something about how you working the nightshift as a security guard was bullshit."

"Because it helped Shelly's real-estate startup. Yup." He looked around his backyard, which was lush and trimmed with a redwood fence. "Think I regret any of that now?"

Mike took a long, slow swig. "No," he said quietly. "I bet you don't."

Whereas thoughts of their parents only needled Mike with old anxieties. Dad griping about Mom's cooking. Mom ignoring the criticism and offering some banality instead. The silent warfare of two unhappy people. Had their marriage always been that way? Had he been too self-absorbed and content with the status quo to notice the rifts and barbs? Maybe sampling a taste of something sweeter and more balanced had altered his perception.

Shelly popped her head through the patio door. "Hey, you two. It's late. You coming to bed, Tom?"

"Sure."

Watching his brother unfurl from his chair was like watching some fantasy made real. Tom held his near-empty bottle by the neck. His other hand interlaced with Shelly's as they said their good nights.

Mike didn't necessarily want kids and a mortgage. That was like speaking Martian. But that connection... That trust they shared... What would it be like to share that with Leah?

His brother was right. Misguided impressions about bygone gender roles were just that. Misguided. Even worse, if he dug a little deeper, he might find his own inadequacies. He'd given Leah a ration of crap during their early days because she was the one with ambition. All he'd had was a bad attitude and a dick to swing around.

Through her career, she'd needed to stand strong against a thousand similar attitudes. Every day was an achievement in the face of that much scrutiny. That she'd excelled was a testament to her determination. That she cracked under the pressure sometimes... Who wouldn't?

He still missed her, and he hated wondering whether she had the guts to see this through.

He found himself rubbing his bare right wrist. "Fuck," he whispered.

The phone vibrated. His heart lurched.

The ID wasn't Leah's.

Banking the flash flood of disappointment, he thumbed the call button. "Tin Tin? Man, what the hell?"

Jon Carlisle's voice was as slinky smooth as always, with a hint of laughter that said he was up to no good. Mike had actually started to like the guy. "So is it true the humidity makes the heat worse?"

"You've never been to Florida?"

"Of course I have. Just making conversation. But now you need to blow that popsicle stand."

"Why?"

"I got a call from our fearless leader. Fang's getting hitched."

"To Cass?"

"Course," he said with a chuckle. "The boy's got it bad. They're doing the deed Saturday. Leave it to those two to agree on a quickie Vegas wedding."

"Fang gonna wear mess dress?"

"Sure thing. It's almost tacky enough to be awesome."

The heavy, cloying heat sat on Mike's chest like a nasty troll. He grimaced, even though Tin Tin's news was good. It was *right*. Major Haverty never looked more content than when Cass, his gentle redheaded pixie, was there by his side.

"Thanks for letting me know, Tin Tin," he said, his throat constricted. "I'll be sure to congratulate him when I get back."

"No way, man. Not good enough. He wants us there. Me and Heather, Leah, you—and as many from the squad as possible. I get the feeling he doesn't want to be outdone by Cass's relatives. Ryan doesn't have much in the way of family, so we're going to make sure his side of the church is filled."

Mike considered his options. Telling Tom and Shelly that he had to duck out two days early wouldn't be pleasant. But his conversation with his brother had shed new light on how he envisioned his future. He was antsy to get back to Vegas, to talk to Leah for real. No more dodging their issues.

Decision made.

"I'll be there," he said.

"Cool. You gonna phone Princess or should I?"

Thud. Just like that. He hit rock-hard emotion again.

Jon had practically become a silent partner in helping Mike impress Leah, but the kid sure as hell wasn't getting anything more than the bare facts.

"You call her, Tin Tin. I'll see you in Vegas."

Mike stood in the Best Little Wedding Chapel and adjusted his cummerbund. To say he was waiting for the ceremony to start would be a lie. He was really waiting for Leah. As soon as all this energetic, happy hoopla settled down, with Fang whisking his new bride away to a casino honeymoon suite, Mike would sit down with Leah.

So many times she had complimented him on the way he kept his body in check, never unleashing his strength until she needed it. She relished how he could hold back for her pleasure. Waiting. Giving over to her pace.

For his own sense of self-preservation, he needed that restraint now. A week had passed and she hadn't called, which meant they were starting on different pages. To get what he wanted, he needed to chill out before he made a complete ass of himself.

Talking. Sharing. That was it.

He enjoyed begging for his mistress, but not for her affection.

Though relatively small, Cass's family was a fun lot. Her older sister had just given birth, which meant a fussy newborn to contend with, but no one snapped. It was all laughter and good-natured teasing—a slightly cleaner version of the trash talk that permeated the squadron.

The chapel was awash with white, from the cinder-block walls to the hexagonal ceiling tiles. A blood-red velvet carpet runner marched between two banks of white wooden folding chairs. The contingent representing Fang on the groom's side was made entirely of airmen, making Mike wonder about Tin Tin's comments about the man's lack of family.

The contrast between that tasteless little chapel and a dozen mess dress uniforms was almost funny, until he glanced toward where Fang stood waiting. The major bobbed his weight onto his heels. Then he checked his watch. Then he straightened his bow tie and the row of medals pinned precisely into place.

Mike followed the red velvet runner to the altar. Well, maybe altar was too impressive of a word. A white garden arch had been decorated with plastic climbing roses. Someone had added the 64th's unit flag to the vines.

"Hey, Strap," Fang said, offering his hand. "Glad you could make it, man."

"Me too. I'm happy for you, sir."

"Don't let Cassandra hear you call me that."

"Not a problem. You look nervous as hell."

Fang grimaced. "I thought a quickie wedding would make it less of a big deal." He shrugged, as if that said it all.

It did, actually. No matter the location, Major Ryan Haverty was a man on the verge of making a lifelong commitment.

Mike couldn't help but take that seriously.

"Fang, my man!"

Tin Tin strolled into the chapel. With one hand he carried two bottles of Cristal champagne by their necks. His other hand was wrapped around the waist of a stunning woman. Clad in an Air-Force-blue silk dress, with her hair done up like a '40s starlet, she was a fantastic combination of sex and elegance— nearly as tall as Tin Tin and probably five years his senior.

"And Strap too," Tin Tin said, catching sight of Mike at the altar. "Back from purgatory, I see. Did you bring me souvenirs?"

"You know, Tin Tin is too awesome of a dog, kid. How about we call you Toto instead?"

A sly, dirty smile crept across Jon's mouth. "Call signs don't matter, my friend. Only who wears a collar in real life. Now, say hello to Heather. Heather Morris, this is our new guy, Captain Mike Templeton."

"Strap Happy, is it?" she asked as they shook hands. "And here I was convinced you were a figment of Tin Tin's imagination."

"Not at all. Flesh and blood." She said the words with a slanted glance at her partner.

"Quit flirting with me, Heather love, or we'll be MIA for Fang's big moment." Handing the champagne to the major, he said, "Really, man, you didn't need to *actually* get married to play bride and groom."

"Shut up, Tin Tin, or so help me I'll run you over with your own car."

"Fine, fine," he said with a negligent wave. "I'll be good. I just had it waxed."

Heather edged nearer to Mike. She smelled exotic, like a flower that couldn't be touched without wilting. Only that wouldn't be true if she was really Tin Tin's girl.

"Where's Leah?" she asked.

"Haven't the foggiest."

The dark-haired woman masked her briefly befuddled expression. "I just assumed she'd be here already."

As if on cue, the chapel door banged open. Leah, as formal as the other airmen in her mess-dress uniform, stood in the doorway. Her hair was loosely bound and slightly disheveled around her doll-like features.

Mike clenched against the rush of seeing her again. Time had stretched and drawn, until *bang*. There they were. Back in the same room, breathing the same air. He did battle against the impulse to go to her.

He had no claim on her and vice versa.

"Yo, Fang," Leah said, her words sloppy at the edges. "There's an adorable redhead out here waiting to get hitched. You ready or what?"

The skin prickled along the back of Mike's neck. Fang and Tin Tin exchanged grave expressions, mirroring a pinched coldness in his gut. If Leah weren't already drunk, she was well on her way.

Chapter Thirty-Five

Leah hadn't had any problem filling her days. Cleaning her house, dinner out with Jon and Heather. There had even been an oh-so-exciting library trip. She really knew how to live.

The whole time, her palms had itched with the need to sprawl all over Michael. Her good boy.

Despite being lost without him—or maybe because of it— she hadn't called. At all. What should she have said?

Sorry I was such a clumsy noob last time? And gee, wasn't it convenient timing that you flew to Florida right after I fucked up?

He'd said it was no big deal. Didn't mean she believed him.

So yeah, she'd needed to take a cab to the wedding. Having two vodka tonics meant her bike was off limits.

When Leah walked in the double doors of the wedding chapel, he was the first person she saw. Michael. She stuck there for a long moment. Her insides tumbled even as her pussy pulsed.

God, he looked good. His hair had grown a bit shaggy again. The golden-brown curled along the top of his neck. He wore the same-ol', same-ol' Air Force dress uniform. After all her years in the service, she would've thought herself immune to it. She wasn't, not when it was on Michael. He looked so slick and put together that he could almost be the groom.

Wasn't that a frightening thought? Her air stuttered in her throat. They were kink. Plain and simple. A girl didn't marry kink and expect to have it all work out.

She touched her tiny gold airplane. The necklace didn't meet regulations, so she'd hidden it under her collar. Better that way. But the delicate gift still shocked her to the core. *Special.* He made her feel special.

Plastering on a smile, she sought out Ryan. The boy looked like a bundle of nerves, practically vibrating. He smiled wanly and stuck out his hand as she ambled up the aisle. "Glad you could make it."

She took his grip but then tugged to toss an arm around him. "I wouldn't have missed it for the world. Cass is a great girl. She's on pins and needles out there, waiting. You two are going to be so happy together."

"What's this?" Ryan leaned back and peered into her face with a faked expression of concern. "Real emotion from Princess Leah? Don't tell me you've gone and grown girl parts."

She balled up a fist and planted it on the major's shoulder. "Fang, don't be an ass on your wedding day. I'm pretty sure it's against the rules."

He pretended to consider, then shook his head. "Nope. I have to be nice to Cassandra. And her parents. That's it."

"You better be nice to her forever. Or I'll chop *your* bits off."

Jon sidled up to them, with Heather at his side. "Now there's the mean girl we know and love."

They shared a round of greetings, until she couldn't put off talking to Mike. As the minister, who looked like he probably did Elvis weddings in his free time, took Ryan to the side, Leah found herself face-to-face with Michael.

Her heartbeat flushed in her ears on the sudden memory of swinging the cane in the hotel room. The way his mouth had pinched down at first, then gone slack as he'd floated away on the feelings.

His hiss when she'd screwed up.

She made herself smile. "Hey, you."

"Hello...Leah." He'd meant her to fill in the blank with *ma'am*. She had.

She wanted to lean up and kiss him. An easy slide of her lips over his—the normal greeting when two people were involved. "How was your vacation?"

"Could have been better," he said as something dark flitted across his features.

Though there was no denying that they *were* involved, she still couldn't put a name on them. Fully half the squadron had turned up for Fang's wedding. Jon knew. Ryan might suspect. But every dickwad she worked with? No thanks.

Besides, she hadn't called him. More to the point, he hadn't called her either. She might want to be on top in the bedroom, but Mike had the perfect fuck-buddy system down to an art. She would've liked to be the one to run. He hadn't given her the chance—bailing for Florida at the first opportunity.

She rocked back on her heels as she racked her mind for something to say. Anything that didn't involve ordering him out to the back alley so she could climb him the way she wanted to.

Goddamn, she needed another drink. Bad.

She'd thought about stashing a flask under her dress jacket but figured Fang would have her head.

The minister started shooing everyone to their seats. She went willingly enough, staking out a spot in the front row next to Heather. Jon stayed at the altar beside Fang. Even the notorious Tin Tin had found his earnest face, apparently taking seriously his role as best man.

Mike slid in next to Leah.

Her nerves shot napalm down her skin. Every inch knew his proximity. Three inches between their elbows. Five between their knees. And a canyon between their lips.

She scrubbed the back of her hand across her mouth. *Such a hot mess.* The second he realized that, he'd bolt faster than he had to Florida. She wouldn't even see his contrails streak across the sky. Hell, he already had. Not calling was a pretty clear signal.

A soft swell of prerecorded music filtered through speakers. At least it was well done, all the gentle chords of the traditional wedding march.

Leah stood along with everyone else, turning to face the chapel doors.

Cass looked beautiful. On short notice she'd managed to find a sleeveless white dress with a tiny hint of train. The real beauty was on her face. Incandescent joy that shone in her eyes as she stared at Ryan—who looked just as joyous. The nerves had all faded away from his expression. Little remained but happy expectation.

Leah's heart clenched for them, and with a more intense version of the jealousy she'd felt while observing Dash and Sunny.

Mike sat in her peripheral vision. His eyes were that bright blue she both loved and dreaded. She knew what to do when they shifted dark—knew how to hold herself, to let the command keep her spine stiff.

This moment... Watching one of her best friends get married ought to be something good. Pure. She felt like a traitor because she wasn't feeling that selfless.

When Cass and Ryan linked hands in front of the minister and everyone else sat down, Leah had to tuck her fingers under her thighs. All to avoid reaching for Mike's hand.

He would let her. Screw the rows of airmen behind her. Screw the week he'd been gone, with her being a stone-cold bitch for not calling. She knew without asking that he'd lace their fingers together, even let her trace a thumbnail over the vulnerable skin at his wrist.

Because he had that calm, Zen-out factor—the cool she loved to shake up when they were naked in bed.

The same reserve that made her feel like shit. She couldn't measure up.

The words of the ceremony were washed under by the blank roar in her ears. Her heartbeat hurtled past the sound barrier. The only thing that cracked through was "I do", and the way Cass and Ryan grinned at each other.

When the minister announced the new husband and wife, Leah exhaled on a shaky whoosh, as if she'd been worried for them.

Ryan curved his hands around Cass's face and bent toward her. She stood on her toes to kiss him back. *Hard.* They were so cute together, like Ken and Barbie but better. More real.

The squadron stood and cheered in full-on military war cries. Cass's side of the aisle stood also, though they clapped more like normal people as the happy couple strolled past arm in arm.

In a tiny reception room, Jon broke out the bottles of champagne and poured dribbles of golden bubbles into plastic cups provided by the chapel. A few rounds of speeches went by, led off by Cass's gruffly overjoyed father.

Leah drifted farther and farther toward the periphery of the room. The little cup of champagne wasn't easing the drawn-crazy buzz that coursed down her spine.

She couldn't take her eyes off Mike. The easy way he fell in with the group. His wide smile. His bright eyes. She leaned against a credenza, plastering her best "I'm happy" smile on her face. She managed to keep it steady even when Jon sidled up next to her.

"Are you going next?" She'd aimed for lighthearted and failed miserably. She needed another drink to cut through her fucking crankypants mood.

Instead of laughing it off as she'd expected, Jon's gaze tracked down Heather. The woman stood with Cassandra, their heads bent together as they giggled. Normal and girlish.

"You never can tell," he finally said.

Leah drained the last dregs of her champagne. Jon always sprang for the good stuff. "Don't tell me you're going all normal like."

He shrugged. "When you find someone who fits you...it's the logical step."

She bumped her shoulder up against him. "Marriage isn't about logic."

"No, it's not." He grinned. His dark eyes narrowed, back to the pervy boy she'd known for so long. "When you're supremely lucky, it's about finding the one person who makes you feel like you're the hottest shit around and makes you feel humble at the same time."

That was Mike, all right, but the humble part sure seemed to outweigh the rest. She set the plastic cup on the credenza, carefully avoiding Jon's gaze. "Tell Ryan that I wish him the best, okay? I don't feel like wading through the crowds to get to him."

Jon grabbed her wrist. "You okay?"

"Of course, Tin Tin," she said with a forced smile. "I'll see you at work."

She left. Walked right out the front doors of the chapel and kept going. She didn't even bother trying to hail a cab.

"Leah," called a voice from behind her. "Wait up."

Her feet stuttered to an abrupt halt, but she couldn't make herself turn around. She didn't need to. The voice was Michael's. She knew it wide awake. Knew it in her sleep. Knew every tone and inflection.

Now he was all rough annoyance. He spun her with a rough hand on her shoulder. "Where are you going?"

As if she actually had any goal in mind.

She pinched the back of her neck, but that didn't free her from the tension. She wasn't able to look at him directly. Too much temptation and risk. She feared that everything she doubted about herself would be reflected in his blue eyes.

"There," she said, pointing at a tiny bar two buildings down. The doorway looked shadowy and cool. Neon blinked in the painted-over front window. The place had once been a more upscale bar, maybe in better days, but now it perfectly fit her mood.

"Wanna go get a drink with me?"

He studied her so carefully, prying apart her secrets and poking at her fears. "Not really. I was thinking we might go back to my place."

Fucking hell, she wanted that. Considering how things had gone down last time, she didn't know if she had that degree of control. She possessed none of the icy calm he'd need from her. She was one hundred percent ragged edges, and half-bombed to boot.

Leah shook her head and ran a hand over her bun, which was starting to slide free. Drinking in a dive bar in dress uniform might not be her best idea ever. She knew she was careening out of control. Best to let Michael see the worst of her now, before they continued to get their hopes up.

"I need a margarita."

She started walking toward the bar, but the ties binding her to Michael were even stronger than she thought. She couldn't resist throwing back a few more words. Just in case. "You're welcome to join me if you want."

Chapter Thirty-Six

Mike banked his expectations. Again.

His skin flashed frigid. A heavy pulse chugged in his ears, and as he crossed the street to follow Leah on her self-destruct course, he put a huge chunk of himself away.

She couldn't even look him in the eye without a haze of alcohol separating them. What sort of future was that?

None that he could stomach. That was depressing as hell.

The dive was a shithole and a half. Dingy beige walls wept an oily sheen. Humid and sickly, the air hung heavily with the stench of cold cigarette smoke. A few patrons turned rusted necks to watch him and Leah make their way to the bar. By comparison, it made Paulie's look like the swank Italian place where he'd taken Leah for their birthday dinner.

Already a lifetime ago.

"Set me up," she said to the emaciated bartender. "Two shots of tequila."

"I'm not drinking, Leah."

"Didn't say you were. And a margarita."

First one shot, then the other, she blitzed herself in high style. By the time she reached for her margarita, which had a strange gray color, her eyes had gone glassy and soft.

"To the happy couple," she said, raising her glass. "Live long and prosper. Or something."

Mike couldn't speak. His heart was squeezing shut. Whatever he'd wanted from this woman wasn't going to happen. Not that night, at least. Maybe not ever. How could he trust someone who had so little stomach for braving the hard shit?

Because that's what this was. The hard part. They were pressed right up against it—the precipice where they'd launch into something new. Time to crash or fly.

Leah bobbled on her barstool, which gave him a preview of the outcome. Flames and wreckage.

"Hey, there," he said, steadying her balance. "Easy."

"You taking care of me, pet?"

He grimaced. That name should've lit him up like an incendiary bomb. Instead it jabbed at him, knife sharp. It was all that they *weren't*. Not right then.

"What I'm doing is keeping you from UCMJ action."

"So gallant, Strap Happy." She flicked the Silver Star pinned to his uniform. "Is that how you got to be such a hero?"

"I haven't done any more than another would."

"Don't believe you," she said, leaning into his arm. "You're Mr. Air Force Stud. That's why I like to see you on your knees."

Mike cringed and instinctively flicked his gaze around the bar. "Are you going to behave?"

"Shh, that's what *I* ask of *you*. I love it when you behave. When you follow my commands to the letter. When I mark your lovely flesh. So fucking hot, Michael." As if she realized her string of lizard-brain babble, she blanked. Stiffened. Waved to the bartender. "Another shot, please."

"Forget it," Mike said to the man. "She's had enough."

"Not by half, pet."

"Cut it out, Leah. I mean it."

But her third shot went down as quickly as its predecessors. As she reached for the margarita, her hand grazed the edge of the glass. It toppled. Frozen lime and tequila spilled across the bar's grimy surface and sloshed onto her uniform.

"Ah, fuck," she muttered. "That's not good."

"Most sensible thing you've said in an hour. Out we go."

Mike grabbed her under the arms and hauled her off the barstool. She protested, even fought a little, but he would always be stronger. They both knew that. It was what made their play so tantalizing. So when he needed them, his muscles were right there, able to restrain her flailing protests.

He wished it were as easy to restrain the wicked turn of his thoughts and how violently her harsh, stripped words pulsed and throbbed in his blood. She'd never given him much. What she'd said at the bar was almost cruel, here, now, when there was nothing to do but endure the moment. No trust to make the most of it.

Five minutes later they were in a cab. Mike's arms had numbed but not in any pleasant way. Just rigid. Inexorable. Holding everything in. This wasn't about sex anymore, and not even about protecting Leah from herself. This was about salvaging, perhaps, something of what they had.

Which meant he told the cab driver to take them to a motel. Any motel.

If they went to his place, they'd be right back in the middle of temptation—and no way in hell would he let her top him. If they slept at Leah's tiny apartment, they'd be on her territory.

She snuggled against his side. He put an arm around her shoulder and pulled her close, kissing the top of her head. Such a fucking mess. The whole damn thing. Because even though they were pressed together as closely as ever, Mike felt himself pulling back. It wasn't safe to be this vulnerable. Cold took the place of calm.

The cabbie dropped them off at a white stucco motel that looked like something out of *Psycho*. Not exactly Caesar's Palace. A rickety railing leaned off the second-floor balcony. Trim that may have once been green had faded to the look of a Midwestern thunderhead. Two letters on the vacancy sign were dark.

As dusk gathered up in night shadows, external floodlights flicked on. Mike guided his stumbling charge, his hand laced with hers, as he reserved a room and hauled her up the external open-work staircase. She listed, her feet dragging. The tequila had hit her pretty hard by the time they reached the room. Whatever hope he'd had for their stay to be decent was extinguished, but it was private.

Leah set about peeling off her uniform. No pretense or seduction. She shrugged out of her tuxedo coat, yanked off the tie and cummerbund, and bent at the waist as she tugged down her trousers.

Mike leaned against the closed door. A single lamp over a scuffed table by the front window cast a sickly yellow pallor over the scene. He hadn't seen her in more than a week, and this was his reintroduction to the graceful perfection of her body. Something out of a prison movie.

She turned to face him as she shook loose the bun barely secured at her nape. A quick flick sent waves of dark silk tumbling loose over her bare shoulders. His one speck of hope was the gold necklace around her throat. She still wore it, and yet his right wrist remained bare.

She eased toward him, unsteadily, wearing only her underwear—a matched set made of perfectly innocent white lace. The look in her dark eyes was anything but innocent.

Unconsciously Mike prepared himself. This wasn't going to be pretty or good or clean.

"Pet?"

"What, Leah?"

"That's not the right answer." Her face twisted around a frown. "I am the ranking officer in this room, am I not?"

"You are. But I'm the sober one."

She blew a strand of hair out of her eyes. "I'll give you that one, Michael."

"Good. Bed, then. You need to sleep this one off."

She didn't back down, instead standing toe-to-toe with him. He pressed his hands flat behind him to keep from touching the soft, warm temptation she presented.

"Just look at you, Michael."

The way her eyes feasted on his face, his neck, his chest was a powerful aphrodisiac. He was still such a sucker for how she made him feel, like some extra-powerful version of himself.

Without warning she bent at the waist. Her hands were at the zipper of his dress trousers before he could register what he saw. Leah's face so near to his cock, tugging down his briefs.

A wrenching shudder worked up his back.

Her hands wrapped around his hard-on. Fingers interlaced, she gave him a rough squeeze. That loosened the frozen tension from his arms. Grabbing the back of her head was the easiest thing in the world. He wound those loose strands around and around, covering his palms, holding her there.

For a split second, he wondered if they'd reversed roles. By all rights he should've been the one to determine what happened next, but the thick sludge of his blood had come to a stop, waiting. Even now, resenting Leah for what she'd done to wreck something fun and exciting, he couldn't punish her the way she deserved.

She knew it.

"I'm in control here, pet," she whispered against his swollen flesh. "And I'm going to prove it."

Her tongue darted out and slicked his head. Again and again she teased him, licking, edging him higher. She didn't even pull against his hold. Like a dare. If he wanted to hurt her, he was going to have to do it all on his own.

Mike didn't have the stomach to hurt her. Never had. The very idea turned his bones to jelly. So he could only use the hair banding his hands as an anchor. A touchstone.

He didn't trust her.

Leah's mouth closed over his head. His balls had drawn up tight. Sweat moistened the thin skin below his navel.

Her mouth popped off. "Spread your legs, pet."

Jesus.

He did it, giving her access to the sensitive stretch of his inner thigh. She petted up with firm, kneading stokes, which pinched just short of pain. Her ass was perfectly rounded where she bent at the waist. The sight of her head bobbing back and forth, his cock disappearing into those perfectly luscious lips, was almost enough to send him over, plummeting toward a hot, shaky release.

Instead he grabbed beneath her jaw and pulled her back. His dick was wet from her saliva, still hard enough to pound nails. The surprise in her eyes turned hard. He didn't give her the chance to taunt him, to command him.

Mike yanked her off the dingy carpet. He'd intended to drag her to the bed and seduce her properly—if there was such a thing at that moment. He lifted her into his arms, but she wrapped around him. A second skin. Her mouth crashed into his, all teeth and lips and rough sweeps of their tongues.

The bed would wait.

Settling Leah hard on the floor, her legs swaying, he yanked down the thin lace of her panties. She moaned, eyes so heavy-lidded and soft. Her mouth still teased him, quirked into a half smile.

"So crude, Michael."

After snatching a condom out of his trouser pocket, he rolled it on. She was back, flush against his body, before he could steady himself. His uniform separated them. He wrapped his hands around her back, palming her ass. The heat of her lips and the wicked scratch of her fingernails along his scalp burned away the last of his control.

He positioned his head at her slick entrance and shoved deep. Leah arched in his arms. Her mouth went slack on a long moan. He pushed her up against the nearest wall. The jolt of her back hitting that implacable surface jerked through them both, right where they joined. Mike found her mouth again, kissing hard. Demanding. Knowing he could only take what she'd already decided to give. That helplessness made him rougher.

Pounding now, he drove her hips against the wall. Her pussy was hot, slick, sucking at him with every thrust. Even then, so near to his completion, he withheld. Fuck, he was waiting for permission.

She shattered in his arms. Her inner muscles clutched his erection. Her release shivered over him in a long, low groan. "Come on, my good boy," she whispered against his ear. "Rougher now. Do it."

Mike pressed his forehead against the wall, tucked beside Leah's sweaty neck. He closed his eyes, thrusting, fucking her, until he finally let go. His orgasm ripped a gasp out of his throat. White heat shot up from his groin in waves of pure, streaking pleasure.

Breathing roughly, with Leah's scent all around him, he blinked clear of the haze. His equilibrium was gone. She'd stretched her toes back to the floor, but Mike didn't have any faith in her ability to stand. Not when he doubted his own legs.

"See, pet," she said, her voice still a little sloppy. A triumphant smile edged her mouth. "Mine to command."

His satisfaction evaporated with those few words. He licked his bottom lip, where he could still taste their kiss. It was flavored with tequila and a dark, sour fear.

Fear that this had been the last time.

Chapter Thirty-Seven

Leah's head hurt like a son of a bitch before she even opened her eyes. She crushed her palms against gritty sockets, trying to secure her brains before they dribbled out in a wet pile. Her tongue was pebbled with the acidic bite of cheap tequila. When she rolled over, her stomach flipped a few extra times.

Fuck. Just *fuck.*

That it had been bound to happen didn't make the reality easier, especially when her stomach might turn inside out any second.

Even through squeezed-shut eyelids, a sudden wash of white light hurt like fucking hell. Carefully, she turned her head and squinted.

Mike stood in the open doorway of the hotel room. His dark blue slacks were hitched low over his lean hips. The plain white T-shirt he'd worn under his dress uniform almost glowed in the Nevada dawn. He smashed one shoulder against the doorjamb, his other hand wedged against the far side, as if trying to hold himself there. His bent head said he didn't even want to look at her.

Leah scoured the back of her hand over her glued-nasty mouth. Couldn't blame him for that one.

The room was dingy. Trashy. Once-white sheets were twisted around her, exposing the dirty mattress. Fast flashes of the night zipped through her head like a photo slideshow. Christ, they'd slept on that? Twined together, desperate to get closer.

Well, *she'd* been desperate to get closer, to wrap around him. He'd tried to get her to lie flat, to simply sleep. Holy shit, he'd held her hair back as she cuddled up to the toilet, ridding her body of the cheap booze.

"Rise and shine for another beautiful fucking morning," she drawled. Her hair was a snarled mass.

"Is that what we're calling it?"

He pushed out of the doorway and shut it quietly behind him. The sudden gloom was easier on her eyes, with the only light coming from a muted television. That didn't make looking at him hurt less.

She read the magnitude of her fuckup in his every sharp motion.

Pushing to a sitting position meant her head hit nuclear levels, but it didn't matter. She wasn't having this conversation lying upside down on a shitty motel bed, much less flat-out naked. The room spun when she put her feet on the ground. Her panties were a lost cause, but she found her bra and trousers.

She ran her fingers through her hair but didn't get very far. The hangover's sharp pinches magnified through her tender scalp. "You know what they say. Start each morning as you mean to go on."

He didn't say anything. Just watched her. Carefully. As if he knew what was coming.

So she'd oblige him. Do them both a favor. Cut it off before giving up more of her heart and smashing more of his. Maybe she should've done it weeks ago.

She found her button-down shirt and pulled it on. "So I was thinking..."

Mike folded his arms over his chest. That wide, lovely chest. "We both know how dangerous that can be."

After running cloudy water from the tap, she splashed it over her face. The mouthful she took to swish out the nasty taste didn't wash it clean—or unstick the words in her throat.

"Get on with it, Princess."

That name crawled the wrong direction down her spine when coming from his mouth. "Do I really have to say it?"

271

"Yeah. You do." He pushed away from the wall, coming toward her. *At* her. So intently focused. His wide mouth had flattened and his eyes were dangerous slits. "Look around, Leah. Is this what you want for us? Shitty dives?"

She gripped the chipped Formica counter. "You know it's not."

"Then stop acting like this is the best we can do. I won't be your dirty secret anymore."

"It's no one else's business!"

Beyond the career she'd fought to protect from just such monumental mistakes, she wanted to guard what they did. It was special. Precious. More than that, it was fragile. If she couldn't get it right when they were alone, how the hell would she manage in front of the whole damn world?

"It's *my* business." His voice was so deep. Harsh. The chill edged into her bones and locked her joints. "I won't be jerked around anymore."

"I'm not trying to jerk you around." She forced herself to breathe or she'd black out. "I'm trying to let you go."

"Fuck that." He moved all the way into her space. Hovered behind her. The tall length of him heated her skin. Their eyes locked in the mirror, through the smeared streaks of cleanser. "You're running scared."

She ducked around him and claimed an open patch of floor at the foot of the bed. "My motives don't matter. Just the results."

Leaning against the bathroom counter, he crossed his arms. The laid-back chill she liked so much was gone, replaced by a severe distance she never would've imagined. His fierce eyes were the pale blue of the sky before snow.

"I think I deserve to hear everything. Why else are we here?"

"I don't need this shit," she spat. Because yeah, that was fear and insecurity colliding in a sickly knot in her stomach. Her hands shook as she did up the buttons on her shirt.

His jaw worked, as if trying to hold back the rest of his words. Yet he'd always been braver. "I used to think my parents had the right idea. You remember me telling you about them, years ago? Mom at home. Dad off to work. How it *should* be— not women flying planes. But what the hell did I know?"

He shoved into the bedroom, prowling like an angered lion. "When I was in Florida, I saw things differently. My brother and his wife have something special. A life I admire. I actually envied their give-and-take, how they share the good stuff and clothesline everything else—together. What I thought was right for a man and woman..." A grimace twisted his mouth. "It was crap, Leah. Completely bastard crap. It was easier to be a chauvinist than stand up for women like you. Frankly, back then I was probably jealous of your ambition. It wasn't in me to fight as hard as you did."

She needed to sit. It wasn't a graceful movement, but she wound up on the bed.

"You're the best damn pilot I've ever flown with. Whatever impression I've given that you weren't good enough—that was *my* shit talking." He made fists so hard that his knuckles cracked. "Are you hearing me at all?"

An absent nod was her reply, but what he said barely made sense. She had been trying to give him an out. *Run away. Fast as you can.* Mike had other ideas. His words were a balm she hadn't realized she craved. Acceptance. *His* acceptance and respect.

He gave it to her *now*? When she stank of tequila and wore the sad remains of her uniform?

"I don't want some lopsided relationship that can't weather the worst," he said quietly. "Top, bottom, sideways—no matter how we do things."

"But see, this is how I do things." She made a grand gesture toward the hellhole motel room.

"Nice to know. The only partner you want is one who'll help you wallow and hide and get off. Why the hell are you doing this? Are you so fucking scared of us? I would treat you like a princess for the rest of my life. You *know* that."

Leah's blood ran cold. The hot, angry knot in her stomach was gone, replaced by chills that spread over her skin. "I don't want to be anyone's princess. Least of all yours."

He shut down. Immediately. Just blanked out, and not in that sublimely relaxed way she'd managed to evoke. He looked every bit the Air Force asshole she'd once thought him, no matter his honest admission.

His shoulders bulked higher. "Message received, Captain."

"What?"

"I knew you were competitive. I just didn't know you'd rather drive us into a ditch than back down."

She scooped up her jacket. With her uniform half-assed pieced together and her hair still a mess, she looked like a recruiter's what-not-to-do poster. Didn't matter.

She stopped with her hand on the doorknob. Her mouth worked over so much she'd like to say. At the chapel, she'd been sure he would take her hand if she offered it. The ice in his eyes said that chance was long gone.

He was right. She'd won the round.

And she was breaking them in two.

"Michael..."

"*Mike.*" He punched the TV's off button with one finger. "Call me Mike. Or Templeton. Or asshat. I don't give a shit. I better not hear *Michael* come out of your mouth again. I can't be held responsible for what I'd say in return."

She shriveled up and died inside. Flat out. Nothing left. "Just...take care of yourself."

A sarcastic twist folded his mouth and angled his eyebrows. "Oh, don't you worry about me, *Princess*. I'm going to be just fine. You worry about how you can keep your shit together when you obviously think so little of yourself."

By the time the next live ordnance exercise rolled around, keeping her shit together was the least of Leah's problems.

She'd lost her mind. Full-out zombified.

Yeah, she went through the motions of her day. Did the PT she needed to, showed up to work on time, gave Fang and Tin Tin hell every chance she got. She'd caught them watching her when they thought she wasn't looking.

Not that she managed to catch them that often. She was too busy trying not to watch Michael. Mike.

Correcting herself, even in her own head, had been harder than she'd imagined.

Two weeks after that horrible morning in the motel, she made the mistake of ducking into the common room to grab a bottle of water from the bar. He was there, and he'd stripped off his T-shirt. So much smooth golden skin. Unmarked.

She hovered. Stayed near the open door. Her throat was dry and she bit her bottom lip. Not hers anymore. Her hands clenched on the need to touch and grab and pinch what he'd once offered so willingly. His back was two thick sweeps of muscles, decorated with the dip and play of little ligaments. Normally unkind fluorescent lights skimmed over his skin like a lover's touch, just as she wished she could touch him. His spine was a shallow divot in the center of his back, calling for her tongue to lick up the length.

It had been bad enough seeing him in briefings. In the office. Even across the food court. This was a cruel sort of punishment, to see so much of him and be allowed to touch nothing.

She'd known better than to get involved with anyone in the squadron again. The first few days after their breakup, she'd been so scared that she flinched every time they passed each other in the halls. As if he would stop and point at her and tell everyone within earshot that they'd been in a relationship.

Except Michael was a better man than that. No, not Michael.

He was Templeton now.

Something hot and stinging burned at the back of her eyes. The ache hadn't eased. Nothing she did, waking or sleeping, detracted from one simple, terrible fact. She had let him go.

The moment he spotted her was obvious enough. His hands froze in the act of shaking out a new shirt. Beautiful blue eyes went cold and his mouth flattened. He shoved his head through the shirt and yanked his flight suit back up with short, sharp moves. Not even a word of greeting—nothing to signal that they were squad mates, let alone former lovers.

Just strangers.

She ran. Again. Ducked right back out the door without grabbing a water and hoofed it back to her office. Thank God it was empty because she really didn't want to deal with Jon being all full-on Tin Tin. It took everything she had to gather her mental shit and get ready to take to the air two hours later.

As her plane cranked up over ten thousand feet, she knew it was for the best. She could have hurt him. Like, for real and for keeps. Obviously she couldn't be trusted the way he needed to trust a mistress. A *partner*.

Yet she clamped the throttle at the thought of him kneeling before anyone else. Or his eyes turning deep blue for another woman. Even the idea of him making jet-fuel coffee while he and a new girlfriend laughed together in his tiny little kitchen was enough to make her shake.

She choked it down. Pushed it away. This wasn't the time or place to be so perfectly aware that it was his fucking plane on her right wing. She knew that dogged, head-down way he flew. He'd die before letting down the other members of the squadron.

They had a mission. Take out Jon's team of three. Be the bad guys.

Leah had that one down to a science.

Even while flying, she couldn't keep her head in the game. That ought to tell her something.

She'd screwed up but hard. Despite that, she couldn't help wondering if he'd take her back. She'd need to suck up her pride and spend an awful long time making it up to him. Maybe she'd start by proving she could handle the real stuff, that she wouldn't duck her head in the sand when she got scared. Because that's what she'd done. She was scared of having something so real that she'd have to fight for it. For them both.

Jon, Fang and Kisser were three clicks ahead, flying like Israelis today. Their target.

Eyes on the prize, goddammit. Before she lost her shit entirely.

Nothing went right. Not in her head, and not with Mike.

They'd just crested the mountains, bearing down on Jon, when Mike's plane jerked in the air. A white plume of smoke streaked from his F-16's only engine.

The radio exploded into chatter. Leah's throat choked down. Adrenaline jacked her pulse into a fierce throb. Her fingertips went tingly numb on fear.

A free fall. Flat spin. Mike's jet spun like a leaf toward the desert floor. Smoke trailed spirals in his wake.

His voice came cold and harsh over the airwaves. After the hours on hours they'd spent in the flight simulator, Leah knew that tone. He was pissed at himself. Frustrated. That was when he made mistakes—compounding, fatal mistakes.

The truth hit Leah with a crushing force, right against her chest. Against her heart, really.

The man she loved was going to die.

Chapter Thirty-Eight

A black haze had swept over Mike's eyes. The dead weight of his hands meant clumsy responses as he jerked the throttle. His thinking brain realized it was panic. Moments became nightmare slow as the spin's G-force controlled his body.

Game over.

No.

No way.

He pushed past his body's cloying shutdown and forced his senses to cooperate. Sight came back first, as he watched dials spin like roulette wheels. The tips of his fingers were icy and his legs numb from the knee down, but he held his body steady.

His hearing... That came back in the form of some sick delusion.

"Michael!"

He jerked. It wasn't a delusion. The panic in Leah's scream was unbelievable.

The whine of sirens drowned her out. He was glad. One thing at a time. That meant shoving *any* fear into a faraway corner.

Warning buzzers and blinking lights were furious now. Each needed his attention. Hours of training in the simulator eased over him like a double shot of whiskey. He was going to puke into his lap any second now, but he'd do it with a clear mind.

He wasn't going to die. Plain as that. Physics could take a fucking leap.

His flight gloves felt overly large so he stripped them off with his teeth. After wiping off the sweat, he found a better grip on the throttle. Stronger. Already doing the impossible, he was six steps ahead of his thinking brain. Reflex and muscle memory took the helm.

Radio chatter dimmed to flight control. Just one voice. That faceless man relayed trajectory data for Mike to compare to his plane's faulty readings. Thoughts bounced at lightning speed. Dials, readings, information up the ass. The whole time, his body wrestled with a dying fighter jet.

Until something shifted.

He wrested a modicum of control from the floundering jet. It slugged more forward than down. Mike fought for each degree. Level out. Regain control.

Altitude was dangerously low. He'd have to make a decision. Quickly. Keep trying to pull out of the spin or eject.

"Strap Happy, respond. Do you have control of the aircraft?"

"Negative, Control."

A gust caught his wing, which would normally be a challenge. At that moment, it was just enough to change the game. The throttle jumped in his hands. He managed a sharp bank to the left. Instead of flipping the aircraft, he spiraled rather than fell.

A mantra struck up behind his brow. *Keep it steady.*

The spiral widened and became more shallow. The heartbeat in his ears was a monotonous thrum, but he pushed past it to keep the flow of information coming.

"Strap Happy, respond," came the voice again. "Do you have control of the aircraft?"

"Still losing altitude, Control. Slowing the rate of descent. Requesting instructions for landing."

"Blue Force barracks runway. Emergency crews standing by."

The Earth's pull dragged and sucked at his fighter. He was flying straight, but he was too low. He blinked past a stream of sweat.

Screw gravity. He was landing in one piece. *Fact.*

The Blue Force runway was miles into the desert, where they trained well away from the city. Less chance of harming other people. It loomed ahead of him like a ditch waiting to be dug. *Nope.* That deadly scenario wasn't worth a thought. Instead, a gift of precision and logic processed everything clearly. Layers of frustration and streaks of fear thinned to wisps.

Leah and the others had peeled away to circle and land behind him. The control tower's lone voice became the center of his world. Trajectory. Wind speed. Distance. He was riding on pure gut instinct. Unconscious data aligned as naturally as when he took a smooth corner on his BMW.

The throttle bucked like a wild animal, but he used his bones and his flesh to fight back. After getting the nose level, he inched it higher. Higher. The fighter's rear wheels stretched toward the tarmac. Streaks of rock whipped past his peripheral vision. Every fiber of his body focused on easing his shaking, ruined machine toward solid ground.

Touchdown.

The force of impact jammed against his chest as the harnesses yanked taut. His head lurched forward. He let it happen. No resistance. Less damage to the spinal column. Wheels squealed. A renewed flash of voices buzzed like cicadas in his radio. The runway narrowed and darkened at the edges, with fire engines at the end of the long, long stretch.

Flaps and brakes. The rear of the plane threatened to launch end over end, but he didn't overburden the machinery. Calm. Slow. Lots of finesse.

His Falcon came to a stop.

A wail of sirens ran up to meet him. Gusts of flame retardant swallowed his view in the cockpit, which made him feel oddly claustrophobic. Rather than fight it, he simply slumped back against the headrest, breathing, letting tides of adrenaline grind his brain to dust.

A member of the emergency response team popped the canopy. "Nice work, sir. Are you injured?"

"No."

"Then out you come."

He allowed the airman to guide him down the ladder. Two medics waited with a blanket.

Shock. Yeah, he could see that.

Someone stripped off his helmet. He sucked in a deep breath of what felt like a hit of pure, cold oxygen. Plane after plane landed along the isolated airstrip. He tracked each one, as if failing to watch them come to a safe stop would curse them with what should've happened to him.

Maybe going nose to nose with death made a guy superstitious. Only when the last F-16 touched down did he let one of the medics ease him down on a gurney.

A feminine shout came from a far distance. "Wait!"

He surged upright without thought. Leah was running across the tarmac with her helmet in hand. She ditched it just before reaching the gurney. He expected her to pull up short and shove that god-awful wall back between them. But she didn't hesitate, didn't flinch. Her body folded against his. Gorgeous curves were wrapped in the utility roughness of her flight suit. She smelled as sweat-drenched as him.

"Jesus, Michael," she said on a sob.

She clung to him—right there in front of everyone, as Fang and the rest of the squadron assembled at the base of the radar array.

Mike was completely at a loss. Shock on top of shock. Out of pure reflex, he cupped the back of her head. She pressed her face more tightly against his neck. Her hands were restless creatures roaming over his back, his shoulders, his arms, as if trying to reassure herself that he was whole.

A hysterical laugh gurgled out of her. "You scared the shit out of me."

"Me too."

Leah bracketed his face with her palms. "You did great."

"Watch it, Princess. Everyone will see you cry."

"I'm not gonna fucking cry, you monster." Yet she buried her face against his chest.

Mike rubbed her back as she shook.

She'd brought their secret into the light. Great. Terrific. Too bad that small miracle had required a near-death experience. So he let her go. Pushed her away, truth be told.

Hurt mingled with fear and understanding as she stepped back. Once. Again.

That's when he gave up. He'd just scraped back from the brink of poof, gone, *splat*. How hard would it have been to say she loved him?

Leah Girardi wasn't the woman he'd believed her to be, which meant she wasn't the woman he thought he loved.

"Sir?"

He looked up to find the medic waiting. "You want me in that ambulance, don't you?"

"Yes, sir."

Mike settled onto the stretcher, looking up to the roof. No amount of deep breathing got rid of his tension. It was twined with his marrow and refused to budge.

Fourteen hours passed. Medical assessments. Precautionary tests. Debriefings. Turned out he wasn't to blame for the near accident, that was for damn sure. Video playback proved as much. The mechanics would need time to find the exact cause. Mike didn't care. He was a zombie. Too much to process.

He slept fitfully as military and medical personnel came and went. Dawn lightened the sky when Dash was finally able to drive him home.

"That was some scary shit, Strap."

Mike let out a long breath. "You're telling me."

They pulled to a stop outside his bungalow. Dash's expression was one hundred percent hardcore. "Don't fucking do it again."

"And you don't fucking do it *ever*."

They slapped each other on the back a few times. Mike trudged up to his porch. Key in lock. Duffle on floor. Every movement was truncated, in reality and in his head. Higher thought would take a day or two to return.

The eerie pink of sunrise added a surreal quality to his living room. The details, however, were just as he remembered—and just as shitty. Two flattened pillows, a jumbled blanket and a discarded pair of briefs looked like accusations. He'd lived on his couch during his off hours, without the guts to sleep in his own bed. His drawer of toys was in his bedroom, as were a hundred erotic, tender memories he wasn't ready to stare down.

Those memories had been of a couple with potential. Maybe even a future.

The truth was much plainer. Mike was a bachelor. Grease-stained pizza boxes and cardboard containers of empty beer bottles proclaimed that with exclamation points.

Jesus.

The worst was his hope. Hope that Leah would've visited him in the hospital room. Hope that she would've been waiting when he was discharged from the hospital. Apparently her outright burst of emotion on the tarmac didn't carry through to the hours and days and years that made up a real commitment.

Fuck it. He'd just survived the impossible. He should be grateful to have a skull, guts and limbs, all in the right places. Even that reminder didn't help. So he showered, barely managing to drag jeans on. Glared at the coffeepot he still hadn't used. Ate cereal while standing at his counter. He sure as shit didn't need to head to base for a couple days, which meant he'd hit the sack pronto.

Back to the couch. *Fuck.*

A knock at the front door made him jump.

Through the peephole, he saw Leah.

Christ, he didn't need this now. But he still opened the door because she was there—because he needed her to be there.

She lifted her head, which seemed like a huge effort. She'd cleaned up, wearing jeans and a kitsch ABBA T-shirt that molded to her breasts. A lightweight Air Force hoodie covered her arms. His necklace encircled her throat, which felt like an insult. Her hair was loose, damp at the ends. Yet to say she had bloodshot eyes and dark circles would both be understatements. She looked completely blasted.

Mike glanced over her shoulder toward his driveway. "Where's the Ducati?"

"Took a taxi from my house." Her voice was a hoarse mess. "My bike ride from base wasn't exactly...steady."

"I just got cleaned up and ate. Now I'm going to sleep. You should go home and do the same. No way am I up for whatever reason you're here."

Leah kept silent but pushed past him, into the house.

"You heard what I said." His tone was biting. Too bad. He was still hurting in ways he hadn't catalogued.

"I heard."

"Whatever, Princess."

He set about cleaning up the pizza boxes and beer bottles. That she was there to bear witness to that telling mess was humiliating. She had to know how she affected him. Did he need to spell it out for her too?

No way could he look at her. Something she said or did would pull him back again, when compromising was no longer an option. So he headed to the kitchen and tossed everything into a recycling bin.

Let her friggin' stand there all day.

"Michael?"

A part of his brain snapped in two. "I told you to shut up with that shit!" He stalked back to the living room. But she wasn't standing.

She was on her knees.

Mike could only stare. His blood drained down through the hardwood floor.

"What the hell is this? You drop by after I just about bite it and decide to screw with me? Wasn't that little display on the tarmac enough of a head-fuck? Get out before I say anything I regret. There's already too much to list."

"Michael, please." She swallowed and looked about ready to puke. He could relate. "I need to apologize."

He could've been punched in the chest and felt less pain. Hope was a goddamn bastard with a wicked right cross.

Her compressed lips were nearly colorless. Her back was rigid, as if supported by an iron spike. Yet her gaze never wavered. "You were right. I've been a complete coward. After trying my whole life to be better and braver than everyone else, I turned chickenshit when it mattered the most."

His nerve endings tingled, like a limb easing back from the edge of frostbite.

"I didn't realize how hard it would to keep from talking to you. Or for you to ignore me. I don't just mean right now. After...after how I screwed up. I crawled out of my skin every time I saw you on base."

Mike fisted his hands. *Stay put, idiot. Don't you fucking move.*

She fidgeted with her fingers, the hoodie's zipper, the pockets of her jeans. "That must've been what you felt when I kept us a secret. To have you so close but not *have* you? Just horrible. And to think I've done that for months to the man I love."

Crossing his arms over his chest was a last ditch means of defense. He was crumbling by the second.

"Michael, nothing has ever scared me so bad as today. To lose you..." A tear trailed down her left cheek. "How could I stand it?"

The crack in her voice marked the end of his control. He closed the distance between them, although his joints had turned to slush. He stood over her because, damn it all, he deserved an apology that pushed her to the edge. He needed to know if she would retreat or hold firm.

From the pocket of her hoodie she retrieved a black velvet box. Her lower lip quavered. The sunlight glimmered across her wet cheeks. Wordlessly, she lifted it. An offering.

"I'd have been at the hospital, except I had to make an emergency trip to the jewelers. Look inside."

Mike swallowed and accepted the box. He opened the hinged lid. Inside was a smooth, lustrous cuff of gleaming copper, unadorned except for the word *Pet* engraved on the inside of the band.

What he'd been waiting for. Only now he needed her words too.

"May I?" she asked.

Soberly, he said, "That's the first time you've asked my permission for anything."

"I hope..."

"You hope what?"

Her dark eyes were big, luminous, shimmering. "I hope I won't screw up so bad that I have to do this again. And I hope you'll take me back."

Silently, he held out his right wrist. Leah sucked in a slow breath. Another fat tear crested the apple of her cheek. Her fingers shook as she fastened the cuff and reverently touched the copper.

"I should've given this to you at our birthdays. I saw it in the shop and...I backed off. Told myself it wasn't perfect enough, when that was just a copout. What you've offered me is so beautiful that I didn't think I deserved you."

The tension he'd thought permanently fused inside his bones seeped away. He could *almost* think again. Without fanfare, he grabbed beneath her arms and hoisted her up. She swayed on unsteady feet and used him as her anchor. He held on tight. As if relief had broken her open, she lost control of her tears. Her sobs could have smashed his heart, except his arms were full of Leah again.

"Enough of that," he said against her temple. "When I told you that I wanted to treat you like a princess, I didn't mean it to take anything from you. It's a give and take—the good we could share. Do you see that?"

She pulled back and raised her chin. Braver now. Clear-eyed, despite the streaks of tears. "I do. Honest, I do. I've been fighting for so long to make my mark... I don't think I believed I could be successful *and* pampered."

"I won't compromise anymore."

"I wouldn't want you to. I won't either."

Heady warmth eased out from his chest. "Then chalk it up to learning the ropes of something neither of us knew dick about."

She swiped at her cheeks. They were close enough to breathe one another's air. "You mean it? Because if you'll let me, Michael..."

The hesitation was yet another request: to use his full name. "If I'll let you?"

"Then I'm yours, Michael. All yours."

His exhalation was painfully deep. "And what about me, ma'am?"

"*You*, my darling pet—you're mine." She wrapped her arms around him. Holding him. Binding them together. "I'm strong enough to believe that now, with all my heart."

Epilogue

Leah adored the look Michael wore when he was washed over with pain—the pain he enjoyed. His eyes lost focus. That lovely mouth of his quirked at the corners, as if he could barely believe it was so good. She brushed a lock of hair back from his forehead.

That she enjoyed seeing his bliss, even when she wasn't the one administering the pain, was a little surprising.

She tugged her chair nearer to Michael's right side, the better to whisper in his ear. His right arm lay across her lap, wrist facing up. She trailed her fingertips over his open palm. "How are you doing, baby?"

He rolled his head slowly to look at her. Watch her. She loved that steady, intense way of his. His smile grew a fraction. "Green light."

She scratched her nails lightly under his hair, over his scalp. He was starting to get a little shaggy again. No matter the warnings Fang had given him over the past months, he kept pushing the regs, letting his hair grow out as long as he could. They both enjoyed when she wrapped her fingers in that silky softness.

"You're my good boy, aren't you?" she purred.

The tattoo artist flicked an amused glance up before going back to work on the inside of Michael's left wrist. The man's shaved-bald head shone in the bright lights of the tiny, private booth.

Leah didn't give a crap. For one thing, the sheer square-footage of ink covering him said he was no stranger to alternative lives. Most important of all, she and Michael were together. What others thought didn't matter so long as they had each other.

That wasn't to say they flaunted the specific dynamics of how they worked, but they didn't hide either. The rather spectacular reveal of their relationship had meant everyone on Nellis talked for months. She couldn't have cared any less. She was proud of Michael, proud that everyone knew the partnership they shared.

She curled her hand under his right wrist, the one that was finished. A possessive flush swept through her once again. Four exquisitely tattooed links of chain marked him as hers. Permanently. The carefully shaded links looked like heavy metal. Perfect and unbroken.

They'd decided against wrapping the design around his entire wrist, figuring that might be a little much. It was enough that he was bound to her. Just like she was bound to him. She wore the paper airplane necklace every single day, except when she was flying.

She traced a fingertip over the top of his cheek, where his faint laugh lines were scored. "You know, pet, you seem to have lost your poker face."

His tongue slicked over his bottom lip as he blinked a few times, obviously trying to gather some semblance of thought together. "Don't need it. I've got you."

She couldn't help but laugh. If it sounded suspiciously like a giggle, she sure wasn't admitting it. "Jesus. Every time I think I've got it under control, you have to go and get more perfect."

"You're obviously delusional, Major."

She stuck her tongue out at him. "I haven't been pinned yet."

"Yeah, but you made the list." He turned his hand and wove their fingers together. "It's just a matter of time."

"There." The tattoo artist set his gun on a side counter. "We're done."

Michael let out a long, slow breath. His eyes were the dark, deep blue that she loved so much.

She swallowed around the knot in her throat. "Can we get a second?"

The guy smirked but ducked out anyway, closing the half-curtain of the booth.

Leah pushed off with her heels and rolled her seat directly in front of Michael. She laced their fingers together, palms up, and tugged forward so that his wrists hovered side by side.

"Beautiful," she breathed. She brushed a kiss over the bottom of his palm, right under the black ink. "Did it hurt badly?"

He shook his head. "Not really."

"But you slid away. A little bit. I liked seeing it." Her thumbnails traced the lines of his palm. If she were the type of person to believe in mystic crap, she might try to figure out where her lifeline wove in with his. A tiny shake went up his arms.

"You've dealt out much worse." The wicked smile that curved his lips said he didn't mind. "It was more than the pain. More like knowing what it meant."

She couldn't stay away from him for long. Sliding out of her seat, she practically crawled up his body until she nestled in his lap. Straddling him.

He was so solid for her. Calm and self-assured. Patient. Always waiting for her cues. Leah folded her hands along the sides of his face and kissed him, letting his strength ground her. The last vestiges of her nerves eased away. She *needed* him. Without Michael, she would've spun out into the stratosphere. Sooner or later.

She nuzzled the length of his neck then grazed her teeth over his skin. "Tell me what it means to you." She already knew, since they'd talked about it long and hard, but that didn't make it any less sweet to hear.

His hands caressed her hips. "It means I'm yours."

The flat-out *rightness* of it jolted under her ribs.

"I love you, pet," she said against his skin. It wasn't the first time she'd said it, but the way it got easier and easier was remarkable. Amazing and perfect. No more fear dragging her down.

"I love you, ma'am."

She wiggled out of his lap then stopped with her hand on the curtain. "Now, I'm going to call him in here. I want you to listen to the aftercare instructions very carefully."

His lips spread in that wide, wicked smile. She'd known the moment she'd seen his smile, years ago, how devious it could make her feel. She just hadn't realized where it would take them and that it could make her feel so strong.

"I will, ma'am."

"Don't you want to know why?"

His gaze flicked down to the tattooed chains at his wrist. "You'll tell me if you want to."

She moved back to the chair, carefully dipping her head to his ear. Close enough that he would feel her breath on his skin, but far enough to keep it a tantalizing promise. "I want to know exactly how long it will be before I can put real chains on your wrists. You'll wear them just long enough for me to make you come so hard that you forget where you are."

He breathed her name then drew her down for a kiss. The sheer emotion in the move let her know exactly how deeply he felt it too. "As long as you're there, I always know where I am. Safe."

Tears prickled at the back of her eyes, but she blinked them away. "We'll keep each other safe, Michael. Together. Always."

Author's Note

The 64th Aggressor Squadron is an active United States Air Force unit assigned to the 57th Adversary Tactics Group, stationed at Nellis Air Force Base in Las Vegas, Nevada. The pilots' objectives are as we've described: to fly as adversaries against allied pilots from around the world, teaching them to better counter enemy tactics. The unit dates back to WWII when it participated in multiple theaters of operation.

Now, the 64th and other "bandits" from the 57th ATG regularly conduct dogfighting simulations in the United States, known as Red Flags, and Maple Flag exercises in conjunction with Canadian Forces. They also add their expertise to the USAF's Weapons School syllabus and travel the country to provide training and test mission support to various units.

All individuals described in this story are fictitious. Research mistakes are entirely our own.

In the meantime, we enjoy assuming that at least one of these dedicated, highly skilled bandits rides a big, mean motorcycle.

About the Author

Katie Porter is the writing team of Carrie Lofty and Lorelie Brown, who've been friends and critique partners for more than five years. Both are multi-published in historical romance. Carrie has an MA in history, while Lorelie is a US Army veteran. Generally a high-strung masochist, Carrie loves running and weight training, but she has no fear of gross things like dissecting formaldehyde sharks. Her two girls are not appreciative. Lorelie, a laid-back sadist, would rather grin maniacally when Carrie works out. Her three boys love how she screams like a little girl around spiders.

To learn more about the authors who make up Katie, visit www.katieporterbooks.com or follow them on Twitter at @carrielofty, @LorelieBrown and @MsKatiePorter.

Desire as reckless as a fighter jet in freefall...
and just as dangerous.

Double Down
© 2012 Katie Porter
Vegas Top Guns, Book 1

As part of the 64th Aggressor Squadron, Major Ryan "Fang" Haverty flies like the enemy to teach Allied pilots how not to die. The glittering excess of the Strip can't compare to the glowing jet engines of his F-16. But a sexy, redheaded waitress in seamed stockings? Now *she* gets his blood pumping.

Cassandra Whitman's good-girl ways haven't earned any slack from her manager ex-boyfriend, or prevented a bad case of frazzle from holding down two and a half jobs. She sure wouldn't mind letting the handsome Southern charmer shake up her routine.

Their wild weekend lives up to Sin City's reputation. Especially when they discover a matched passion for roleplaying. For Cass, it's an exciting departure from her normal, shy persona. But for Ryan, it triggers memories of a time when his fetish drove away the woman he loved—leaving him reluctant to risk a repeat performance.

Except Cass refuses to settle for ordinary ever again. She's about to show the man with hair-trigger hands that she's got a few surprise moves of her own.

Warning: This book contains dirty-hot roleplaying, featuring an all-alpha fighter pilot and an ambitious waitress with a fabulous imagination. Also: dressing-room sex, a plaid schoolgirl skirt, and a sprinkling of spankings.

Available now in ebook and print from Samhain Publishing.

SAMHAIN
P U B L I S H I N G

It's all about the story...

Romance

HORROR

Retro ROMANCE

www.samhainpublishing.com